**Praise for Denise Swanson's Scumble River mysteries**

"Swanson's Scumble River mysteries are marvelous."
—Jerrilyn Farmer

"It's no mystery why the first Scumble River novel was nominated for the prestigious Agatha Award. Denise Swanson knows small-town America, its secrets and its self-delusions, and she writes as if she might have been hiding behind a tree when some of the bodies were being buried. A delightful new series."
—Margaret Maron

*Murder of a Snake in the Grass*

"Swanson's Skye Denison, amateur sleuth, is an endearing and realistic character. . . . A fast-paced, enjoyable read."
—*The Herald News*

"This book is delightful. . . . The characters are human and generous and worth following through the series."
—*Mysterious Women*

"A well-written, nonviolent, enjoyable story which captures the essence of the small Midwestern town."
—*Mystery News*

*continued . . .*

## Murder of a Small-Town Honey

"A delightful mystery that bounces along with gently wry humor and jaunty twists and turns."
—Edgar Award–winning author Earlene Fowler

"A lighthearted, entertaining mystery."
—*Fort Lauderdale Sun-Sentinel*

"A charming, insightful debut mystery."     —Carolyn Hart

"The start of a bright new series. Swanson captures the essence of small-town life in Scumble River, and Skye is a likable heroine."     —*Romantic Times*

"A likable new heroine reminiscent of some of our favorite childhood detectives—with a little bit of an edge. . . . A fresh, delightful and enjoyable first mystery."
—The Charlotte Austin Review

"Skye is smart, fiesty, quick to action and altogether lovable."     —I Love a Mystery

"A charming debut novel that rings with humor, buzzes with suspense, and engages with each page turned . . . an impressive first novel worthy of praise."
—*The Daily Journal* (Kankakee, IL)

"With a light touch, [Swanson]'s crafted a likable heroine in a wackily realistic small-town community with wonderful series potential. I suspect we'll be seeing a lot more of Denise Swanson and Scumble River."     —The Mystery Morgue

# Murder of a
# Barbie and Ken

*A Scumble River Mystery*

# DENISE
# SWANSON

A SIGNET BOOK

SIGNET
Published by New American Library, a division of
Penguin Group (USA) Inc., 375 Hudson Street,
New York, New York 10014, USA
Penguin Group (Canada), 90 Eglinton Avenue East, Suite 700, Toronto,
Ontario M4P 2Y3, Canada (a division of Pearson Penguin Canada Inc.)
Penguin Books Ltd., 80 Strand, London WC2R 0RL, England
Penguin Ireland, 25 St. Stephen's Green, Dublin 2,
Ireland (a division of Penguin Books Ltd.)
Penguin Group (Australia), 250 Camberwell Road, Camberwell, Victoria 3124,
Australia (a division of Pearson Australia Group Pty. Ltd.)
Penguin Books India Pvt. Ltd., 11 Community Centre, Panchsheel Park,
New Delhi - 110 017, India
Penguin Group (NZ), 67 Apollo Drive, Mairangi Bay,
Auckland 1311, New Zealand (a division of Pearson New Zealand Ltd.)
Penguin Books (South Africa) (Pty.) Ltd., 24 Sturdee Avenue,
Rosebank, Johannesburg 2196, South Africa

Penguin Books Ltd., Registered Offices:
80 Strand, London WC2R 0RL, England

First published by Signet, an imprint of New American Library,
a division of Penguin Group (USA) Inc.

First Printing, November 2003
10   9

Copyright © Denise Swanson Stybr, 2003
All rights reserved

Ⓟ REGISTERED TRADEMARK—MARCA REGISTRADA

Printed in the United States of America

PUBLISHER'S NOTE
This is a work of fiction. Names, characters, places, and incidents either are
the product of the author's imagination or are used fictitiously, and any resemblance to actual persons, living or dead, business establishments, events, or
locales is entirely coincidental.

The publisher does not have any control over and does not assume any
responsibility for author or third-party Web sites or their content.

To Center Cass District 66, particularly the staff of Lakeview Junior High and especially Sue Guinand, Sue Hagansee, Madeleine Maguire, Barb Albrecht, Karin Snodgrass, Julic Peterson, Valerie McCaffrey, Carole Adams, Barb Ulie, Becky Foellmer, Jan Heckman, Marilyn DeYoung, Mary Ann Grembler, Nona Jones, Erika Sullivan, William Ward, and fellow school psychologist Heidi Santucci, who have supported me by buying books, coming to signings, and letting me know they're proud of me.

# Acknowledgments

My sincere thanks to:

Ellen Edwards and Laura Blake Peterson for their continued support of my writing career.

The booksellers who have hand-sold my books, the librarians who have ordered them for their collections, and the readers who have read them.

Cindi Baker for putting me in touch with Robin Partin, and to Robin for filling me in on the details of Drug Court in Illinois. Any mistakes I've made about the procedure are my own fault.

Linda Rutledge for liking my books well enough to want her friend to be a character in this one.

And hugs and kisses to the Deadly Divas for their help, especially Susan McBride.

Special thanks to my personal assistant and Der Webmeister, Dave Stybr, for supporting me in countless ways and for composing the *Scumble River Legend.* How many mystery series have their own signature music?

# CHAPTER 1

*"Will you walk into my parlour?" said a Spider to a
Fly . . .*

—Mary Howitt

Skye Denison's eyes popped open as a scream ripped
through the elegant living room. She had been half doz-
ing, hidden behind a huge schefflera, when what sounded
like a screech owl brought her to full alertness. She peeked
through the plant's dense foliage, and was disappointed to
see that the shouting was just a result of her hostess, Barbie
Addison, awarding the next door prize.

The object of all the fuss appeared to be a circular piece
of rubber about the size of a small saucer. Skye scratched
her head; surely Barbie wasn't giving away diaphragms.

The mystery was solved when a loud voice exclaimed,
"Oh, Hilary, you'll love it. This is the best jar opener I've
ever found. Of course, as Barbie's been demonstrating, all of
the Instant Gourmet's products are wonderful."

Skye snorted, and eased back behind the plant. This con-
trived testimonial had been imparted by Barbie's best friend,
Lu Ginardi, another Instant Gourmet dealer.

Skye had hoped that the shriek was a result of something a little more serious, something like a fire alarm, something that would cause the house to be evacuated, and the guests to be told to go home. A product-demonstration party was the last place she wanted to be on a snowy Monday night, or any night for that matter.

She looked at her watch. Seven-thirty. Judging from past experience, it would be at least another ninety minutes or more before she could make her excuses and escape to her quiet cottage. She just hoped she could remain out of sight until that time.

No such luck. Barbie was heading in her direction. Skye frantically searched for an escape route. Damn. Barbie was in front of her, and the living room wall was at her back. She was trapped.

"Skye, what are you doing hiding over in the corner?" Barbie demanded, her hands on her hips. She was one of those flawless women who always looked like she had just stepped out of the beauty shop or off the pages of a magazine. Her champagne-blond tresses had never experienced a bad hair day, her makeup never smudged, and her burgundy cashmere turtleneck and matching wool pants encased a perfect figure that never gained a pound.

Skye shrugged. "Just taking a little breather." She mentally shook her head, and wondered, for perhaps the twentieth time since meeting Barbie and Ken Addison, how a mature woman could stand to go by the name Barbie, especially when she was married to a man named Ken. It was just too cute.

"I'll bet you're feeling a little shy." Barbie perched on the arm of Skye's chair. "You haven't been a Bette for very long, have you?" She answered her own question. "No. Of course not. Simon only joined the GUMBs in August, and it took him a while to persuade you to become a Bette."

Barbie was referring to Simon Reid: Skye's boyfriend, funeral home owner, coroner, and a recent member of the

Grand Union of the Mighty Bulls. When he had told Skye he was joining the GUMBs, he'd claimed it was to network with the other businessmen in town—but more and more he'd been sucked into the social activities of the club.

When Skye confronted him, he had pointed out the scarcity of places to go or things to do in Scumble River. Its size—fewer than three thousand people—and location—the heart of the Illinois prairie—limited the available forms of entertainment to watching the corn grow, sitting at a bar, or riding around the back roads with a six-pack. There was one restaurant, a run-down bowling alley, and four taverns. The closest movie theater was in Laurel, forty-five minutes away.

Using this logic, Simon had convinced Skye to join the GUMBs' ladies' auxiliary, the Gumbettes. But no one had warned her about the dark side of the Bettes. No one had told her that almost every member peddled some sort of useless product, which they sold from their homes at high-pressure sales events disguised as parties. And worst of all, no one had even suggested that as soon as she joined the club, her name would be inked in at the top of each and every guest list.

As far as Skye could tell, the other Bettes dabbled at selling—content to have a party once in a while, make a few dollars, and earn the most recent hostess gift—but Barbie appeared to be intent on creating an empire full of her clones, all selling Instant Gourmet.

"No reason to be bashful." Barbie interrupted Skye's thoughts. "Now that you're a Bette, we're all your friends."

Skye wondered about Barbie's definition of friendship. The only things these women seemed to have in common were rich husbands, big houses, and membership in the GUMBs, an organization that wouldn't even give them equal status with the men.

Abruptly, Barbie popped up and grabbed Skye's hand,

dragging her out of her chair. "Come on. We're about to play another game. It's a great way to get to know everyone."

Skye's nose twitched and her eyes watered. Barbie's musky perfume engulfed her, closing her sinuses. She sneezed, then smiled weakly and tried to edge back to her seat. "Maybe I should sit this one out. I had a tiring day at school."

Barbie ignored her words and turned to the other women, announcing, "You all know Skye's the school psychologist in town, right?" She looked back at Skye. "So, whose little darling went berserk today?"

Before Skye could answer, there was a loud crash, and all eyes turned toward the sound. Joy Kessler stood with her hand covering her mouth. Shards of glass and greenish-yellow liquid oozed over the hardwood. The sharp odor of tequila permeated the air.

Joy's gaze briefly met Skye's. The message was clear: *Don't you dare tell about my son.* Skye tipped her head in a half nod. Joy quickly looked away as she knelt and tried to soak up the mess with a napkin, saying, "I'm so sorry. The pitcher just slipped."

Barbie's face went stiff. She whipped the linen napkin out of Joy's hand and hurried into the kitchen. Her irritated walk spoke volumes. She was back in an instant with a mop. Once the floor was restored to its original pristine shine and the mop disposed of, Barbie responded to Joy, who had continued to babble apologies throughout the cleanup.

"No harm done. At least you didn't get any on my Aubusson carpet."

Joy fanned herself with her hand and sank into a chair. "Thank God!"

Barbie turned to Skye with a determined smile. "You were going to tell us about your day."

"Sorry." Skye kept her face neutral. "I can't talk about it." Barbie's lips thinned with irritation, and Skye quickly added, "I'm sure you understand the importance of confidentiality, being married to a doctor and all."

"True, Ken knows everyone's secrets, that's for sure." Barbie preened for a moment, then got back to business. "Okay, ladies, let's play Fashion Designer. There are twenty of us, so split into groups of five. I have wonderful prizes for the winning team."

Skye found herself in her hostess's bedroom with several women she hardly knew. They had been given a partial roll of wallpaper, twelve safety pins, and the instruction to make an outfit using one of them as the fashion model. Skye suddenly realized they were all eyeing her.

"I think it would be easiest to make an outfit for the smallest member of our team," Skye said hastily, trying to get off the hook. Her generous figure was never the smallest in any group.

Hilary Zello, the winner of the jar opener, said, "Oh, no, honey. The object of this game is to make your team's model look the funniest, so we tend to pick . . ." She trailed off, obviously thinking better of what she was about to say. Suddenly her eyes lit up—clearly an idea light bulb had gone on in her head—and she continued, "We tend to pick the newest one to our little circle. Which would be you."

"Thanks, but really, I'd rather not."

"Now, don't be like that, sweetie. It's all in good fun. You aren't an old party pooper, are you?" For someone who appeared to be quiet and pleasant, Hilary was relentless.

Skye shook her head. It crossed her mind that she could be out the bedroom's French doors, across the patio, and in her car before anyone would think to stop her. Of course, that would probably be a major social faux pas.

"Good. Strip to your underwear and stand still."

"Shit!" Skye said underneath her breath. It looked like she was about to be dressed in wallpaper, and it was all Simon's fault. Why had she ever let him talk her into joining the Bettes?

Skye understood only too well the limitations of Scumble River, but the GUMBs and the Gumbettes were not the answers. She sighed and closed her eyes. She was now officially living the life she had tried to run away from.

The day after she had graduated from high school, Skye had fled her hometown. She had managed to stay away for more than a decade, but had finally been forced to come crawling back two and a half years ago after being jilted, getting fired, and maxing out her credit cards. She'd been stuck in Scumble River ever since.

Skye's thoughts were interrupted by a sharp jab in her butt. She jumped and Hilary murmured, "Sorry, angel, the safety pin slipped. We're almost done."

Another minute or two crept by while Skye planned her revenge on Simon, then Hilary said, "Done. Go look in the mirror."

Skye made her way to the gilt and brocade dressing table on the far side of the enormous bedroom. As her reflection came into view she gasped.

Sheets of wallpaper had been secured from her waist to her ankles. Additional pieces were wrapped mummylike around her torso. And the whole thing was topped off with a flowing veil that hung from the crown of her head to her derrière. She looked as if *I Dream of Jeannie* and *The Flying Nun* had been mutated into one TV show, and directed by someone on LSD. *Ridiculous* was too kind a description.

Once again, Skye contemplated fleeing. She could probably make it out of the house without being caught, but her car keys were in her purse, which she had foolishly left in the living room.

Before she could formulate an alternate plan, her team led her out into the living room where she was lined up with the other "models." One wore a paper evening gown, another a maid's uniform, and the third a peignoir set.

Skye cringed. No way could this evening get any worse. The flash of a camera proved her wrong. Whoever had just taken her picture would have to either hand over the film or die.

Back in the bedroom, after the judging was completed, Skye tore off the wallpaper. She had tried to be a good sport. The other women seemed to be enjoying themselves. Even the ones who had been dressed up like Skye had laughed and pranced around as if they were having a great time. What was wrong with her?

She shrugged. This wasn't the time for self-analysis. Right now she had to get dressed, paste a smile on her face, and return to the party.

After putting on her black pants and red twin set, she scanned the area for her shoes. One lay near the side of the bed, but its partner was missing. Skye got on her hands and knees and lifted the dust ruffle.

At first she didn't see anything in the darkness. Finally a glint from the decorative buckle on her loafer caught her eye. It had somehow gotten shoved to the very center underneath the king-size bed. She couldn't reach her shoe from where she was, and she certainly couldn't fit under the bed. There had to be another solution.

Skye thought a minute, then went to the walk-in closet. Wow! Barbie had enough clothes to outfit all of Scumble River and most of the next town over. Unfortunately, they were all on padded satin hangers. Shoot! Now what?

Just as she was about to turn away, she spotted a sheaf of dresses in dry-cleaning bags. She grabbed a wire hanger from one of them and straightened it out.

Back on her knees, Skye shoved the curved end as far as she could, and felt it thud against something solid. She put her head horizontal to the floor and peered into the murky depths. What had she hit?

After several seconds, her eyes focused and she noticed a dark opaque plastic box. The shadows made it nearly invisible. Skye briefly wondered what it contained, but quickly returned to the matter at hand, retrieving her shoe.

Skye thrust the hook toward the errant loafer. Within seconds, she pulled it out. She wrinkled her nose. Phew! Barbie's perfect world obviously did not extend to places guests weren't expected to see. A dust bunny the size of Harvey the rabbit clung to the toe of her shoe. Skye frowned. Since when did she care about how clean others kept their houses? Great, she was starting to think like her mother.

What next? Would she get a sudden urge to wash windows, scrub toilets, and iron clothes? Skye shuddered, pushed that thought away, and continued dressing.

She was dragging a comb through her hair when Hilary burst through the bedroom door. "Hurry. Barbie's about to give out the grand prize."

"Great." Skye forced a false perkiness into her voice. "I'm right behind you." She followed the excited woman into the living room, and joined her on the sofa.

Something smelled delicious. Skye's mouth watered. The odor of onion, cheese, and dill drifted from the front of the room. Barbie stood by a long table covered by a crisp white linen cloth, with platters of food exquisitely arranged across its surface. Silver candelabra and crystal vases of roses completed the picture-perfect display.

"Before I award the grand prize, I'd like you to taste the superb fare you could have each and every day if you sign up for the Instant Gourmet program."

Skye licked her lips, then blinked. Once again, appearance seemed to be more important than substance. The portions were all small enough to have been cooked in an Easy Bake oven. Maybe that was how all these women stayed so thin: they thought two bites constituted dinner.

Barbie's smile was predatory as she continued. "Each dish comes fully prepared. All you need to do is pop it into the microwave for a few minutes. If you buy the entire system, you will not have to grocery shop or plan a menu again.

You pick up your week's worth of meals on Wednesday afternoon, and are set for the next seven days."

Oohs and aahs came from all sides of the room. The guests descended on the food, and there was silence as everyone dug in.

After a few minutes, Barbie announced, "The first three people to sign up for the deluxe package get one week free."

Several women rushed toward her.

Barbie turned to the rest of the crowd. "If you sign up tonight for any program, I will personally give you a ten-percent discount." She paused. "Of course, the best deal is to become a distributor like me. Then you get your own meals at cost."

Skye looked around. Most of the guests were now clutching pens and balancing clipboards on their knees. She noticed that Joy, Lu, and Hilary were helping the others fill out their order forms. They were already part of Barbie's Instant Gourmet army.

Barbie's gaze swept the room and a smug smile lifted a corner of her mouth. "Now for the grand prize." She reached into a basket and pulled out a ticket. She quickly scanned it and announced, "Our winner is . . . Skye Denison. Congratulations! You've won a month's worth of Instant Gourmet food."

As the applause wore down, Barbie said, "Just complete this paperwork."

While Skye filled in the required information, Barbie and the rest of the guests started to drift into the foyer. Goodbyes wafted into the living room as Skye reached the last page of the contract.

Why did they want her credit card number? Wasn't this supposed to be free? She paused and read the small print. Ah, she had to agree to buy a month's worth of food in order to get the free month. Skye chewed the end of the pen. She knew from other parties of this sort that she was expected to make a purchase. But a whole month was too much.

She crossed out the original amount and substituted an order for the trial package—a week of food for one person. Skye winced as she wrote a check for fifty-seven dollars and forty-three cents. This stuff had better be good—at that price she certainly couldn't afford to buy any other groceries.

Okay, she had fulfilled her duties as a guest and bought something, so where was Barbie? Skye listened. It sounded as if her hostess was still in the foyer talking to someone.

Skye put her clipboard with the others, grabbed her purse, and made her way out into the hall. She could hear raised voices, then the sound of a hand striking flesh, and finally a door slamming.

Rounding the corner, Skye saw Barbie holding her cheek and asked, "Are you okay?"

The blonde's hand flew from her face and she forced a short laugh. "Fine. I just bumped into the closet door. I'm such a klutz."

"As long as you're not hurt." Skye knew Barbie was lying, but wasn't sure if she should force the issue. "I guess I'll get going, then. Unless you want to talk." They weren't that kind of friends, and it really wasn't any of Skye's business, but she felt she had to offer Barbie the chance to open up.

Barbie ignored Skye's words. Instead she handed Skye her coat, turned the key in the deadbolt, and opened the front door. Snow gusted against the glass storm door and the wind rattled its hinges.

Skye shot a puzzled glance at the elaborate lock. This was Scumble River, Illinois, not New York City. Why did the Addisons have such a substantial piece of hardware guarding their door?

Catching Skye's look, Barbie explained, "Our insurance company insists we have extra security because of my extensive jewelry collection and the pharmaceuticals that Ken keeps on hand." She pointed to an alarm box. "So we had everything they wanted installed. We just don't turn it on, and we leave the inside key in the deadbolt." She laughed, and echoed Skye's earlier thought. "After all, this *is* Scumble River."

"Right. Nothing exciting happening here." Skye moved toward the door. "I had a nice time," she lied. "Thanks for inviting me."

Barbie stepped closer, and at first Skye thought she was about to tell her the truth about the slap, but Barbie only said, "If you'd like to make some extra money in your free time, you ought to consider selling Instant Gourmet. As a distributor you can really make a killing."

# CHAPTER 2

*Look homeward, Angel . . .*

—Milton

What was a hooker doing on her front step? As a school psychologist whose first job had been in New Orleans, Skye thought she had seen it all. But a woman who looked like this one, showing up at her isolated Illinois river cottage on a snowy Tuesday evening the week before Thanksgiving, definitely made her revise her opinion.

When Skye had moved back to her hometown, she had fully expected to live a very quiet life—after all, Scumble River was barely a dot on the map. And although several past events had already proved her wrong, a trollop on her porch was a spectacle she hadn't anticipated.

Bingo, Skye's black cat, rubbed against her ankles as she took another look out the window. The woman's obviously dyed hair tumbled in scarlet ringlets from beneath a white Stetson. A fringed miniskirt barely covered her essentials, and there was a vast expanse between its hem and the red vinyl, high-heeled cowboy boots that had not been designed to wear in a Midwestern blizzard.

Skye spoke to the feline. "I should pretend not to be home."

The cat regarded her with bright golden eyes, but offered no opinion.

Another round of pounding pushed Skye's curiosity quotient over the top, and she impulsively flipped on the outside light while opening her front door a few inches. Being nosy but not stupid, she kept the safety chain firmly in place. "Yes?"

The woman blinked a couple of times, probably surprised by the sudden brightness, then smiled widely. "You Skye Denison?"

Skye nodded, wondering if she should have denied the identification.

"Hi there, honey. My name's Bunny. I'm your Simon's mother."

Skye was sure there was some mistake. "Simon Reid, who owns the funeral home and is the coroner?" This trashy-looking woman couldn't be Simon's mother. He was one of the classiest men she had ever met, while this female was decidedly at the other end of the well-bred scale. Besides, she was sure Simon had said that his mother had died when he was fourteen. This woman didn't look dead—rode hard and put away wet, yes, but not dead.

"Yep, that's Sonny Boy."

Skye stood in silent disbelief until a sharp wind blew a plume of snowflakes into her face. Bingo's sharp yowl, the needles of ice, and the redhead's shivers all worked to snap her into focus. She unchained the door and swung it open.

Bunny adjusted the tote bag on her shoulder, then twisted and bent over, hoisting a large worn suitcase off the sidewalk behind her. Skye narrowed her eyes, but the older woman seemed not to notice as she maneuvered her luggage into the cottage and dropped it on the foyer's hardwood floor. Melting snow immediately formed a puddle.

Without stopping, Bunny strolled into the living room, a

wave of stale cigarette smoke and alcohol fumes drifting after her. She shed her fuchsia fake fur jacket and dropped it on the floor before settling on the sofa. Skye followed her and perched on one of the two director's chairs that faced the couch.

Bingo padded in after them and began sniffing the older woman's ankles. She reached down to pet him, but he moved a few inches out of her reach, his expression none too happy—he didn't like anything, or anyone, new coming into the house. Bunny sighed and sat back, saying, "I love kitties. Mine passed away a few months ago, and I miss her so much."

"I'm sorry to hear that. It's really hard to lose a pet." Skye commiserated, then paused, not exactly sure where to go from there. Finally, she said, trying to regain control of the situation, "So, Mrs. Reid, is Simon expecting you?"

"Call me Bunny." The redhead's attention was focused on a small hand mirror she had dug out of her purse as soon as she sat down. "What? No."

"Wasn't he home when you called him? Did you leave a message saying you were coming here?"

"No. Not exactly."

"So, we should call him, then." Skye felt as if she were talking to someone who hadn't quite mastered the English language. "Let him know you're here."

"No. Later." Bunny finished fixing her hair, and moved on to applying lipstick.

Skye waited for Bunny to explain. When she remained silent, Skye said, "Mrs. Reid, I'm afraid I don't understand. It almost seems like you don't want me to call your son."

"Bunny, my name's Bunny. You're making me feel old with that Mrs. Reid stuff."

"Bunny, why don't you want me to call Simon?"

"It's sort of a long story."

"I have a feeling you'd better take the time to tell it."

"Well, I tried to check into the local motel." Bunny

briefly looked away from her image. "Charlie, the nice man at the Up A Lazy River Motor Court, was so upset he didn't have a cabin for me. Said a lot of people had checked in at the last minute. Because of the weather being so bad and all, they were afraid to keep driving."

"I see." Skye had no idea what this had to do with her or why she couldn't call Simon.

"So Charlie said you wouldn't mind putting me up for a few nights—just until he gets an opening."

"My Uncle Charlie sent you?" Skye was getting more and more confused. Why had her godfather sent this strange woman to stay with her? And why wasn't she staying with her own son?

"Yes, he was ever so sweet." Bunny rummaged around in her purse, then looked up. "Damn, my gold compact is missing. I wonder what happened to it?"

Skye wouldn't be distracted by lost makeup. "But I still don't understand why we aren't calling Simon."

"Hey, could I use your little girls' room? I gotta tap a kidney pretty quick."

"Sure, it's off the foyer." Skye gestured the way they had come. Bingo, startled by her sudden movement, ran into the bedroom. He would probably spend the rest of the night hiding in his favorite spot under the bed. Too bad she couldn't join him.

Bunny jumped up, grabbed her purse, and scurried toward the foyer. She stopped before entering and said, "Boy, a cup of joe would sure hit the spot."

Skye sighed. It was hard for anyone raised in the rural Midwest to turn down a request for refreshments, even from an unwanted, uninvited visitor who was already making herself too much at home.

By the time Bunny emerged from the bathroom, Skye was back in the living room. A tray with a thermos, cups, sugar and creamer, spoons, napkins, and cookies waited on the coffee table.

After pouring for Bunny, Skye continued to lean forward. "So, how about we give Simon a call now?"

"That's not a good idea."

"Why?"

"Well, he's not really expecting me." Bunny's gaze was fastened to her cup, as if she could read the coffee grounds like tea leaves.

"All the more reason to call before it gets too late. This way, he has time to get a room ready for you." Skye hadn't been a school psychologist for several years without learning how to keep reluctant teens going in her preferred direction. Somehow, despite her age, Bunny seemed to fit the adolescent category.

"The truth is I need to sort of gradually let Sonny Boy know I'm in town." Bunny fluttered her false eyelashes at Skye. "I'm sure you understand. Sometimes a woman has to help a man into right thinking."

"Right thinking?" Skye did not like the way this was sounding. "What does Simon need to be helped into right thinking about? Is there a problem?"

"Maybe a teeny little one." Bunny selected a cookie and took a dainty nibble. "These are yummy. Homemade, right?"

"My mother made them. They're chocolate-topped shortbread." Skye answered automatically. "What's the teeny problem?"

"Well, it's been a long time since I've seen Sonny."

"Uh huh."

"And, to tell the truth, we didn't part on the best of terms last time."

"Okay."

"So I sort of need to ease into seeing him. Maybe run into him somewhere." Bunny's pink tongue darted out and licked the icing from the cookie she was holding.

"I see." Skye didn't see at all. "Are you from around

here? I mean, would it be natural to just bump into him at a store or something?"

"Yes . . . no . . . I was born in Laurel, but I blew that Pop-sicle stand the minute I turned eighteen," Bunny said, a far-away look in her eyes. "I didn't care where I ended up, as long as it was some place where a traffic jam wasn't con-sidered ten cars waiting to pass a tractor."

Laurel, the county capital, was the largest of Scumble River's neighboring towns. "But Simon grew up in the city, didn't he?" Skye felt as if she were trying to take a social history from an unwilling parent. "So you ended up in Chicago?"

Bunny shrugged. "I lived there a while. I've lived lots of places."

That explained the way she mixed idioms in her speech. "Most recently, where?"

"Las Vegas." Bunny looked relieved. "I lived there for the past twenty years."

"Let's see if I have this straight. You're Simon's mother, but you haven't seen him in a while. You grew up around here, but haven't lived here in years." Skye waited for Bunny's nod. "Okay, then, what brings you here now?"

"Thanksgiving, of course. I always told him I'd be home for the holidays."

"You just didn't say which ones, right?" Skye muttered under her breath. No way was this woman telling the whole truth. Should she pursue that avenue, or move on to why Bunny was at her house? Self-defense won. "There's still something I don't understand." Bunny stiffened, but relaxed as Skye continued, "Why did Uncle Charlie send you here?"

"Why, honey, because he figured since I'm going to be your mother-in-law, you wouldn't mind me bunking in with you for a few days." Bunny grinned. "A chance for you to get on my good side, so to speak."

Mother-in-law! Had Charlie lost his mind? Skye knew that both he and her own mother, May, desperately wanted her to get married. And they both thought Simon would nicely fit the role of husband. But if they were telling people that she and Simon were engaged, she would have to kill them. Any jury of her peers—her peers being single females over thirty with interfering families—would never find her guilty.

Skye refocused on the woman sitting across from her. Bunny's face held a bright, expectant look. Skye tried to come up with something tactful to say. Instead she blurted out, "Simon and I are not engaged."

Bunny leaned forward and patted her hand. "Oh, I know it's a secret. But Charlie said when he found out you and Sonny had spent the weekend in Chicago together, he knew you'd be making the announcement soon." Bunny reached for another cookie. "Don't you worry. I'm sure Sonny Boy will make an honest woman of you before too long."

Skye's head was pounding, and she felt the area under her right eye start to twitch. "I'm really sorry, Mrs. Reid, but Uncle Charlie was wrong. Wishful thinking on his part, understand?"

"If you don't want to call me Bunny, you could call me Mom, but I told you, cut the Mrs. Reid crap."

Skye had a brief vision of calling this woman Mom, and how well her own mother would react to that. "Mrs. . . . . Bunny, look, I'm really not your future daughter-in-law, and we really ought to call Simon."

The redhead shrugged, her suspiciously firm breasts hardly moving. "If you want to keep it a secret, I understand, but couldn't you just let me stay with you for a night or two without calling Sonny?"

"I'm sorry, it just doesn't feel right to keep this from Simon." Skye always got into trouble whenever she tried to keep secrets from the men in her life.

"But . . ."

Skye watched the other woman's face crumple, and hurried to continue. "And, you know, I don't even have a guest room. There's just this room, the kitchen, and my bedroom. There's nowhere for you to sleep."

Bunny bounced up and down a couple of times on the sofa. "Honey, this little old couch will do me just fine."

"But Simon has a really nice guest room, with a queen-size bed and everything."

Bunny raised an eyebrow. "And how do you know that, Missy, if you and him aren't getting married?"

Even though Skye suspected that Bunny, of all people, had no right to question where anyone else slept, she felt herself blushing and stammered, "He showed it to me once. I didn't stay there or anything."

The sly grin that appeared on the redhead's face confirmed Skye's thought.

"Anyway, I have to call Simon. I'm sorry."

Bunny trailed Skye into the kitchen, and sighed as Skye punched his number into the telephone. After four rings Simon's voice answered. "I'm not available at this time. Please leave a message after the tone." She tried the funeral home number and his cell phone, and got similar announcements. She told all the machines to have Simon call her, but didn't say why. It was too confusing to explain in a short message.

"Looks like Simon's not home yet," Skye said, looking at the clock. Only seven. It seemed later. "When I talked to him yesterday, he said something about a meeting in Chicago. He must not be back yet."

"Sure. I know Sonny would never cheat on you, honey."

Skye opened her mouth, but shut it without speaking. What was the use? She had learned quickly that Bunny heard only what Bunny wanted to hear. Instead she asked, "Did you have supper? Are you hungry?"

"A little. I had a big lunch, but I could go for something light." The older woman patted her flat stomach. "Gotta watch my figure, or no one else will."

Skye frowned. Was that an insult? For most of her life,

she had starved herself on less than eight hundred calories a day and managed to keep her weight within society's expectations, but a few years ago she had decided to get off the diet roller coaster. Now she ate sensibly, exercised, and accepted the fact that she would never make the cover of *Cosmopolitan*.

Usually she was okay with her more curvaceous appearance, but occasionally someone would say something, and it would throw her self-esteem off balance for a moment or two. "Bunny, I'm sure you didn't mean to imply that no one could be attractive if they weren't a size six, right?"

The older woman looked at Skye, her eyes widening. "Oh, no, honey. You're a beautiful girl. Those emerald eyes and that long curly chestnut hair probably have men panting on your steps all the time. I'm sure those extra pounds don't make a bit a difference for you."

"Thank you, but my goal in life isn't to have men panting at my door. I'm perfectly happy on my own. I don't need a man to make my life complete."

"That's sure different from my day. But then, everything is different from when I was young." Bunny's voice grew nostalgic. "In the sixties, we took acid to make the world weirder. Now the world is weirder than we can handle, and we take Prozac to make it normal." She was silent a second, then shook her head and straightened her shoulders. "Oh, I forgot to tell you, something's wrong with your toilet."

"What?" Skye wondered if this was Bunny's way of changing the subject.

"It didn't seem to want to flush, and now I can still hear it running."

Skye cocked her head. Yes, she could hear it, too. She rushed toward the bathroom. What in the world had Bunny done to it? It had always worked okay until now.

Flinging open the door, Skye was just in time to see the water in the bowl start to overflow. She leaped to jiggle the handle, but the water kept rising.

She pushed Bunny aside and ran for the plunger, which was stowed in the bathroom off her bedroom. Returning, she again had to push the older woman out of the way. Why was Bunny so fascinated with a plumbing problem? Could she have flushed something she didn't want Skye to see?

The ringing of the telephone momentarily stopped Skye's efforts to unblock the toilet, but she quickly resumed plunging and said to Bunny, "Could you get that?"

The redhead paused and listened as the phone rang for the second time, then shook her head. "It might be Sonny."

"For crying out loud." Skye thrust the plunger's wooden handle at Bunny. "Then you use this, while I answer it."

Bunny backed away as if Skye had tried to hand her a pile of poop. "Ew, no way."

The phone rang for the third time.

"Fine." What was a little more water? The bathroom floor already looked like Lake Michigan. Skye tried to edge past Bunny who had resumed her position in the doorway.

The phone rang for a fourth time and the answering machine picked up.

Skye could hear Simon start to talk. "Hi, I got your message. Where are you?"

Missing this phone call was not an option. She pushed at Bunny, who now seemed to be deliberately blocking her way. The two women struggled, the plunger held horizontally between them like some sort of jousting pole.

Simon continued, "I'm stuck in Chicago. I'm going to check in to a hotel. The snow has closed down most of the roads, and I don't want to chance trying to drive home." There was a high-pitched beep, then he said, "Damn, the battery on my cell phone is dying."

With a mighty shove, Skye finally managed to move Bunny and raced toward the phone. She was just in time to hear "I'll talk to you tomorrow. Bye."

Bunny had followed her into the kitchen and cooed, "Oh, you missed Sonny. That's too bad."

Skye gritted her teeth.

Bunny widened her eyes and twisted a strand of hair around her finger. "Guess that means I'm staying here tonight."

Skye took a deep breath. "I guess so."

"So, when do you think you'll get my bathroom cleaned up?"

"How about never?" Skye muttered as she left Bunny standing in the kitchen. "Is never good for you?"

# CHAPTER 3

*Man shall not live by bread alone.*

—New Testament

"A choo! Achoo! Achoo!" Without lifting her head from the pillow, Skye grabbed a tissue from the nightstand and blew her nose.

"God bless you," a voice called.

She sat up. When had Bingo learned to talk? Oh. She sank back down on the mattress and pulled the covers over her head. She had forgotten her houseguest. What in the world would she do with Bunny?

She'd think about that later. According to the clock, she had fifteen minutes before she had to get up for work. Closing her eyes, Skye made her mind go blank.

After what seemed like seconds later, her radio alarm clicked on and the announcer said, "It's six o'clock on a snowy Wednesday morning. Most roads are impassable. The following schools are closed . . ."

Skye listened intently.

Half a dozen names into the list the DJ said the magic

words, "Scumble River Elementary, Junior, and Senior High Schools."

Technically, if her district was closed, Skye should have received a phone call, but she was on the very bottom of the phone tree, so it came as no surprise to hear the news from WJOL first.

Skye switched off the radio and snuggled back under the covers. A bout of sneezing woke her up a half hour later. Her head was completely stuffed up and her throat hurt. Wonderful. She would spend her day off sick in bed.

"You really ought to take something for that." Bunny's voice blasted through Skye's closed bedroom door. "Then we could both get our beauty sleep. Time may be a great healer, but it's a lousy beautician." It was obvious that Bunny would not be an easy houseguest.

Skye reluctantly got up and shuffled into the connecting bath. She mounted the two steps leading up to the oversize soaking tub, turned on the faucet, and poured in some foaming oil.

Although she loved everything about her little cottage—the unusual octagonal shape, the deck reaching from the left of the front door, around the side, and all along the back, and the small center cupola that acted as a skylight—in many ways, the master bathroom was her favorite part.

As the tub filled, she crossed to the medicine cabinet and took out a box of cold tablets. She popped two pills from the blister pack, ran a glass of water, and swallowed the green capsules. Oops! Skye squinted. The directions said for nighttime use only. Oh, well, she was just going to lie around all day anyway.

After stripping off her pajamas and putting them into the hamper, Skye climbed into the bathtub. An oval window was set high on the wall, positioned so the tub's occupant could lie back and look outside. This morning the only thing to see was snow pelting the glass.

She settled back, adjusted the foam neck pillow, and let

her eyes drift shut. She was dreaming of the beach when she first became aware of the cacophony of noises—the phone was ringing, Bingo was yowling, and Bunny was cursing. What the heck was going on?

Skye reluctantly emerged from the soothing water, toweled dry, donned her robe, and braced herself to face whatever chaos had erupted on the other side of her bedroom door. As she stepped over the threshold and got her first good look, she groaned.

Bunny had certainly made herself at home. Clothes and makeup were everywhere. Red satin bikini panties and a matching bra were draped over a lamp, hand lotion oozed out of its bottle onto the coffee table, and Bingo was wrapped in what looked like a lime-green marabou boa.

Skye leaned against the wall. Her head was spinning, and she wasn't sure what was causing her dizziness—the mess or the cold medicine. She could hear Bunny's voice from the kitchen. Who was the woman talking to? It had better be a hotel reservation clerk.

Bingo freed himself from the feathers and rubbed against Skye's leg. She scooped him up and he started to purr. "Are you hungry?"

The purring grew louder, and she carried the cat into the kitchen, where an odor of burnt toast greeted her.

Bunny waved as Skye entered and put her hand over the receiver. "I'll just be a minute." Stretching the cord to its maximum length, she disappeared around the corner into the foyer and lowered her voice.

Skye fed Bingo, then filled the teakettle and put it on the stove to heat. Bunny had done a number on the kitchen, too—unwashed dishes filled the sink, a pool of coffee spread over the counter, and the table was littered with the remains of breakfast. As Skye waited for the water to boil, she began to clean up.

Bunny materialized from the foyer just as the last spoon was washed and put into the draining rack. She pointed to the dishes. "I was going to wash them as soon as I finished my phone call."

Nodding, Skye asked, "Any luck?"

Bunny looked confused. "What?"

"Did you find a room?"

"Oh, no . . . ah . . . all the hotels are still full. The snow and all."

Both women looked out the window. The snow had stopped falling, and the sun was out.

"You can try later today," Skye said. "It looks as if the plows will start opening the roads soon."

"Right, or maybe tomorrow." Bunny didn't meet Skye's gaze. "Ah, hey, guess I'll go take a shower." She had already turned to go when she said over her shoulder, "Your mom's left three or four messages on your machine. You'd better call her back. She sounded kind of cranky the last time."

Skye played back her mother's messages. The first one was: "Skye, this is Mom. Pick up the phone."

The next one said, "Skye, where are you? I hope you haven't been in an accident. It's snowing out."

For the last one, May's words had become intensified. "Skye, if you're lying dead somewhere, I'll kill you. Call me right now."

Skye scooped up the receiver and dialed. Her mom answered before the first ring was completed.

"Hi, Mom. I'm fine."

"You don't sound fine. You're sick, aren't you? Did you drive into a ditch and have to walk home?"

"No, I've just got a little cold."

May sighed. "Why weren't you answering your phone? Did you have a fight with Simon?"

"No, I was in the bathtub."

"For two hours? I've been calling since six-thirty."

"Sorry. I had my bedroom door closed and the humidifier going. I couldn't hear the phone." Skye tried to divert her mother. "Are you working today?" May was a dispatcher for the local police department.

"No, thank goodness. I'll bet the station is flooded with car accident calls. I'm just glad you're home safe and sound. With the schools closed, you can have a nice quiet day."

Skye thought of Bunny and wondered about the accuracy of her mother's last statement. "Why were you trying to get me?"

"Your father's out with the tractor plowing the family's driveways. He should be back soon. I'll send him over in the pickup if you need to go to the store or anything. You shouldn't drive your car on these roads."

Skye drove a '57 Chevy Bel Air. It was huge and not designed for icy streets. "Thanks, Mom. I do need to get a few things." She didn't mention her houseguest, as she wasn't sure what May's reaction to Bunny would be.

"You go get ready, then. Dad should be there in half an hour or so."

Jed's old blue truck rattled to a stop in Skye's driveway. Knowing her dad's opinion about being kept waiting, she was ready for his arrival and ran out of the door before he could cut the engine. She hopped in, buckled the seat belt, and said, "Good morning."

Chocolate, her father's Labrador retriever, wagged his tail and licked her face. She scratched him behind the ears. The aroma of wet dog filled the cab.

"Morning," Jed mumbled as he put the vehicle in reverse. "Where to?"

"Walter's." Skye named the closest grocery store.

As they pulled away, she realized that the only car in the driveway was her own. How had Bunny arrived? Skye lived more than a mile from town. Surely, the older woman hadn't walked to her cottage in the middle of the snowstorm.

A wave of dizziness pushed the question of her houseguest's transportation from Skye's thoughts. She laid her head on the back of the seat and closed her eyes for a second. Woo. That cold medicine must be strong. Her head was swimming, and she felt as if she might pass out. Not wanting her father to notice and tell her mom, she made small talk. "Did you get everyone's driveway cleared?"

"Yep." Jed's steel-gray crew cut was hidden by a bright orange cap with the earflaps folded up. His jacket was open, revealing a red plaid flannel shirt, and his hands were bare. No Scumble River man ever buttoned a coat or put on a pair of gloves until the mercury stayed below the zero mark on the barn thermometer for at least a week.

Jed's faded brown eyes squinted as he gazed out the windshield. Only citified wimps wore sunglasses. He had a summer face—tanned and leathery—which looked out of place in contrast to the snowy landscape.

Skye took a deep breath. Good, the wooziness was passing. "What's the temperature?" She tightened the wool scarf she had wound around her throat, and adjusted her earmuffs.

"Radio said it was hovering around the mid-twenties."

"That's too cold for November." She put her gloved hands to the truck's heating vent. "If this keeps up, we're all going to freeze come January."

"Can't do nothing about the weather."

Skye shot him a look. "That's not what you say in July when the crops need rain."

Jed and Skye rode in silence past mountains of snow and ice-encrusted trees. A few hardy souls were out with shovels and blowers, but most of the houses they passed were silent, the snow surrounding them pristine, untouched by footprints.

"Dad."

"Yeah?"

"I want to get a basic set of tools so I can fix little things around the cottage. What should I get?" Skye asked, thinking about last night's toilet emergency.

"You only need two tools—WD-40 and duct tape. If it

doesn't move and it should, use the WD-40. If it moves and shouldn't, use the duct tape. Anything more complicated than that, call me."

Skye rolled her eyes. Her father's view of women was somewhat antiquated. As Jed turned right on Basin Street, Skye glanced to the left. The downtown area looked cleansed by the whiteness. The spire of St. Francis Catholic Church seemed to float above the commercial buildings. And the businesses themselves sparkled as if dusted with a teenager's glitter powder.

They pulled into the grocery store parking lot. Cars were everywhere. Skye didn't see one open space.

Jed grunted, "I'll drop you off and wait in the truck. Don't take too long."

Skye unbuckled her seat belt and jumped out as soon as her father coasted to a stop in front of the entrance. She paused. Oh, that had been a mistake. The sudden movement made her feel light-headed again. Once the world stopped spinning, she hurried inside and halted abruptly. Where was the line of shiny steel shopping carts that usually occupied the space between the door and the checkout stand?

As she moved farther into the store, her question was answered. The aisles were wall-to-wall people, and they were snatching items from the shelves as if their very survival depended on seizing the last roll of toilet paper.

What had gotten into everyone? Skye spotted her cousin Gillian fighting with some Jabba the Hutt look-alike over a loaf of bread. As she watched, they tugged at opposite ends until the plastic split and slices flew all over.

The man quickly gathered them up, shoved them into his cart, and snarled, "Who lit the fuse on your tampon?"

Gillian burst into tears and screamed, "Pregnant women don't use tampons, you idiot." She was a tiny blonde with big blue eyes, wearing a yellow maternity top with ruffles running down the sleeves and matching stretch pants.

Skye rushed to her cousin's side and put her arms around her. "What's going on?"

Gillian sagged against Skye and sobbed, "That monster stole the bread right from my hand."

Skye tried to soothe her cousin. "That's awful. If brains were chocolate, he wouldn't have enough to fill an M&M."

Gillian sniffled. "Go say something to him."

"That's not a good idea." Skye attempted a little humor. "After all, I can't have a battle of wits with an unarmed man." She patted her cousin's shoulder. "Besides, the store will get more bread tomorrow."

"But Irvin wants French toast for lunch today." Gillian hiccupped. "And they're predicting more snow. We might not get more food for days."

Skye bit her lip. She was getting along better with her cousins than she had since she was a teenager, which meant she couldn't tell Gillian what Irvin could do with his yen for French toast. Instead she said, "Well, let's see what's left."

The two women turned to face the nearly empty shelves. Skye, being close to seven inches taller than her cousin's five-foot height, spotted a package of hamburger buns shoved to the back of the top shelf. She snagged it and put it into Gillian's cart.

"What am I supposed to do with that?" Gillian frowned.

"Use it in my mom's recipe for Puffy French Toast. It'll work fine."

"Irvin doesn't like me to try new recipes."

Skye counted to ten. "Okay, I'll take the buns. Why don't you call your mom or my mom or your sister and see if one of them has any bread in the freezer?"

"Hey, that's a good idea. Mom always keeps a couple of emergency loafs."

Skye gave Gillian a quick hug. "You okay now?"

The blonde nodded.

"I've got to run. Dad's waiting in the truck." As Skye made her way through the store, she managed to scoop up a few items, but tempers were short. She didn't feel well enough to fight for food, so she gave up and headed toward the front to pay for what she had. When she joined the checkout line, she heard more raised voices.

"What do you mean, I can't write a check? I've been writing checks here for ten years." The speaker was Theresa Dugan, a well-dressed, attractive woman in her early thirties.

Theresa was a teacher at the elementary school, and Skye and Simon were on a bowling team with her and her husband on Friday nights.

The cashier's face was impassive. "Sorry. Walter said cash only today."

"Then I'd like to speak to Walter, please." Theresa's voice was pleasant but firm.

"Sorry, he's not available." The teenager behind the register popped her gum.

"Hey, lady, either pay or get out of the way." The same man who had stolen Gillian's bread was in line between Skye and Theresa. He looked familiar, but Skye couldn't remember where she had seen him before today. He said to the cashier, "I've got cash, and I'll take her stuff."

Skye rapidly counted the money in her wallet. She had forty-two dollars, more cash than usual. She took a quick total of her own meager purchases; they should run about fifteen dollars.

"Theresa." Skye raised her voice over the man bellowing in front of her. "Would twenty-seven dollars help?"

The woman turned toward Skye with a puzzled look in her brown eyes. "Oh, Skye, I didn't see you there," Theresa apologized. "Are you sure, about the money I mean? That, along with what I have, should just about cover it. I'll pay you back Friday."

"Sure, no problem." Skye handed the bills to her.

The man swore, and shot Skye a malevolent glare.

After Jabba the Hutt checked out and Skye was paying

for her groceries, she said to the checker, "Do you know who that guy was that just left?"

The teen popped another bubble. "Yeah, that's Nathan's dad."

"Nathan who?"

"Nathan Turner."

Ah. Now Skye remembered where she'd seen him before. He was a member of the GUMBs. Although he didn't hang out with the same group she and Simon did, she had heard his name mentioned and seen him at an official meeting or two.

Jed was listening to the radio and petting Chocolate when Skye climbed back into the pickup. She looked at her watch. It was almost ten-thirty. "Sorry I took so long. The store was mobbed. Did you see Gillian?"

"Yep." Jed put the truck in gear. "Any place else?"

Skye was about to say no—she really didn't feel very well, sort of fuzzy and not able to think straight—when she remembered it was Wednesday. "Well, if you have time, I am supposed to pick up my Instant Gourmet order at Barbie Addison's today."

"Where's she live?"

"You know those big houses south of here after the curve?"

"By the cemetery?"

"Right. Barbie's is the biggest one."

"Okay." Jed turned left.

"Dad, do you know a Mr. Turner?"

"Big guy?"

Skye nodded. "He resembles one of the less attractive mountains."

"That'd be Nate Turner. He owns Turner Landscaping." Jed looked at her. "Why?"

"He was being a jerk at the grocery store."

"Yep, that's him. He's a couple of hubcaps short of a

Buick." Jed shook his head. "Stay away from him. He's a mean son of a—"

The rest of Jed's comment was drowned out by a snow-plow rumbling past them in the opposite lane.

Skye pointed. "There, on the left. That's the Addisons'."

As her father guided the truck down the long driveway, Skye viewed the house with fresh eyes. She'd been inside on two or three occasions to play bridge or attend a party, but she had always arrived at night, and the sheer size of the place hadn't been as noticeable in the dark.

In the stark sunlight, the enormous brown multilevel house looked liked an airplane hangar. It was easily six thousand square feet, and that was without the three-car, double-width garage that was bigger than Skye's cottage.

"I'll only be a minute. I've already paid, so Barbie just has to hand me the package," Skye said to her dad as she slid out of the truck cab.

She walked past the two vehicles already parked in the driveway and up the front steps. Twin evergreen wreaths with shiny gold bows hung on the Addisons' big double front doors. Barbie was obviously getting a jump on her Christmas decorating—she was well-known for the extravagant displays she put out for every holiday.

Skye rang the bell and waited. No answer. She rang it again and once more. Still no response. Swell. Barbie must not be home. She was turning to leave when she saw a small engraved brass sign that read: INSTANT GOURMET PICKUPS IN REAR.

The drive and front steps had been cleared, but the sidewalk leading around back hadn't. There was a single set of footprints marring the snow, and Skye tried to walk in them to avoid getting her new leather boots wet.

Winter had come early to Scumble River. They'd had frost in early October, sleet on Veterans Day, and it looked as if it would be a white Thanksgiving.

Unlike her mother, who adored snow, Skye was not a fan

of the white stuff. She did not like anything that got in her way, made her late, or ruined her expensive shoes.

Today was a good example. What a waste of time. And despite what scientists said, she was convinced that snow, not germs, caused head colds.

As Skye followed the footprints to the garage's side door, she noticed that the Addisons' backyard looked like a Christmas card, and the air smelled of pine and chimney smoke.

She knocked, and watched as the door swung inward. It obviously had not been latched. She could hear "Jingle Bells" playing and called out, "Barbie."

Nothing.

She tried again. "Barbie, it's Skye Denison. I'm here to pick up my order."

There was no answer. Skye stepped through the door. It felt as if she had entered a maze made out of cardboard boxes. The entire three-car garage was stacked with bins, crates, and cartons as far as Skye could see. Calling Barbie's name, she followed the narrow path that appeared to lead toward the back.

As Skye navigated the labyrinth, she read the various labels —cheddar broccoli soup, garlic mashed potatoes, lemon pepper penne rigate, Caesar pasta salad. These were all side dishes. Where were the main courses kept? She rounded a corner created by cases of vanilla almond oat cereal and stopped.

She had come to a clearing. Three chest-style freezers were lined up against the wall that the garage shared with the house. That must be where the entrees were stored.

A row of long tables held open cartons of food arranged assembly-line fashion down the center. On one end, stacks of round boxes covered in glossy apricot paper were empty, ready to be packed with the Instant Gourmet meals. The other end held the lids, three-foot lengths of peach wire-edged ribbon, and big fluffy bows. The finished products were piled on a round table off to the side. Skye shook her head. No wonder this stuff was so expensive. The packaging probably cost more than the food.

She scanned the area. Where was Barbie? Skye could still hear music, and the door leading from the garage to the house was open. Maybe she had gone inside while Skye was walking from the front door to the garage.

As Skye moved forward, she noticed an alcove off to the side containing a desk and filing cabinet. Drawers hung open and papers littered the floor. Something was starting to feel wrong.

Beads of sweat popped out on her upper lip and forehead. Why was it so hot? Should she leave and get her order some other time? No. She wanted to get this over with—her cold was getting worse by the minute, and she didn't want to have to come back.

Hesitantly, Skye climbed the three stairs leading into the utility room. The sound of the washing machine ending the spin cycle and turning off startled Skye. There was still no sign of Barbie. Surely she wouldn't have left in the middle of doing laundry. "Barbie, are you here? It's Skye Denison."

Skye entered the kitchen. On her left was a breakfast nook. To the right, a row of cabinets formed a peninsula dividing the area and blocking her view. As she edged past the counter, she could see the section of the room previously concealed. The cupboard doors stood gaping. Dishes and glasses were shattered on the linoleum, and food was smeared on the counters.

In the midst of this mess, a large male body lay on its stomach in the middle of the floor.

# CHAPTER 4

*. . . fools rush in where angels fear to tread.*

—Pope

Skye ran over and crouched down. "Dr. Addison, Ken, are you alright?"

There was no answer or movement. She put her fingers to his neck to check for a pulse. Instead of skin, her hand encountered a stiff, slippery material. A piece of peach ribbon was knotted tightly around his throat.

She had to get it off. She tried to slip her fingers underneath, but it was tied so firmly that the wire edges were cutting into his neck. Scissors, she needed a pair of scissors. Where would Barbie keep scissors?

A knife. There were plenty of them scattered around from the emptied drawers. Skye grabbed one and tried to slide the blade between the ribbon and his throat, but it was immediately evident she wouldn't be able to do it without slicing into his flesh.

With the ribbon wound so tightly, could he still be alive? Clamping her fingers around his wrist, she tried to find a pulse. Nothing. His hand flapped limply as she laid it by his

side. It had a bluish tinge. She finally took a good look at
him. His skin was purplish, with a waxy overtone, his lips
were pale, and his eyes had a curiously flat appearance. He
was dead.

She wished she could think straight. Should she turn him
over? He was such a big man she wasn't sure she'd be
able to budge him. Besides, she shouldn't disturb the crime
scene. A phone. She had to call the police. Frantically, she
looked around. The receiver was missing from the kitchen's
wall unit. She rushed into the adjoining den.

This room had also been ransacked. Sofa cushions were
sliced open and stuffing was spilling out; chairs were up-
ended, their bottoms slashed; and pictures were torn off the
walls, their glass smashed. Either the killer was in a rage or
looking for something. Maybe both.

The killer. What if he were still here? She had to get out
of the house. The front door was closest. She ran past the
curving stairway, through the hall, and into the foyer. The
inside key Barbie said was always kept in the deadbolt was
missing. Had the murderer taken it and locked the door from
the outside as he left?

Skye hoped that was what had happened, because she
wasn't getting out this way, and since it now looked like she
had to retrace her path and go out the garage, she didn't want
to run into the murderer. She started back toward the den,
but had only made it to the staircase when she heard the thud
of heavy footsteps. Which way were they coming from? She
couldn't tell. Skye took a deep breath and tried to think.
Should she hide, try to get out a window, find a weapon?

All three, she concluded. If she could make her way to
the kitchen, she could grab a knife, see if the French doors
would open, and, if not, hide among the cartons in the
garage. But what if that was where the killer was?

She had to make a decision. Better to go down fighting
than stand there and make it easy for the murderer. She tip-
toed over to the foyer's dining room entrance and peered

around the corner. It was empty. She slipped in, eased the pocket door closed, and darted across the room, pausing at the door to the kitchen, which was slightly ajar.

She could no longer hear the footsteps—or anything else, for that matter. Had the killer left the house? Just as she started to push open the door a hand wrapped around the edge. Without thinking, she yanked the door shut. A grunt of pain rang through the wood.

Great. She had just pissed off the killer. Now what should she do? She needed another way out. Monday night, when she had been forced to change clothes in the master bedroom for the Fashion Designer game, she had noticed French doors leading to a backyard patio.

Skye bolted back across the dining room and flung open the pocket door. As she ran into the foyer, she slammed into something solid and unyielding, then felt a blow to her head and crumpled to the wooden floor.

Everything was dark. What had happened? Shit! The killer must have hit her. Was he standing over her right now ready to plunge a knife through her heart?

Her eyelids flew open. Sprawled opposite her was her father. Without speaking, Jed struggled to his feet, grabbed Skye by the arm, and jerked her upright. Silently, he pulled her through the den, kitchen, and utility room.

As they entered the garage, Skye stopped. Her head was spinning, and she thought she might throw up. "Dad, wait, I need a minute."

Jed kept his grip on her arm. "First get to the truck."

"Just a second." Skye freed herself from her father's grasp and leaned back against one of the freezers. She put both hands on her thighs and dropped her head between her arms.

"We gotta go."

He was right. Skye took a deep breath and put her palm on the freezer to help her stand upright. What? Instead of the cool metal she felt . . . oh, my God, it was hair. She leaped away from the appliance, then reluctantly looked back. Yes, she could see a sheaf of blond tresses caught between the top and the chest.

"Dad." Her voice broke. "Come over here a minute."

Jed grumbled as he joined her. "Yeah?"

Skye pointed to the hair, and he sucked in his breath. She put her fingertips under the lip of the lid and started to lift.

"Don't," Jed said.

But it was too late. The lid opened with a whoosh and Barbie Addison's face loomed into view. A peach ribbon was wound tightly around her neck. She looked like a gift-wrapped doll.

Skye snatched Barbie's wrist. No pulse. She put the back of her hand to Barbie's lips. No breath.

Suddenly, Jed grabbed Skye and hauled her away from the freezer. He continued to pull her behind him, not stopping until they were in his truck with the doors locked.

Skye gasped for air while Jed snatched his shotgun from the rack behind the seat, wrenched the mike from his CB, and put in a call to the police.

"They're both dead." Skye sagged against the backrest.

"Yup. Saw the doc when I came through the kitchen looking for you." Jed took a red hanky from his pocket and wiped his face. "Why'd you slam the dining room door on my hand?"

"I thought you were the killer." Skye looked anxiously at her father. "Are you all right?"

"Yup." He sat straight, his eyes scanning back and forth, the gun cradled in his arms.

"Why did you hit me in the foyer?" Skye asked, touching the tender spot near her hairline.

"Didn't. You ran into me and we bumped heads."

"Oh."

A minute or two passed in silence. A painful sense of comprehension was beginning to replace the shock she'd felt when she first saw the bodies—Ken and Barbie Addison were dead, and someone had killed them. Skye realized how precariously close to crying she was. She buried her face in Chocolate's brown fur and hugged the dog, forcing the tears to stay unshed. Her father had been through enough. She wouldn't add a sobbing female to his ordeal.

A squad car squealed into the driveway, lights flashing and siren screaming. Walter Boyd jumped out and headed toward the pickup. He was the chief of the Scumble River Police Department, a handsome man with warm brown eyes, curly black hair with just a touch of silver, and a striking year-round tan. His crisply starched police uniform emphasized his muscular chest and arms.

Although they had never dated, Skye and Wally had a history that wasn't easy to explain. She'd had a crush on him when she was a teenager and he was a rookie cop, but when she came back to Scumble River as an adult, he was married. His wife had left him about the time Skye had become involved with Simon. They had a *The King and I* sort of relationship—attraction without fulfillment. Recently they had taken to pretending that the attraction never existed.

Wally conferred briefly with Jed and Skye, then spoke into his radio. Officer Roy Quirk was next to arrive, with two county cruisers roaring in soon afterward. Before entering, the lawmen surrounded the house, peering into windows and creeping around corners.

The police took a long time to search the premises. As Wally later explained, they had to make sure the killer wasn't hiding anywhere and that there were no more bodies tucked away.

Skye watched as one of the deputies started to string yellow plastic tape around the perimeter of the property. She knew that an evidence technician from the county would arrive soon. He'd have his work cut out for him, going over such an enormous crime scene.

Finally, Wally came out of the house and spoke to Jed

and Skye. "It's all clear." His breath hung in the frigid air like a cotton ball. "Jed, Quirk's going to talk to you for a couple of minutes, then we need for you to go to the station and make a formal statement."

Jed said, "Gotta drop the dog off at home first."

Wally nodded. "Fine. Skye, you come with me." He jerked his head toward the cruiser. "Let's go sit in my car."

She followed him, toting her bags of groceries along with her. The front seat felt like a block of ice, and she shivered.

He started the engine and turned the heater to full blast. "What were you and your dad doing here?"

"I had to pick up my Instant Gourmet order, and Dad was driving me because the roads were too icy for the Bel Air."

"Instant Gourmet?"

"It's a product Barbie sells, I mean sold, at parties she held in her home."

"Like Tupperware?"

"You are so behind the times. But, yes, like Tupperware."

Wally stroked his chin. "Why would she bother selling stuff like that? It couldn't be for the money. She was married to a doctor—they had to be rolling in dough."

"That's a question I had, too. I'll be interested to hear what you find out."

"You mean you haven't heard any of the ladies talking about it?"

"No. Which is unusual—gossip being the most powerful commodity in Scumble River. The 'ladies' have been strangely quiet on that subject." Skye paused. There was something else she wanted to tell Wally before she forgot. "That reminds me. Monday night, at the party Barbie hosted where I ordered the Instant Gourmet food, Barbie and one of the other women must have had some sort of fight. I heard someone slap her as they were leaving, but I didn't see who it was."

"I'll keep that in mind." Wally made a note on the pad he

took from his breast pocket, then said, "Now, tell me what happened from the minute you got here."

Skye started with her knock on the Addisons' front door and described her movements up until she found the first body. Then she said, "I blame the cold medicine I took earlier this morning. I knew I shouldn't go into the house after finding the garage empty, but nothing seemed real."

Wally's expression was skeptical, but he didn't challenge her statement. Instead he asked, "What happened then?"

As she finished describing her movements, a hearse glided into the driveway and Xavier Ryan, Simon's assistant at the funeral home, climbed out of the driver's seat.

"Didn't Simon make it back from Chicago yet?" Skye asked Wally.

"No. He's on I-55. We beeped him and he called back from a pay phone at a gas station along the way. Traffic is tied up with accidents, and he's not sure when he'll get here." Wally nodded toward Xavier as he entered the house. "We were going to wait, but there are some samples that Simon wants taken ASAP."

Skye's thoughts flew to Bunny. Simon would probably be too busy to see her today. It seemed she'd be getting a short reprieve. Too bad the Addisons hadn't been as lucky; fortune had certainly smiled at them in every other aspect of their lives, but it had not protected them when it really counted.

Her gaze swept the imposing house and expensively landscaped grounds, and she said, "Isn't it ironic that one moment Barbie and Ken could be on top of the world, the rulers of all they surveyed, and the next instant they could be murdered like some homeless couple living in an alley in Chicago?"

# CHAPTER 5

*Let the dead Past bury its dead.*

—Longfellow

Skye stumbled out of the squad car, waving listlessly to Wally as he reversed the cruiser and pulled away. Her throat hurt, and in the hours she was at the police station, she had developed a hacking cough. Her plans for the immediate future were a hot cup of tea, another hit of cold medicine, and bed. Although she was afraid that when she closed her eyes, all she would see would be Barbie and Ken with those hideous ribbons cutting into their throats.

Her first hint that, even if she could put the Addisons out of her mind, sleep was not in her future came when she noticed Charlie's car in the driveway. Wonderful. She loved her godfather, but right now the last thing she wanted was more company. Swallowing a sigh, she plodded up the front steps, pushed open the unlocked door, and went inside. Voices and music drifted from the back of the house.

Skye plunked the bags of groceries on the kitchen table and trudged back into the foyer, pulling off her gloves, unwinding her scarf, and shrugging out of her coat as she walked. Her boots were more of a challenge. She had to sit on the hall bench to remove them. The moment she sat down, a wave of weariness washed over her and, for a second, she contemplated just staying there and letting the world revolve without her. A burst of annoying laughter made her change her mind.

In her stocking feet, she moved noiselessly into the great room. Uncle Charlie and Bunny were dancing. Shoot. This couldn't be good. Uncle Charlie never danced.

He wore his standard uniform of gray twill pants, limp white shirt, and red suspenders. His clothes varied only by the length of his sleeves—short for summer and long in the winter.

It took Charlie and Bunny several moments to notice Skye. When Charlie finally saw her he stumbled, let go of Bunny, and took a step backward. Bunny raised an eyebrow at Skye, and gave a tiny shrug. Charlie was probably not the first man who sought her out in private but disavowed her in public. Bunny looked from Skye to Charlie and said, "I need something to drink. Anybody else want something?"

Skye nodded at the redhead. "Hot tea would be wonderful. Thanks."

Charlie shook his head.

After Bunny left the room he hesitated for a second, then swooped Skye into a suffocating bear hug. At six feet and three hundred pounds, he overwhelmed most people.

Intense blue eyes under bushy white brows scrutinized her face. "You don't look so good."

"Thanks a lot." She struggled free of his hold. "I have a terrible cold, maybe the flu."

"Why aren't you in bed?"

Skye quickly told Charlie about the murders, but refused to answer any of his questions. After the hours she had spent at the police station, she couldn't face talking about it anymore. Instead she said, "Did you come by to tell Bunny that you have a room for her?"

The big man looked sheepish. "No, the motor court is still full."

Skye's lips thinned with irritation. "The roads are clearing up. Why aren't people checking out?"

Charlie edged toward the foyer. "It's way past noon, so I have to charge 'em for the day, and the highway patrol is still advising against travel because more snow is predicted within the next hour or so."

"Swell." Skye walked Charlie to the door. She lowered her voice. "Why did you send Bunny here?"

He looked chagrined. "She needed somewhere to stay, and I got the feeling money was a problem. She asked me if she could send a check later."

"But why me? We don't know anything about her. She could have murdered me in my bed."

"I think you could whip her." Charlie grinned. "Considering your past experiences with subduing criminals."

"You make me sound like Buffy."

"Who?"

"Buffy the Vampire Slayer from TV."

"I don't reckon Bunny's the undead." Charlie frowned. "She seems pretty lively to me."

"But why didn't you just give her directions to Simon's house?"

"She said she couldn't stay with Simon."

"Why?" Skye demanded.

"I didn't ask." Charlie pulled big rubber boots on over his shoes.

"If you wanted to be a Good Samaritan, why didn't you let her sleep on your couch?"

"That wouldn't be proper. Your mom would have a fit." Charlie looked shocked. "Anyway, half a good deed is better than none."

Skye huffed. "But why me?"

"She just seemed sort of, I don't know, desperate. And, after all, you are a psychologist."

"I'm a school psychologist. I'm not allowed to counsel people over twenty-one." Sometimes Uncle Charlie's faith in her frightened Skye. "You know, this puts me in a really awkward position with Simon."

"Things will work out." Charlie donned his jacket, opened the door, and stepped outside. "No matter what, she is his mother."

Skye fed her houseguest, then planted her in front of the TV. She could still hear Bunny's complaints about the lack of cable as she escaped into her bedroom. Skye closed and locked the door, then went into the bathroom and swallowed a couple of cold tablets. She'd meant to buy some daytime pills at the grocery store, but with all the shoppers acting so crazy, she had completely forgotten.

The pillow's cool smoothness beneath her cheek felt wonderful as she stretched out on the bed. She let her thoughts wander while she tried to drift off to sleep. She was just beginning to doze when the doorbell rang.

Bunny wasn't in the great room when Skye walked through on her way to answer the door. Where was she? A quick peek in the kitchen and bathroom revealed she was nowhere to be seen. Could she have locked herself outside?

Skye pushed aside the curtain and looked out the window. It was Simon. She flung open the door and pulled him inside. Snow swirled around him as he stepped into the foyer.

The elegant black wool overcoat he wore emphasized his tall, lean physique. Ice crystals melted on his auburn hair, making it shine and picking up the golden highlights in his hazel eyes. He gathered her into his arms and buried his face in her curls.

They stood for a moment, enjoying the comfort of each other's embrace. Then she sneezed.

"Bless you."

"Thanks. I've got a cold."

"Did you take anything?" Simon cupped her chin.

She nodded. "Yes, and it makes me groggy."

That seemed to end the conversation, until they both spoke at once.

"Why—"

"What—"

Simon indicated that she should go first.

"What are you doing here? I thought you'd go straight to the crime scene, and be tied up for the rest of the day."

"I was worried about you, and wanted to know why you needed to talk to me yesterday. It sounded like there was something more than you missing me." Simon kissed her on the temple. "And I heard you were the one who found the bodies."

Skye bit her lip. The situation with Bunny would be hard to explain, so she'd start with discovering the Addisons. Sad to say, but sometimes the dead were easier to deal with than the living.

Simon wrapped a chestnut ringlet around his finger. "How are you and Jed doing? Wally told me the whole situation was brutal."

"Let's just say I tried to take a nap, woke up screaming, and realized I hadn't fallen asleep."

"Poor baby."

Skye allowed herself to savor his concern for a moment before easing out of his arms. She had to tell him about Bunny right away, before it started to look like she was hiding something. Speaking of hiding, where was Bunny? Skye took a quick look around. The cottage appeared to be empty.

"Simon?"

"Mmm?" He took off his coat, hung it up, and moved into the great room. "What happened in here? It looks a Victoria's Secret store exploded." He sat on the sofa after moving a pair of black silk stockings.

"That's what I want to talk to you about." Skye followed

and sat on the chair opposite him. "I had a surprise visitor last night."

"During the snowstorm?"

"Yes, she just appeared on my doorstep. It was almost as if someone cast a spell and poof, there she was."

"Who?"

There really was no good way to break this to him. She might as well just blurt it out. "Your mother."

"My what?" Simon sprang off the sofa. "No. That's not possible."

"Well, that's what I thought. I was sure you had told me your mother was dead." Skye stopped. Wait a minute. Could Bunny be an imposter? She hadn't asked to see the woman's identification. Had Uncle Charlie? Probably not. "Is she . . . dead, I mean?"

"She is to me."

"Oh." Skye chewed her lip. "So, then technically it is possible that my houseguest is your mother."

"Houseguest?" Simon swiveled, looking around the room. "You invited her to stay with you?" His tone sharpened. "Why?"

"I didn't exactly invite her. She just sort of moved in." Skye noted Simon's frown and hurried to explain. "You weren't home. I wasn't able to get hold of you. What was I supposed to do, turn her out into the snow?"

"Why didn't you answer the phone when I called?"

"Your mother," Skye said. Simon glared at her, and she edited her answer. "Bunny, that is, broke my toilet. I was fixing it, and somehow she and I got tangled in the doorway, making me miss the call."

"Typical Bunny behavior." Simon began to pace, his anger apparent in his stride. "So, where is she?"

"Uh, I don't know." Skye got up and checked the bathroom and kitchen again. "She was watching TV last time I saw her. I was napping in my bedroom when I heard the bell, and when I came out to answer the door, she wasn't here."

"Maybe she left."

"She wouldn't leave her stuff." Skye gestured around the room.

"No. Maybe she went to town for something."

"That's another funny thing. I noticed this morning there was no car in my driveway. I meant to ask her how she got here but I forgot. If she left, someone would've had to pick her up." Skye looked into the foyer. "And her coat's still hanging on the hall tree."

"She'll turn up. Don't worry about Bunny. She can take care of herself."

"What are you going to do when she does?" Skye drew him down on the sofa and curled up next to him.

"Send her back to wherever she came from."

"She said she's been living in Las Vegas."

"That's what she always wanted, bright lights, fast living, and no responsibility." Simon rested his head on the back of the sofa and stared at the ceiling.

Skye hugged him. "Why did you say she was dead to you? What happened?"

He sighed. "Dad was a high school basketball star."

"From Scumble River, right?"

"Right. Bunny was from Laurel. They met at a game. She saw him as her ticket out of small-town life."

"And your dad?"

"He was mesmerized by her." Simon's voice had an edge to it. "He had a basketball scholarship from Loyola, and she convinced him to marry her and bring her along."

"What happened?"

"Dad wrecked his knee, lost his scholarship, and dropped out of college. He ended up operating a crane at the steel mills. She went to work as a go-go dancer at a club. Things were okay until she got pregnant."

"Your dad wanted her to quit her job and be a full-time mom?" Skye guessed.

"Exactly, but that was the last thing she wanted. And

Bunny always got what she wanted. She went back to dancing right after I was born. My dad said he'd walk in at five-thirty after his shift at the mill, and she'd hand me to him, then head downtown to the club."

Skye squeezed his hand. "That must have been rough on them both, having such different dreams."

"Rough on Dad, you mean. Bunny ignored his wishes completely. She stuck around for a couple of years, but left when I was three."

"Was that the last time you saw her?"

"Oh, no." The skin across his prominent cheekbones tightened. "That would have been too easy. If she had just divorced Dad, let him get remarried, and disappeared for good, maybe I could forgive her."

"But she didn't?"

"Every few months she would pop in with a toy, take me to the zoo or a movie, and promise that she was coming back for good real soon."

Skye could feel his hurt. She squeezed her eyes shut to stop the tears from falling. "But she never did?"

"No. Later I found out that she came to visit only when she wanted money from Dad."

"Your dad never tried to divorce her?"

"He loved her until the day he died."

Skye kissed his cheek, knowing there was nothing she could say to ease his pain.

"I was fourteen the last time I saw her. We hadn't heard from her for nearly five years before that. Then one day I came home after school, and there she was sitting on our front steps." Simon was silent for a while, then said, his voice thick and unsteady, "She really fooled me that time. She said she was tired of being on the road, and she was getting too old to dance, and she wanted to come back."

"What happened?"

"Dad and I welcomed her home like the prodigal mother.

She stayed almost a month. Then one day she was just gone."

"No note? No good-bye?" His expression told Skye that something worse was coming.

"She didn't leave a thing," Simon's face hardened, "but my dad had given her access to his bank account. She took ten thousand dollars from it before she disappeared."

Skye gasped.

"And that was the last time you saw her? She never tried to get in touch?" Skye knew the answer, but had to ask.

"That was it. To me, my mother died that day."

Skye gave him a few minutes to process all that had been said before she spoke. "Maybe your mom did, but Bunny is still alive. And sometimes happiness comes through doors you didn't even know you left open."

Simon put his hand on her cheek. "You're too soft-hearted, but that's why I—"

The moment was shattered by a loud thump, a yowl, and Bunny's voice yelling, "Damn it."

They ran into the kitchen, and were just in time to see Bunny come flying out of the utility room.

She skidded to a stop, ignored Simon, and said to Skye, "Your cat just ruined my last pair of pantyhose." Bunny put her hand out. "You owe me five bucks."

Skye's mouth hung open, but no words came out.

Turning to Skye, Simon shook his head. "And some doors should be nailed shut, sealed behind concrete, and the earth in front of them spread with salt."

# CHAPTER 6

*It's no use crying over spilt milk:*
*it only makes it salty for the cat.*

—Anon.

"Sonny Boy?" Bunny studied him. "It *is* you!" She flung herself into Simon's arms. "Sonny, my baby, let me look at you."

Derision washed over his features, and Simon peeled her off his chest, casting her aside as if she were a piece of lint he had removed from his jacket. "What in blue blazes are you doing here?"

"Is that any way to greet your mother?" Bunny smoothed her hip-hugging cranberry velvet skirt.

"Answer the question." The color of Simon's face was beginning to match his auburn hair.

"I came to see you, of course."

"How did you find me?" he asked flatly.

"I went to the old house, and when I saw you had sold it, I figured you'd ended up in Scumble River. You're just like your dad. I never could convince him that the only difference between a rut and a grave was how deep it is." She shrugged. "See, no big mystery."

Simon crossed his arms. "What do you want?"

"Why, to spend Thanksgiving with my only son. What else could I want?"

"Please." Simon imbued that single word with a paragraph's worth of meaning. "Thanksgiving isn't until a week from tomorrow. Besides, what about the last twenty Thanksgivings?"

"There's no time like the present." Bunny retied the bow on her midriff top. "I'm not getting any younger and . . ." she trailed off.

"Never mind." Simon rolled his eyes. "Look, whatever you're selling, I'm not buying. Pack your things, and I'll drive you to Joliet or Kankakee. You can catch a bus from there."

"But, Sonny, I want to spend some time with you." She looked up at him and twisted a red curl around her finger. "I know I haven't always been the best mom."

Simon snorted, and Skye sneezed. When she tried to leave the kitchen to get a tissue, Simon grabbed her hand and held tight. She blew her nose on a paper napkin and stayed by Simon's side.

Bunny continued as if nothing had happened. "But I've always loved you. And I read this article that said a real good dose of quality time is better than just plain old time. I came so we could have some of that quality time together."

"Look, I'm not Dad. You can't come prancing back anytime the urge strikes you and think I'll welcome you with open arms." Simon's face resembled Mount Rushmore. "If you don't want a ride to the bus station, fine. But you aren't staying with me, and we certainly won't be spending any kind of time together, quality, quantity, or quark."

Skye shook her head as Bunny sidled up to Simon. The redhead did not know when to stop.

Bunny put her hand on Simon's arm and said, "But, Sonny—"

At that moment the doorbell rang. Skye was relieved to escape to the foyer. She looked out the window. The woman standing on her steps was someone Skye recognized from around town, but she couldn't put a name to the face.

She opened the door. "Yes?"

The slim brunette held out her hand. "Hello. I'm Kathryn Steele, the new owner of the *Scumble River Star*. Call me Kathy. Are you Skye Denison?"

"Yes," Skye answered, cautiously. What was the newspaper's new owner doing here? She supposed it must be about the murder, although the former owner would never have printed anything about that. He saved his pages for ads and high school sports' scores.

"Can I come in?" Kathy edged around the door and closed it, saying, "Let's not let out all the heat."

"Did you want to talk to me?" Skye looked toward the kitchen. Maybe some time alone would be good for Simon and Bunny. "Would you like to sit down?" Kathy seemed like a nice enough person.

"That would be lovely." Kathy gestured to the great room. "In here?"

"Yes." After they were seated, Skye asked, "So, what can I do for you?"

"I understand you and your father discovered the Addisons' bodies this morning, and were the ones to call the police." Kathy flipped open her steno pad and clicked on her pen. "That must have been awful. How did you feel?"

"I think awful about covers it." Skye wasn't about to give a blow-by-blow description of her and Jed's not-so-excellent adventure.

"Why were you there?"

Skye explained about the Instant Gourmet pickup.

Kathy didn't seem to be interested in Barbie's activities

as a saleswoman. Instead she asked, "I understand that you knew Dr. Addison personally."

"My boyfriend and I belong to the same club he and his wife did, and we played bridge with their group."

"But weren't you and he especially close?" The newspaperwoman arched a perfectly shaped eyebrow.

"What?" It took Skye a minute to figure out what the woman had just insinuated. "Dr. Addison and me? No! Not at all. What would give you that idea? As I said, my *boyfriend* and I traveled in the same social circles with him and his wife. That's the extent of our relationship."

Before Kathy could ask another question, Bunny sauntered into the room. Skye was actually glad to see her until she opened her mouth.

"Hi, I'm Bunny Reid. Simon Reid's mother."

Skye heard a strangled curse and looked past Bunny. Simon stood behind his mother, his hands curled into fists.

Kathy looked from mother to son. "I see the resemblance. I'm Kathryn Steele, the new owner of the *Scumble River Star*." She rose and extended a flawlessly manicured hand to Simon. "Call me Kathy. So, you're Simon Reid. I'd love to talk to you, too."

Skye narrowed her eyes. Kathy was looking at Simon like he was a Godiva truffle and she had a serious craving for chocolate. Time to put a stop to that. Skye walked over to Simon and slipped her arm through his. "This is the boyfriend I mentioned."

"Are you here to write a story?" Bunny asked, oblivious to the undercurrents. "I'm in show business and could sure tell you some juicy stuff."

Simon paled. "Bunny, I'm sure Ms. Steele doesn't have time for tall tales. Let's go for a ride, and let her and Skye finish their conversation."

Bunny stood firm as Simon tried to pull her from the room. Skye's head pounded. Why had she let the newspaperwoman into her house?

Kathy sat back, her full red mouth curved into a smile. "I'd love to hear your stories, Bunny."

Bunny settled next to Kathy on the couch and started talking. Simon sat in the director's chair facing them, nervously jiggling his foot. Skye stood by his side.

She bent down and whispered in his ear, "Why don't you leave? You don't really want to hear all this."

He shook his head and whispered back, "It's like a car wreck. I want to look away, but I can't."

Bunny leaned back and crossed her legs, finishing a story about her and a notorious Las Vegas gambler. "So, I said to him, 'Johnny, I'll shave my pubic hair in a heart shape for you the day you twist your weenie into a poodle dog shape for me.'"

Simon groaned, and Skye suppressed a giggle.

Kathy scribbled furiously, then flipped back through her notes, and frowned. "You seem to have known more famous people than Forrest Gump. How old did you say you were, Bunny?"

Bunny winked. "Let's just leave it at somewhere between thirty and a Wal-Mart greeter."

Kathy appeared to mull over Bunny's answer, then got up and smoothed her beautifully tailored red wool suit. "Regardless, you've had quite a life."

Bunny walked the newspaperwoman to the foyer. "Well, Kathy, I always say that every woman should have a past juicy enough to look forward to retelling in her old age."

Skye watched as Bunny waved her new friend out the door, then said to Simon, "Now what do we do?"

The bell immediately rang and Bunny flung open the door. This time it was Skye's turn to grow pale.

Her mother, May, pushed past Bunny, and marched straight to Skye. "What in the name of heaven is going on around here?"

\* \* \*

May had not been happy with Skye's explanation of the day's events, and had taken an instant dislike to Bunny.

Now, Bunny and Simon sat in chairs opposite May and Skye. Skye examined both mothers. May was fifty-seven, and Skye guessed Bunny to be about the same age—more from references to her experiences than from her appearance. Both were about five-two, but May had an athletic build that reminded Skye of the cheerleader her mother once had been, while Bunny looked more like an aging *Playboy* centerfold. May's short salt-and-pepper hair took less than five minutes to style each morning. Skye didn't even want to think about Bunny's long red curls.

But the biggest difference was the eyes. May's emerald eyes shone with a sense of well-being, even when she was bawling out Skye for keeping secrets, while Bunny's hazel eyes had a haunted look that never quite went away, even when she was laughing. Maybe Skye should point that out to Simon. Or maybe she should mind her own business.

May whispered into Skye's ear, "Her fake eyelashes are longer than her skirt."

"Mother," Skye warned.

Bunny settled back in the recliner and smiled at May. "Charlie told me so much about you."

"That's funny, because he didn't mention you at all." May bared her teeth in what was supposed to pass for a smile.

"That naughty boy."

"Yes, Charlie has certainly been a naughty boy." May turned to Skye. "Tell me again about finding the Addisons' bodies."

Bunny tsked. "I can't believe you didn't tell me about that as soon as you got home. When that newspaper lady told me about it, I just about swooned."

"What newspaperwoman?" May asked Skye.

Skye explained about Kathryn Steele.

May fumed. "Let me get this straight. You and your father find two dead bodies, Simon's mother moves in with you, it's all going to be in the *Star*, and you didn't think to call me?"

Skye hedged. "I figured Dad would fill you in about the bodies, and I thought Simon should be the first to know about Bunny, and the newspaper thing just happened a minute before you arrived."

"I see."

"Besides, I thought for sure Uncle Charlie would have let you know." Skye sneezed and searched her pocket for a tissue.

"God bless you." May reached into her purse and handed Skye a Kleenex. "Don't worry, Charlie's on my list, too. Along with your father."

Skye didn't need to ask what list May was referring to, because she already knew it was the one she frequently occupied. Instead she asked, "What did Dad do?"

"He came home, got his gear, and went hunting with the dog. Didn't mention one word about finding the Addisons." May crossed her arms.

"How did you hear about it?"

"I stopped at the police station to get my check—I forgot to take it last time I was at work—and everyone was talking about the murders." May frowned. "You and your father made me look like a fool. I had to pretend to know all about it."

Before Skye could respond, Bunny bounced out of her chair. "May, honey, it sounds like you had a really hard day. How about the two of us get gussied up and go have a drink? I noticed a couple of real nice-looking cocktail lounges in town."

Cocktail lounges? Skye wondered which of the four taverns in Scumble River qualified as a cocktail lounge.

After a long interval during which May's mouth kept opening and closing but nothing came out, she finally managed to say, "Tempting as that sounds, I better go home and cook that no-good husband of mine dinner."

Bunny leaned close to May and declared, "My motto is always yield to temptation, because it might not pass your way again."

Skye wondered just how many mottos Bunny had.

May shook her head, got up, and grabbed Skye, pulling her toward the foyer. "I'd like a word with my daughter, alone." And just in case they hadn't gotten the message she added, "Bunny and Simon, you stay there." As soon as they were out of earshot, May ordered, "Get rid of that woman."

"She's Simon's mother. What am I supposed to do, throw her into the snow?"

"Mmm. That would be quite a show. We could call it Harlots on Ice." May's smile was not at all sweet. "Simon wouldn't care if you threw her out. Heck, he'd probably sell tickets."

"That may be how he feels now, but you can't truly believe that sometime, maybe in the distant, distant future, he won't hold it against me."

"Mmm. You could be right." May thought about it. "I guess you can't really *kick* her out, but she's got to go. I know, I'll stop by and tell Charlie he has to find a cabin for her ASAP. I want to have a word with that man anyway."

Skye kissed her mom and opened the door. "You do that."

May paused as she was leaving. "I don't understand how someone like her could have a son like Simon." May tsked. "That woman is an egg short of a carton."

"Sometimes I think a lot of people around here are a little scrambled." Skye waved to her mother as May climbed into her car.

Skye shut the door and turned, but the phone rang before she could return to the great room, so she detoured into the kitchen and grabbed the receiver. Wally's voice greeted her. "Hey, Skye. Is Simon at your house, by any chance?"

"Yes. I'll get him for you."

"Thanks."

Skye fetched Simon, and went back to sit with Bunny.

Bunny said, "Your mama's real nice. I think we'll be pals."

Skye's mouth dropped open. Was Bunny totally clueless? How had the woman ever survived in a place like Las Vegas? "It takes Mom a while to warm up to new people," Skye warned.

"But I could tell we really made a connection."

Skye didn't know what to say, so she seized the first thought that whizzed past. "What would you like for dinner tonight? I could make pasta or maybe a nice Cornish game hen?"

The choices at the grocery store had been both limited and a little bizarre. It was too bad the police were keeping the Instant Gourmet meals as evidence. After all, she had already paid for it. But then again, the thought of eating food that had been at a murder scene was pretty revolting.

"I'm sure Sonny will want to take us out," Bunny said.

"No, *Simon* won't." Simon leaned against the wall between the foyer and the great room. He walked over to Skye. "That was Wally. They need me at the crime scene, and then I have to arrange for the bodies to be autopsied. I'll probably be tied up until fairly late."

"That's what I figured."

"I hate sticking you with her. I promise I'll sort things out tomorrow." Simon turned to his mother. "I hope you'll be a considerate houseguest, and not give Skye any trouble."

"Why, Sonny, you don't have to worry about me. I've changed. My wild oats have all turned to shredded wheat."

"Right, and General Mills has just been made admiral."

# CHAPTER 7

*Out of the mouth of babes . . .*

—Old Testament

Skye balanced two boxes full of testing equipment, a stack of file folders, and a clipboard as she walked down the hall and into the elementary school's oldest wing on Thursday morning. The smell of mildew hit her full force, making her eyes water and her nose twitch, but she didn't sneeze. She hoped this meant her cold was getting better.

As she passed a row of windows, she glanced outside and flinched. The sun's rays bouncing off the totally white landscape was blinding. More snow was predicted for later that afternoon, and the roads leading out of town were still hazardous due to drifting.

But for now, the local streets and parking lots were clear, and school was in session. Skye hoped that meant all the kids scheduled for preschool screening—or, as she liked to call it, preschool screaming—appointments would show up and she wouldn't have to try to reschedule thirty-two three- and four-year-olds.

Shivering, she stepped back from the window. Now if the

heat would just kick in, they'd be in business. School district policy mandated that the furnace be turned down to sixty degrees during the night, and this part of the building was the last to warm back up.

Previously this wing had been rented out to a church group, but they had found a better facility and moved during the summer. The school board was now trying to figure out whether to bring it up to code for classroom use or to tear it down and start over.

It was not the best location for preschool screening—it gave parents a unfortunate first impression of the school district and the cheerless atmosphere made the kids ill at ease—but Skye had learned that conditions were rarely ideal when one worked in public education.

She had asked the custodian to position rolling bulletin boards in the middle of the two large rooms. She set up the various testing equipment—cognitive, fine-motor, gross-motor, and speech/language—in these four smaller spaces, then took the files out to the registration area by the doorway. A card table served as the check-in counter and faced several folding chairs that constituted the parents' waiting area.

Skye sat at the table and started to sort the folders according to time of appointments. A cold draft made her look up. That was odd. The door remained closed, and she didn't see any open windows. She blew on her fingers to warm them, glad she had worn a heavy cardigan with a turtleneck underneath.

Where was everyone? The preschool screening team should be here by now. Suddenly she was aware of an unsettling silence. Usually schools were full of noises.

Abruptly she flashed to the scene at the Addisons'. It had been awful finding them like that. They certainly weren't the first murder victims she had encountered, but something about this discovery bothered her more than the others.

Skye chewed her lip. Why? What was different this time?

Maybe just the sense of rage and violence that hovered in the atmosphere, like the charged air before a tornado touched down.

"Skye. Skye, are you alright?" A voice finally penetrated her dark thoughts, and Skye jumped, knocking over the stack of files she had been working on. The speaker was Abby Fleming, the school nurse.

She gathered up the scattered folders. "Sorry, yes, I'm fine. Just daydreaming." She craned her neck. Abby was tall—five-foot-ten—with the athletic build of a pro tennis player. "You ready for the onslaught?"

"As ready as I'll ever be."

"Did you find a good spot for your equipment?"

"Yep." Abby took a barrette from the pocket of her skirt and clipped back her white-blond hair. "I've got the vision test and audiometer set up in the pastor's old office."

"Great. I'll use the other office to score the tests and explain the results to the parents." Skye looked at her watch. It was quarter after eight. "Where's the rest of the team? The first group of kids is scheduled to arrive in fifteen minutes."

"Relax." Abby pointed down the hall. "Here they come now."

As soon as the four women spotted Skye, they surrounded her, demanding information about the Addisons' murders. She answered their questions, then listened to them talk about the victims.

One of the kindergarten teachers stated, "It was obvious from the day they moved here that they thought Scumble River was beneath them."

"How long ago was that?" Skye asked. She knew the Addisons hadn't been living in town when she left.

"I think it was about ten years ago," the other kindergarten teacher offered.

"Where were the Addisons from originally?" Skye thought she recalled Barbie talking about missing the East Coast, but couldn't remember for sure.

"Somewhere in Connecticut, but they lived in Winnetka just before moving here."

"So they don't have any family in the area?" Skye asked.

"No. And no children. Barbie made it clear they didn't have children because they didn't want them, not because they weren't able to." Before the teacher could elaborate, a gust of wind and a blast of crying signaled that the first parent and child had arrived.

Skye refocused her thoughts on the task at hand. "Does everyone know what they're supposed to do?"

The two kindergarten teachers and the special education teacher nodded, and went in search of their stations.

Belle Whitney, the speech therapist, grinned. "Gee, I wonder what I should do? Maybe the speech and language tests?"

Skye smiled back. "Got it in one guess." Belle wore her ash-blond hair in elaborate curls, with a big bow at the back. Her pale pink dress had rows of lace around the neck, sleeves, and hem. Even her eyeglass frames sported loops and curlicues. She looked like she was auditioning for the role of either Scarlett O'Hara or a wedding cake, but in fact, she was a great speech pathologist and the kids loved her.

Belle fluttered her fingers. "Later."

Other parents and children quickly followed. Appointments had been scheduled at fifteen minute intervals, and everyone was kept hopping. Most of the preschoolers could be jollied through the experience with soothing words, stickers, and promises from their parents of later treats, but some viewed the screening as if it were an alien abduction and they were about to be probed.

Skye found herself trying to wheedle one such munchkin. "Come on, Zach. Let's go play some fun games."

He looked at her through slitted eyes, folded his arms, and refused to budge.

"You can earn five stickers."

He shook his head.

"Your mom told me she would take you to McDonald's for a Happy Meal if you tried your best."

For a moment Skye thought she had him, but instead he opened his mouth and howled, "Moooom . . . meeee."

His mother came running and knelt beside him. "Please, honey, go play the nice lady's games."

"Don't wanna." His bottom lip quivered.

Skye asked, "What type of concerns did you have about your son?"

"Concerns?" The woman seemed confused.

"For example, does he have difficulty pronouncing certain words, or have you noticed problems with cutting or coloring, or delayed speech?" Skye zeroed in on her best guess. "Or maybe behavioral issues?"

"No." The mother looked insulted. "Of course not. I brought him in because he's gifted."

"I'm sorry, but that's not what preschool screening is for. We're looking for children who might need some extra help, so that when they start kindergarten they won't be so far behind."

"But I want him to start kindergarten next year. He only misses the cutoff by a few days. His birthday is the end of August."

"We do have a procedure for that. You'll need to talk to Mrs. Greer, the principal. She'll tell you what to do to see if your son qualifies for early entrance. We look at those children in the spring."

The mother's galled expression said that her time had been wasted. She hustled her son into his coat and out the door without another word.

The screening team took a lunch break at twelve-thirty. Skye had arranged for her mother to drop off Italian beef sandwiches, chips, and a fruit platter. It was waiting for them when they sat down. They wolfed down the food, having only twenty minutes before the afternoon appointments started, and rushed back to their stations.

Belle and Skye, the last to return, walked down the hall together.

"So, are you looking into the Addisons' murders?" Belle asked.

"No. Why should I?" Skye wondered why she was asking.

"You seem to be good at solving mysteries," Belle answered, then commented, "Ken Addison was my doctor for a while."

"But you changed to another physician?"

Belle nodded. "I felt he didn't have my best interest at heart, and when I went for a second opinion, that doctor didn't agree with his treatment plan at all."

Skye wondered what was wrong with Belle, but didn't feel she could ask since her colleague hadn't volunteered her diagnosis. "Are you okay now?"

"I'm getting there." Belle paused, then said, "But if you do decide to investigate the murders, a talk with Dr. Addison's office manager could be a real eye opener."

"I'll keep that in mind," Skye promised as the two women went back to work.

The afternoon passed quickly, and it was after three by the time Skye ushered out the final parent and child. The rest of the team had already left, and Skye felt as if she were ready to drop from exhaustion. Her cold had returned with a vengeance and she had started coughing again. Dealing with three- and four-year-olds was an intense experience—seven hours of being constantly on. It wasn't like an office job where you could take a break to make a phone call, get a cup of coffee, or go to the bathroom whenever you felt like it. There was no putting a preschooler on hold.

Skye was packing everything away, dreaming of a hot bath and a good book, when she realized she had forgotten that she was supposed to be at the high school at three-fifteen. She had a meeting with students interested in working on the newly formed school newspaper.

\*     \*     \*

"Hi, my name is Bitsy Kessler. I'm a sophomore and I want to be on the school paper because I think it would be fun to, like, you know, find out things about people and then tell other people what you found out."

Frannie Ryan snorted. She was a size fourteen in a size six world and took a lot of flack from the other kids because of it. She had a sharp mind and an even sharper tongue, and didn't suffer fools gladly.

Skye shot her a censorious look. Frannie rolled her eyes but kept quiet, except to offer her name when it was her turn to introduce herself.

Frannie was Xavier Ryan's daughter, and Xavier worked for Simon. Skye had first met Frannie when a popular classmate was killed. She had gotten to know Frannie better a couple of months ago when she and Justin Boward, found a body during the Scumble River bicentennial. Frannie and Justin had come to Skye with their discovery and helped her solve the case.

Justin, next to introduce himself, was tall and skinny with thick glasses that hid his best feature, sparkling brown eyes. Skye had first started seeing him for counseling when he was in the eighth grade. He had gained a lot of confidence since then. Instead of being withdrawn and hiding his intelligence, he had become a leader among his small group of friends. Skye counted him among her few true successes.

The rest of the would-be newspaper staff consisted of two boys and three girls who were all part of the crowd Justin and Frannie hung out with.

"It's nice to see you all." Skye tried to make everyone feel welcome. "Our first order of business is to come up with a name for our paper."

Bitsy's hand shot up. "I think we should call it the *Scumble River High School Scallion.*"

*Where is Trixie when I need her?* Skye thought. Trixie Frayne was Skye's best friend and the cosponsor of the student newspaper. Unfortunately, she had been called out of town Tuesday afternoon—her husband's mom had been rushed to the hospital. Trixie had phoned Skye yesterday evening to say her mother-in-law had died, and she wouldn't be back until after Thanksgiving.

Skye focused back on the matter at hand. Keeping her face expressionless, she said, "Interesting suggestion." Her training as a psychologist came in handy at times like this. "Any others?"

"You mean something besides calling our paper after an onion?" Frannie asked with a smirk.

Skye knew she had to set the right tone before things got out of hand. "I was wrong. We have to do one other thing before we name the paper. You all need to know what I expect of you."

She sucked on her cough drop and deliberately waited until the silence grew uncomfortable, then said, "I want you all to practice random acts of intelligence and senseless acts of self-control. Everyone understand?"

Frannie tucked a strand of her wavy brown hair behind her ear. "You want us to be nice to each other."

"Right." Skye smiled at the girl. She hoped that as Frannie's self-confidence grew, the teen wouldn't feel the need to be so hard on her peers.

It took a lot of negotiation and suggestions, but after several names were proposed and dismissed, the group finally agreed to call the student newspaper the *Scumble River High School Scoop*.

Skye checked the time. It was nearly five o'clock. "Here's your homework assignment." She waited for the groans to subside. "I want each of you to come up with ideas for three stories and a column."

Bitsy's hand shot up again. "Like, when're they due?"

"I want them in my mailbox by next Wednesday." Skye looked around the circle. "That way I can go over them during Thanksgiving vacation. We can meet the Tuesday after that and discuss who's going to do what."

As the teenagers shuffled out, Skye noticed Bitsy edge Frannie out of the way and take Justin's arm. Bitsy twisted a copper ringlet around her finger and her kelly-green eyes stared intently at Justin as she asked, "Do you want to work on our story ideas together?"

Justin appeared surprised, and he didn't answer until they had moved out of Skye's hearing.

Skye watched as Frannie stood by herself a moment, then joined the other girls and whispered, "Do you think her mother named her Bitsy because she couldn't spell Bimbo?"

They all giggled and moved away.

Skye tapped her desk with her pencil. So much for her speech about random acts of kindness.

The temperature had dropped again while she was inside the high school, but at least no fluffy white flakes were falling. As she walked to her car, Skye reminded herself she had to stop at the grocery store on the way home and check to see if they'd received any shipments of food. If they hadn't, she and Bunny would be eating Bingo's Fancy Feast for supper.

The phone was ringing when Skye got home.

It was Simon and after they exchanged greetings, he said, "How's your cold?"

"I took some medicine that seems to have stopped my coughing and help me breathe easier."

"Good. Wally asked if you and I would go to the emergency meeting the GUMBs are holding tonight. He wants us to see what everyone is saying about the Addisons. He's not a member, and even if he were, no one would talk freely in his presence."

"True. But how did I get drafted?"

"Well . . ." Simon faltered. "I might have mentioned that

you were a member of the women's auxiliary and that you were really good at getting people to open up."

"I see. Interesting. Does this mean both you and Wally want me to help investigate the Addisons' murder?"

Simon took so long to answer that Skye thought they'd been disconnected. Finally, he said, "Well, yes, I guess it does." There was a trace of laughter in his voice. "Maybe you should ask Wally to put you on salary as the official police psychologist."

"Maybe I should." The idea had some merit. She'd have to think about it.

# CHAPTER 8

*The King is dead. Long live the King!*

—French proclamation

The GUMB Assembly Hall was an old brick building that had been the Scumble River Grand Hotel back in the town's coal mining heyday. The GUMBs had purchased it several years ago and have been renovating it ever since.

The place was buzzing. As Simon and Skye paused in the vestibule to hang up their coats and take off their boots, they could hear a cacophony of raised voices.

"Am I glad to see you two!" Charlie clapped each of them on the back. "I cannot believe how pathetic this organization has gotten."

"I didn't realize you were a member." Skye couldn't recall ever seeing Uncle Charlie at a meeting or function since she'd joined.

"There're a lot of us old-timers who are members but stopped coming around when the new guard started changing things." Charlie scanned the room. "Looks like we might have to take it in hand again. It'd be a shame if these bozos brought the whole club down with their idiocy."

Skye followed Charlie's gaze. They were standing in what had been the hotel's ballroom. Folding chairs filled the center. A small stage took up the front of the room, and a mahogany bar stretched across the back. Supposedly Ulysses S. Grant had drunk there, but Skye was skeptical. A lot of places in Illinois claimed to have quenched Grant's legendary thirst.

Small knots of men were scattered around the periphery. Many were red faced and gesturing wildly. A group of women gathered in the back, talking in lowered voices.

Skye gave Simon a meaningful look. "I see someone I need to speak to. Save me a seat."

As she joined one of the clusters, she was just in time to hear Hilary Zello say, "Ken had a real short attention span. He could get bored in the middle of surgery. He needed a mistress just to break up the monogamy."

Several of the women tittered, but no one corrected Hilary's malapropism.

The five women in the circle all had a sameness about their appearance that came from having unlimited time and money to spend on themselves. Their hair was all some shade of blond, their nails manicured into pink or red ovals, and their clothes the most costly Marshall Field had to offer.

Skye knew most of them, at least on a superficial level. She had gone to school with Lu Hershaw Ginardi, Barbie's best friend. Lu, a senior, had taken an instant dislike to freshman Skye. Skye never quite figured out what she had done to attract her wrath, but Lu had taken every opportunity to torment her. She still seemed barely able to tolerate Skye's company.

Another, Joy Kessler, was the mother of one of Skye's problem students. She nodded to Skye before saying to everyone, "Marriage is tough. I admired Barbie for sticking with Ken despite his extracurricular activities. There are worse habits than infidelity. My first husband and I divorced over religious differences. He thought he was God, and I didn't."

"That's why I believe in starter marriages," countered a woman Skye didn't know. "It's like practice—short-lived, no kids, and no regrets."

Skye rolled her eyes with the rest of the group, then asked, "Were Barbie and Ken involved in any groups other than the GUMBs?"

Lu answered, "Between the GUMB activities and Ken's medical practice, there wasn't a lot of time for anything else."

"Did Barbie ever work, other than selling Instant Gourmet?"

"She was a flight attendant when she met Ken, but she quit when they got married." Lu frowned, as if suddenly remembering she was talking to someone she didn't like. "Why do you want to know?"

"Just curious," Skye answered. "So they didn't entertain a lot, except for the Instant Gourmet demonstrations and the GUMB bridge evenings?"

"I would say most of their parties were for business purposes." Lu narrowed her eyes. "Any more questions, Miss Snoopy?"

Skye shook her head, realizing it was time to back off. She had gleaned what she could from this clique.

She had moved a few feet away when she felt a hand on her shoulder.

Theresa Dugan, the teacher she had loaned money to at the grocery store, stood smiling at her. "Skye, you don't usually come to the business meetings."

"Theresa, hi. I decided it was time to get more involved. Do you go to all of them?"

"We try to get to most." Theresa gestured to a man standing a few feet away with two other business types. "Ted thinks it's important to have a say in how things are run."

"I agree. Do you think they'll ever let the women members vote?"

Theresa made a face. "No, that's why they keep us as auxiliary members, so they won't have to."

"We should do something about that someday."

"Yes, we should," Theresa agreed. "Say, I wanted to thank you again for rescuing me yesterday at the store. Here's the money I owe you."

Skye tucked the cash into her purse. "That was such a stupid policy. Glad I could help."

Theresa glanced back at the women Skye'd been listening to. "I hope you weren't offended with the chatter back there."

"Not at all. I enjoy a good gossip as much as the next woman."

"I know what you mean. It can be sort of fun." Theresa frowned. "But occasionally I think some of them have turned pro."

"Pro?" Skye had no idea what she meant.

"A pro gossip will never tell a lie, if the truth will do more damage."

Skye snickered. "That's a good one."

"Well, I'd better get over there before they start talking about *me*." Theresa left with a wave. "See you at the bowling alley tomorrow night."

It was harder to eavesdrop on the men. Skye would stick out like a prom dress on a basketball player if she entered the unofficial male-only area as a participant. But no one would question her standing next to Uncle Charlie if she kept her mouth shut.

Skye sidled up to her godfather, and he put an arm around her before speaking to the men. "This feels a lot like Déjà Moo: I've heard all this bullshit before."

A tall, rawboned man with thinning mouse-colored hair frowned at Charlie, then said, "As I see it, it'll boil down to two choices." He paused and made eye contact with each individual in the group.

Skye recognized the speaker as Tony Zello, Hilary's husband. His father, old Doc Zello, was the Denison family physician. Tony and his dad had shared a practice with Ken Addison.

She whispered to Charlie, "He seems awfully sure of himself."

Charlie shook his head. "Tony's sure he's right, even when he isn't."

Zello cleared his throat and glared at Charlie and Skye before continuing. "As I was saying before I was so rudely interrupted, it'll come down to a contest between that blowhard, Nate Turner, or our reliable town lawyer, Bob Ginardi. Obviously, we want Bob to win."

Bob had pulled a fast one on Skye's grandmother's trust, so Skye was not one of his biggest fans.

All eyes turned to the handsome man standing next to Zello. Muscles rippled under his camel crew neck sweater as he reached up and ran a hand along the side of his sleek black hair. Ginardi had been a football star in high school, and still looked the part. "Thank you, Tony. I believe I could do a good job as acting Imperial Brahma Bull for the Grand Union of the Mighty Bulls. I would be honored if you gentlemen would vote for me."

Heads nodded, and the men pressed forward to shake Ginardi's hand and reassure him of their support.

The crackle of the public address system being activated drew everyone's attention, and a voice announced, "Would you please be seated? The meeting is about to begin."

Skye spotted Simon standing toward the back, and started to head toward him. Charlie gripped her arm and guided her to a chair in the front row, gesturing to Simon to join them.

While everyone was getting settled, Skye told Charlie

about Nate Turner's behavior at the grocery store and asked, "What do you think of him?"

"The gates are down, the lights are flashing, but the train isn't coming."

"Then you're supporting Bob Ginardi?"

"That's the problem. Bob's a charming man, with plenty of smarts, but he tends to cut corners, as we found out with your grandmother's trust."

Simon leaned around Skye and said to Charlie, "The guys I was talking to seemed to think there might be a dark horse candidate. Do you know anything about that?"

"Could be."

A man mounted the stage. He tapped the microphone, which squealed in protest, then spoke. "Thank you all for coming. It's a sorrowful occasion that brings us together today. Our brother GUMB has been slain, and although I would like to stand up here and extol his accomplishments and virtues, I must instead turn to the urgent matter of who will now lead this great and glorious organization."

"We come to bury Caesar, not to praise him," Skye murmured to Simon. "Who is that pompous boor?"

He squeezed her hand and grinned. "That's Quentin Kessler. He owns Kessler Dry Goods. I'm surprised you don't know him."

"I know *of* him, but I don't think I've ever seen him before," Skye answered. "I know he's Joy's husband, but he's never been with her around me." She asked, "Why is he running things? I thought there was no assistant head honcho."

Charlie answered her. "He's the secretary-treasurer."

The meeting was long and tedious. Several men got up and spoke. None of them made much sense.

Skye muttered to Simon, "It sounds like English, but I can't understand a word they're saying."

Finally the floor was open for nominations.

Both Turner and Ginardi were named. Kessler looked around and asked if there were any further candidates.

The room hummed when one of the older members slowly rose to his feet, leaning on a cane. "I nominate Charlie Patukas."

Voices from all parts of the audience seconded the nomination. Skye looked at her godfather, who was grinning.

No other names were put forward, and it was decided that the vote would be held a week from Saturday. A crowd quickly formed in the vestibule, as everyone tried to be the first to retrieve their coats and boots. Simon and Skye stood to one side, waiting for the more impatient people to clear out.

Simon was telling her about a new restaurant opening up in a nearby town when Skye heard someone say, "Who does that old fart think he is? You don't have a thing to worry about, Bob. The day those dinosaurs start running the GUMBs again is the day I wear a pink tutu to the office."

Skye searched the area to see who had spoken, and she saw Tony Zello and Bob Ginardi huddled together.

"Did you hear that?" Skye demanded.

Simon nodded. "If they really think that, they're seriously underestimating Charlie and his pals."

"Some drink from the fountain of knowledge. Others are waiting for the water to turn into wine," Skye quipped.

When they got into his car, Simon said, "Wally wants us to stop by the police station and fill him in. Is that okay?"

"Sure. He usually works the day shift. He must really be anxious to hear our report."

Simon put the Lexus in reverse. "I don't think he has any other leads at this point."

The police station was nearby, as was everything else in Scumble River. Skye's parents lived just outside the city limits northeast of town, and she lived just inside the limits on the southwest side. It still took her less than ten minutes to go between the houses at peak travel time. Even if the light at Basin and Kinsman Streets was red, it took only a minute or two longer.

Scumble River's police department was housed in a red-brick, two-story building bisected by a cavernous garage. The dispatcher's area and the interrogation/coffee room occupied half of the first floor. The chief's office was at the top of the stairs. There was a rarely used holding cell in the basement—most prisoners went directly to the Stanley County jail in Laurel.

City hall offices were on the other side of the structure, with the town library on their second floor. Recently there had been talk of the library getting its own building. Skye hoped the librarian wasn't holding her breath. Although, maybe, at the next town meeting, the librarian should hold it until she turned blue and fainted——it was probably the only way the city fathers would authorize that kind of money for something as frivolous as a place to house books.

Few other vehicles were present when Simon eased his car into a spot next to May's white Oldsmobile. During the day the parking lot would be full, but hardly anyone used it at night.

Wally was sitting in the dispatch area with May when Skye and Simon entered the station. May immediately spotted them and buzzed them through the security door and behind the half-counter, half-bulletproof-glass partition.

Simon said to Wally, "The GUMB meeting just let out."

"Anything interesting?" May asked Skye.

"Uncle Charlie is running for grand pooh-bah."

"He told me." May's expression was smug.

Skye figured Charlie had used that information as a bribe to get out of the hot water he was in with May due to the Bunny incident.

Wally entered the conversation. "Who else is running for Ken Addison's position?"

"Nate Turner and Bob Ginardi," Simon answered. "I thought the lines were firmly drawn, but with Charlie's hat in the ring, things will get messy."

Everyone nodded.

"You two hear anything else?" Wally looked from Skye to Simon.

"I suppose you know that Ken Addison couldn't keep it in his pants." May's quick intake of breath made Skye rephrase her comment. "I mean, it appears he had several affairs."

"If it weren't for how the bodies were found, I'd wonder if Barbie hadn't killed the good doctor herself," May commented.

"Right, but I doubt Barbie would strangle herself with ribbon, then climb into the freezer," Wally said.

"Poor Barbie." Skye tsked. "Bad enough she had to put up with a husband who slept around, but now it's starting to look like she might have been killed because of his cheating ways."

"Who was his current mistress?" Wally asked.

"Now that you mention it, it's odd that no one said who it was." Skye scratched her head. "But I bet I can find out pretty easily, either at bowling tomorrow night or the dance Saturday."

"That would be a real help." Wally frowned. "Just be careful. Remember, one of those people you talk to may be the murderer."

# CHAPTER 9

*Snips and snails and puppy-dog tails . . .*
—Robert Southey

Friday morning Skye sat in her office at the junior high staring at the stained white ceiling tiles. The janitor had originally used the space for storing cleaning supplies. Its windowless walls were painted yield-sign yellow, and the whole room was no bigger than a walk-in closet.

Skye had attempted to dispel the claustrophobic effect by arranging old curtains around a travel poster. But there was nothing she could do about the faint smell of ammonia that lingered, despite the pine-scented air fresheners she plugged into the only outlet.

Still, she was grateful for the private office. Not having to share, or beg, for a room every time she came to the building was a luxury for which many school psychologists would give up their Christmas vacations and summers off.

Skye took a sip of hot tea and pushed a damp tendril back into her French braid. She'd had time that morning for her daily swim, but hadn't been able to get her hair completely dry before reporting for work.

She looked at her watch. There was a half hour before her meeting with Joy Kessler. She should start writing a psych report, but instead her thoughts were drawn to last night's GUMB meeting and the questions it had raised.

Closing her eyes, she concentrated. What had she learned so far? Number one, Ken Addison was the male version of a slut, and number two, both Turner and Ginardi wanted to be head GUMB. Were either of those enough of a motive to commit murder?

Wally had said that he was waiting for results from the medical examiner and the crime scene techs. He hoped their reports would give him a time of death and identify some of the fingerprints that had been found in the house. But surely there was something else they could do in the meantime.

Skye hadn't been close friends with the Addisons, hadn't even liked them very much—they were too plastic, too perfect, too phony—but she had eaten their food, played bridge with them, and been invited to their house. By doing so she had entered into an unwritten social contract. One that said I accept your hospitality, and in exchange I agree to have a certain amount of regard for you. This regard included making sure that their murderer was caught and punished.

On a legal pad, Skye started listing what she knew about the Addisons. She noted that Barbie spent a lot of time and money on her house and appearance. She shopped mostly in Chicago or Oakbrook, and thought it was tacky to buy things on sale. In Ken's column, she wrote that he expected Barbie to be flawless at all times, but especially when they entertained.

Skye chewed the end of her pen, remembering one bridge party when Barbie's soufflé had fallen just as she brought it to the table. Ken had called her an incompetent fool and stomped out of the room. Barbie, in turn, had taken her anger out on the guests.

While Skye was still absorbed in the memory of the Addisons' failed dinner party, there was a knock on her office door. She jumped at the sound, but quickly called out, "Come in."

The door creaked open and Joy Kessler's face appeared in the gap. "Sorry I'm late."

"That's okay. Please, come in. Have a seat." Skye gestured a welcome. She had brought a second chair into her tiny office, and didn't want to attempt the ungraceful maneuver of climbing over it to shake hands.

Joy stepped into the room, closed the door, and dropped into the metal folding chair. "Thank you so much for agreeing to see me."

Joy had the wholesome good looks of a Sears catalog model. She wore her dark blond hair in shoulder-length waves, and her light makeup emphasized a pale gold complexion. She was dressed in mushroom-colored wool slacks and a taupe silk blouse. The large gold beads around her throat looked real.

"I'm happy you were able to come in. Alex seems to be having a difficult year."

Joy draped the coat she had been carrying over her lap, and smoothed the brown leather with her fingertips. "I don't know where to start."

"Why don't you tell me a little about him? I've watched him in a couple of classes and looked at his file, but I'd like to hear your observations."

"He's always been full of energy and curiosity. As a baby he never slept more than two hours at a time. He still is a restless sleeper."

Skye nodded. This was consistent with what she had observed, and what the teachers had reported. "How did he adjust to kindergarten?"

"Not very well." Joy twisted her purse strap. "The teacher said he was smart, but couldn't sit still, and he bothered the other students."

"That still seems to be a problem," Skye said.

"He seems to be getting worse. We thought once he got to junior high he'd start to mature, but . . ."

Skye nodded sympathetically. "Summer magic. Sometimes kids really grow up during that June, July, August between elementary and middle school."

"There was no magic for us. Summer was a nightmare." Joy shuddered and took a deep breath before saying, "Did you know that if you attach a dog leash to the ceiling fan and hold on, a forty-two-pound boy in a Superman cape can fly?" Tears spilled from her brown eyes. "At least until the fan comes crashing down from the ceiling."

Skye bit the inside of her cheek to keep from laughing at the picture that popped into her mind.

"And I'll bet you had no idea that if you tape a paint can to the blades of a ceiling fan, there's enough liquid inside to spatter all four walls of a twenty-by-twenty-foot room."

"Oh, my." Skye was dying to ask if this was the same fan or a different one, but controlled herself. "What did you do in response to these incidents?"

"We've tried punishing him by taking away television, by grounding him to his room, and having him go to bed without supper—nothing works." Joy grabbed a tissue from the box on the desk. "We've tried rewarding him with stickers and trips to McDonald's." She shredded the tissue, the pieces falling like snow around her ankles. "It's like he can't stop himself."

"I see." Skye hurriedly jotted down some notes.

Joy suddenly laughed, a hysterical edge making it sound tinny and off-key. "Actually, we've learned quite a bit while raising Alex. We now know that while the clothes dryer has no effect on earthworms, it does make the cat dizzy, and dizzy cats throw up twice their body weight."

Now that Joy had started talking, it seemed she couldn't stop. "We've also discovered that garbage bags do not make good parachutes, marbles in a gas tank make a lot of noise when the car is driven, Play-Doh and microwaves should never be used in the same sentence, and Krazy Glue really is forever."

"Alex seems very imaginative." Skye wanted to start on a positive note. "What I've noticed most is his impulsivity, and that he seems driven."

Joy tilted her head. "Driven?"

"Almost as if there's a motor inside him that never shuts off."

"Yes! I see that, too."

"From what you've described and from his behavior at school, you may want to consult a physician and explore the possibility of attention deficit hyperactivity disorder." Skye handed Joy a folder. "Here's some information on ADHD. Why don't you and your husband look it over, and see if you think Alex has similar characteristics?"

"No, I can't do that." Joy moaned. "My husband would never agree to drug our child."

"The doctor may not suggest medication."

"Quentin won't want me to even take him to the doctor. He isn't too happy with Tony Zello."

"Why's that?"

"Ever since he and Ken started doing that research project of theirs, Quentin feels that they've neglected their patients."

"What kind of research were they doing?"

"I have no idea," Joy answered. "But if you really want to know, you should talk to Yolanda Doozier. She runs their office."

"Oh, thanks for the suggestion." Joy was the second person to suggest Skye should talk to Addison's office manager. Skye filed that bit of information away to think about later. Right now it was time to focus on the issue of Alex's behavior. "The fact that your husband has lost confidence in Dr. Zello shouldn't influence your decision to consult a doctor. It would actually be better if you saw either a pediatric psychiatrist or pediatric neurologist. ADHD is more in their area of expertise."

"Isn't there anything you can do?"

"Definitely. I'll work with you and his teachers to design a behavior plan." Skye consulted her appointment book. "How about next Tuesday at nine o'clock? The sixth-grade teachers have their planning period then, so they could meet with us, too."

"That would be fine." Joy stood up. "I just don't know what to do. Quentin is going to be so upset if I even suggest that Alex has something wrong with him."

Skye eased out from the cramped space behind her desk and patted the woman's shoulder. "I've learned that whenever I decide something with an open heart, I usually make the right decision."

Joy sighed and put her coat and purse over her arm. "I just want Alex to behave himself."

"I know. We'll work on helping him do that." Skye folded up the chair Joy had been sitting on to make a path to the door. "By the way, I met your daughter the other day. She signed up to be on the student newspaper, and I'm one of the faculty sponsors."

"Bitsy's never given us any trouble—she's popular, gets good grades, and follows the rules. Why can't Alex be like that?"

Skye patted the woman's arm. There was nothing she could say to that.

After Joy left, Skye sat back down at her desk and studied her notes. Poor woman. She had a long, hard road ahead of her.

Skye shivered. Why was she still sitting in the Bel Air instead of going into her nice warm cottage? Because she didn't want to deal with Bunny. She sank lower in the driver's seat, and considered restarting the engine and backing out of the driveway. But where would she go? Neither Simon nor her mother would be sympathetic.

May had called Skye at work that afternoon, and she had made a point of telling her that she had just stopped at Skye's cottage and found "that woman" still snoring on the couch. Skye was afraid to ask for further details, such as why May had gone to the cottage in the first place, and if Bunny was still asleep—or alive—when May left. The depth of her mother's hostility toward Bunny surprised her. May usually liked everyone.

Sitting in the car like this was ridiculous. Skye inhaled deeply, which started her coughing. It was time to stop being a coward and go inside before she made her cold worse. She got out of the Chevy and approached the door, sneaking up as if a sniper were behind it. The knob turned easily. No sign of life in the foyer, but Skye could see flickering light and hear canned laughter coming from the great room.

Bingo rubbed against her legs and demanded his supper. Skye detoured to the kitchen, filling the cat's bowl with his favorite flavor of Fancy Feast and giving him fresh water.

Finally, she walked into the great room. Bunny was sprawled on the couch painting her toenails. She looked up briefly when Skye entered and said, "How was your day?"

"Fine. Yours?"

"Okay. I called around about some jobs that were listed in the paper."

"Any luck?" Skye asked.

Bunny shrugged. "We'll see."

Skye moved toward her bedroom. "Simon and I are going bowling tonight. There's pizza in the freezer and lettuce in the fridge. Make yourself dinner whenever you're hungry."

"Okay." Bunny sighed wistfully. "I love bowling."

"Really?" Skye changed the subject, afraid Bunny would demand to go with them. "By the way, any progress on finding a motel room?"

Bunny became fascinated with applying the red polish perfectly to her big toe. "Not so far."

"Did you call Charlie today to see if he had a vacancy?"

"I'll do that as soon as my nails dry."

"Don't forget." Skye looked at her watch. It was already nearly six. "Simon's picking me up soon. I have to go get ready."

Simon parked his Lexus between a Lincoln Navigator and a BMW X5. Skye snickered, and he asked, "What's so funny?"

"I was just thinking that I'll bet the only time the Gold Strike's parking area looks like a luxury used-car lot is during the GUMBs' Friday night bowling league. Pickups and Fords are more the norm here." Skye got out of the Lexus and edged over to Simon's side. The asphalt was clear but slippery. "It still surprises me that you like to bowl."

"Hey, I was the teen champ of the Strike and Spare." Simon took their bowling bags from the trunk, and they walked toward the entrance.

Skye pointed to a weathered sign in front of the building and said, "I think the For Sale sign is going to disintegrate before anyone buys this place."

"Probably," Simon agreed, then asked, "Is *she* still staying with you?"

"Yes. I called the highway patrol, and they don't advise driving to Kankakee or Joliet yet. They said the snow was blowing and drifting in a lot of the open areas, so even though Scumble River streets seem okay, the ones leading out of town aren't. Charlie didn't answer when Bunny called to see if he had a room open at the motor court, but she promised to keep phoning him."

"Maybe I could rent a snowmobile or a dog sled or something." Simon shouldered one of the double doors open and waited for Skye to enter.

"She'll be gone soon," Skye soothed. "You should talk to

her before she goes." Skye knew they'd been down this road before, but she also knew that sometimes things had to be said several times before people who were hurting emotionally could hear them.

Simon turned right as he came through the door. He stopped in front of an orange-and-brown cube-shaped locker, and put their bowling bags on the wooden bench bolted to the floor in front of it. "I don't want to talk to her or about her anymore." He took off his jacket and handed it to her.

Skye decided not to pursue the subject, for now. Instead she took their coats across the aisle and hung them in the alcove next to the rest rooms and pay telephone.

As they walked through the bar and grill, music from the jukebox became louder. Gary Lewis was crooning "Save Your Heart For Me" to the nearly empty Formica tables and vinyl chairs that were scattered across the width of the area.

The odor of frying hamburgers and sliced onions permeated the air. Skye's stomach growled. She hadn't had time to eat supper before Simon picked her up. She'd order something after they got started.

She and Simon stepped down into the bowling lanes and joined their teammates, Theresa and Ted Dugan, at number five. They settled on the green plastic bench and exchanged greetings.

While Skye changed her shoes, Theresa said, "School was tough today. It's hard to keep the kids' attention when the week has been interrupted."

"That's one of the reasons I really don't like snow days."

"Is the other because we have to make it up in June?"

"Yes." Skye got up to roll a couple of balls. She was the weakest player and needed the practice. "I hate that."

"Are you planning to do any traveling this summer?"

"Nothing firm yet, but I'd really like to go somewhere," Skye said over her shoulder as she approached the lane. "It's been years since I had a real vacation." She looked down at the hardwood floor and found her mark, but before she could step forward, an angry voiced stopped her.

"Excuse me. I was here first." Lu Ginardi was on the adjacent lane.

Skye gestured with her free hand for Lu to go ahead.

Lu waited to make sure Skye wasn't about to move, then made her approach and released the ball. A strike. She shot Skye a triumphant look and flounced over to her seat.

Skye really wished she knew why Lu disliked her so much. Skye rolled a spare, which was good for her but seemed pathetic after the other woman's stellar performance.

On the opposing team's bench, the Ginardis and the Zellos had their heads together, whispering. Skye wondered what they were talking about. It could be about tactics, but what kind of strategy was there to bowling? Still, they must know something. They were in the number one spot.

When Skye sat back down, Bob Ginardi said to Simon, "Is your team ready now?"

"Sure. Let's get started."

During the first two games, Simon, Skye, Theresa, and Ted all bowled well above their average. As they started the third game, they were ahead by almost fifty pins. Neither the Ginardis nor the Zellos were taking it well. Skye and Theresa were trying to carry on a normal conversation and ignore the other team's pointed comments.

"Boy, I should have followed your example the other day," Skye said. "I'm just about out of food, and the store shelves are still nearly empty."

"Even with all the stuff I got Wednesday, my cupboards are just about bare again," Theresa agreed. "Three growing boys require a lot of nourishment." She shook her head. "I keep thinking of all those Instant Gourmet meals at the Addisons'. Do you think there's any way that food could be distributed?"

"No. Chief Boyd said they need it for evidence. After that

it becomes a part of the estate, and the next of kin will have to deal with it."

"What a waste."

"It's a good thing I was able to get a few things yesterday." Skye retied her shoe. "I don't mind cooking if I have the ingredients, but I'm no Martha Stewart. I can't whip up a three-course meal from refrigerator mold and leftover Halloween candy."

"Cooking isn't my thing either," Theresa said. "I read recipes the same way I read romances. I get to the end and think, Well that's not going to happen."

Skye laughed and Tony Zello leaned across the aisle, frowning. "Could you two be quiet? Some of us are trying to concentrate."

Theresa and Skye rolled their eyes, then watched as Tony's wife, Hilary, picked up her ball and approached the alley to take her turn.

Tony shouted out instructions. "Keep your arm straight and look at your mark."

Hilary took a deep breath and nodded. Lines formed at her mouth, and she stared at the pins.

As Hilary released the ball, Skye heard a familiar voice and then a loud wave of laughter. She cringed, turned, and stared.

Bunny was holding court near the bar. Skye watched as the redhead leaned toward another tackily dressed woman and announced, "Darling, my philosophy is if the shoe fits . . . buy it in every color."

Charlie stood beside Bunny with a silly grin on his face. So that was how Bunny got to the bowling alley. May would have a fit when she found out Charlie had taken Simon's mother out on a date.

It was Skye's turn to bowl, but her attention was focused on the table behind her. Her ball rolled into the gutter, and the other team perked up.

When Skye returned to her seat after throwing her second

gutter ball, Simon gritted from behind clenched teeth, "She's here."

"Ignore her. She's probably doing this to get your attention."

He visibly forced himself to relax. "You're right."

"Good. Go get a strike."

He hugged her and got up.

Skye scanned the area. Oh, no. Charlie was gone, and Bunny was leading a pack of men to a nearby table. Her hips swayed like a Chevy with bad suspension, and the men were nearly drooling. She wore a short black skirt with a slit up the back and a chiffon top with a neckline that plunged deeply into her silicone valley.

One of the men handed Bunny a drink, then ran his finger down her cleavage. She laughed and batted his hand away.

How much alcohol had she already consumed? Her face was red and her gestures exaggerated. Skye glanced at Simon, who was getting ready to roll his second ball. After that he'd turn around and see what his mother was up to. Skye wondered what to do. Hiding in the bathroom held a great deal of appeal.

Where was Charlie? He had brought Bunny, so he should be keeping an eye on her. Skye excused herself to the Dugans, and edged out of the bowling area.

Nate Turner, the guy running against Charlie for head honcho of the GUMBs, leaned against the bar with a beer in one hand and a shot glass in the other. As Skye passed, she heard him say to the bartender, "I married Miss Right. I just didn't know her first name was Always." The bartender smiled weakly, and Skye wondered how many times the man had heard that old joke.

Skye finally found Charlie coming out of the men's room. "Why did you bring Bunny here?" she demanded.

"She was bored. You leave her by herself all the time. What do you expect?"

"Hey, she wasn't exactly an invited guest, remember?"

He shrugged. "What's the harm? She wanted a pizza. We'll eat, have a couple of beers, and leave. It's not your problem."

"Except it is." Skye realized her voice had risen and she made herself calm down. "While you've been occupied with other things, Bunny's been knocking back drinks like they might reinstate prohibition tomorrow and virtually doing a strip tease for several of your dearest friends." Skye pointed at Bunny's table. "Simon will have a cow when he gets a load of her behavior."

"Oh, I'd better get over there, huh?"

"Good idea," Skye said. Usually Uncle Charlie was the one in charge, but somehow Miss Bunny's presence was making him act like a big goofball.

Skye and Charlie arrived just as Simon walked up to his mother. The laughter at the table died as if a switch had been thrown.

Simon stared at the men until one by one they made their excuses and left. Finally he said, "I see you've set aside this special time to humiliate yourself in public."

"What?" Bunny pushed a red curl out of her face. "But I've always loved bowling. I used to take you when you were little."

A pained expression darted across Simon's features. "I remember."

"Did you know I was the women's champ at the Las Vegas Lucky Strike three years running?"

"How would I know that? It's not like you ever wrote me a letter." He took Skye's hand. "Let's go."

The Dugans were waiting for them. Theresa said, "Everything okay?"

"Peachy," Skye answered.

From that point on, Simon bowled poorly and Skye did worse. The other team ended up winning by two pins. Skye was relieved to see that Bunny and Charlie were gone by the time they finished changing shoes and gathering their things together.

As they got ready to leave, Skye said to Simon, "I'll meet you by the door. I have to use the bathroom."

Bob Ginardi and Tony Zello were waiting for her as she exited the ladies' room. Tony said, "Can we talk to you a minute?"

"Okay." Skye didn't really trust either man, although she had no good reason for being leery of Tony—she really liked his father, old Doc Zello.

They drew her over to a corner and Tony continued, "We were really impressed with how you solved the murder during the bicentennial. The way you handled that saved the town a lot of embarrassment."

"Thanks."

"We'd like you to do the same thing for the GUMBs," Tony said.

"Oh." What were these two up to?

"We want you to figure out who killed the Addisons, but keep anything else you find out quiet," Bob chimed in. "For the good of the organization."

"Like what?" Skye asked.

"Oh, anything you find out that doesn't have to do with the murder." Tony forced a laugh. "Everyone has some skeleton in their closet they'd rather didn't rattle too loudly."

"I understand." Skye thought quickly. Wally would probably want her to agree with the men's plans in order to keep tabs on them. "Okay, I'll do a little poking around and see what I can come up with."

"Wonderful," Tony said.

The two men shook her hand and walked away. Now this was an interesting twist. What did Tony and/or Bob have to hide?

# CHAPTER 10

*The boy stood on the burning deck . . .*
—Felicia D. Hemans

Skye was surprised to see Frannie and Justin leaning against the Bel Air's hood Saturday morning when she came out of the bank. After the Bitsy incident, Skye would have bet big money that Frannie wouldn't be talking to Justin for a while. Clearly, the girl was more enlightened than Skye gave her credit for.

"Hi, Ms. D." Frannie waved a red-mittened hand. "Got a sec?"

"Sure. But let's sit in the car. My cold's almost gone, and I don't want to take any chance on bringing it back."

As soon as they were settled and the car's heater was blowing full blast, Justin said, "We've been thinking about a story for the first edition of our newspaper."

"Good. Any ideas?" Skye could see they were itching to tell her what they had come up with.

"We've been hearing some interesting stuff about that murdered couple." Frannie bounced up and down in her excitement.

"And?" Skye didn't need to ask how the teens had heard about the Addisons' private lives. If gossip were an Olympic event, Scumble River's citizens would win the gold, silver, and bronze medals. Every man, woman, child, and pet had probably been fully informed regarding the Addisons' history within hours of Skye and Jed finding the bodies.

"We want to cover that story for the paper," Justin said, leaning forward and looking around Frannie to Skye.

"I don't think that's a good idea." Skye definitely didn't want Frannie and Justin involved. Last time, they had been too close to the line of fire for her comfort level. "The school newspaper should cover stories that the town paper doesn't, and believe me, the *Star* is covering the murder."

"But we want to come at it from a different angle," Frannie said. "We want to write about it from the kids' point of view."

"Let me think about it." Skye did not like the sound of their proposal, but couldn't immediately come up with any good reason to object. "I'll get back to you guys in a few days."

After a few token protests the teens left. As Skye put the car in gear and pulled into traffic, she wondered how she could stop the pair from sticking their noses into something that might be very ugly, not to mention extremely dangerous.

Skye made a face. Had Wally and Simon felt the same way about her in the past when she'd investigated? She shrugged. This time it was different. Both men had asked for her help.

Simon and Wally had opened the door, and today she was going to walk through it. Since both Belle and Joy thought Ken's office manager, Yolanda Doozier, had important information about his medical malpractice, Skye wanted to talk to the woman ASAP.

A call early that morning to the medical clinic had informed her that Yolanda didn't work Saturdays, which meant Skye would have to seek her out at home. One good thing about living in a small town: Skye knew exactly where that was. Yolanda, her great-grandmother, and younger brother, Elvis, all lived in an farmhouse east of town on State Road.

When Skye turned right on State Road, it was deserted. Neither cable TV nor gas lines ran this way, and electricity was often iffy in bad weather. Most of the families who had once lived in this area had long since moved to town. Skye passed fields wearing their winter coat of white and a couple of collapsed barns that looked like dinosaur skeletons.

The Doozier house was the only residence for miles. As she slowed to pull into their driveway, Skye felt a twinge of frustration. The lane hadn't been plowed, and it was obvious from the pristine snow that no one had driven in or out of there since before Wednesday's huge snowfall.

Where were Yolanda, Elvis, and their great-grandmother, MeMa, staying? Skye closed her eyes and concentrated. She should be able to figure this out. Where would they go? Skye hit her forehead with the palm of her hand. Earl's, of course. Somehow all Dooziers eventually ended up at Earl's.

The patriarch of the Doozier clan, Earl, lived with his wife, Glenda, and his son and daughter, Junior and Bambi, north of town near the river. His nephew, Cletus, and younger sister Elvira lived with them, too. Dollars to donuts, when the snow got bad, MeMa, Elvis, and Yolanda packed up and moved in as well.

It was touch and go, but Skye finally managed to turn the Bel Air around without landing in a ditch. She retraced her route until she came to Kinsman Street, where she turned right, then right again on Cattail Path. This road hadn't been plowed, but car tires had flattened the snow until it was a slippery sheet of ice. She slowed the Chevy to a crawl.

City services didn't often venture into this part of town—

when they did, machinery, tools, and sometimes people turned up missing.

Scumble River was originally built in the fork between the two branches of the Scumble River. Since then it had spread along both banks. The group of people who lived along this bank of the river was known as Red-Raggers. These were not folks who appreciated uninvited guests.

Earl Doozier was the king of the Red-Raggers.

Skye had visited the Dooziers three times in the past two and a half years. The first time was to obtain a consent to reevaluate Junior Doozier for special education services. The second was when Junior and his father had fished her out of the river. And the third was to ask Earl and his wife some questions about an incident they'd witnessed during the Scumble River bicentennial. She hoped she was now on good enough terms with the family for Yolanda to talk to her. She knew that no Doozier would ever willingly give information to the police.

When Skye pulled into the Dooziers' rutted driveway, she was relieved to see signs of occupancy—tracks in the snow and various vehicles scattered in and near the garage.

The house itself was dilapidated to the point of looking third world. Gray snow covered the front yard. Cars up on cinder blocks and old appliances were scattered around like lawn ornaments. A sign had been added since the last time she had visited. Tacked to a post at the end of the lane, it said: TRESPASSERS WILL BE SHOT. SURVIVORS WILL BE PROSE-CUTED.

Even in the cold air, Skye could smell animals, and the growls coming from the backyard were anything but welcoming. She was trying to remember if she had actually ever seen the Dooziers' dogs when Junior burst out the side door.

He had a red crew cut, and a wide jack-o'-lantern grin lit up his freckled face. "Miz D., what are you doing here? You okay?" He had come to her aid on more than one occasion, and now considered himself her personal guardian angel.

"I'm fine, thanks. How about you?"

"I'm bored."

Skye dug into her purse for one of the little treats she always kept there for the various kids she worked with, and pulled out a McDonald's Happy Meal toy. She handed it to Junior. "Is this any fun?"

"Sure. Wait until Cletus sees what I got." He started to run off.

Skye stopped him with a hand on his shoulder. "Is your Aunt Yolanda staying with you?"

"Yeah, she's here. Come on."

Junior led her through the side door, past a small entryway, and up a few steps leading to the kitchen. The odor of stale beer and the sound of angry shouting permeated the air.

Earl Doozier, heavily tattooed and wearing only sweatpants, stood nose-to-nose with a raven-haired beauty whose lush curves made the twisting Scumble River look as straight as the Mississippi. She sported a heart-linked ankle bracelet, and a rose tattoo peeked from her cleavage.

Skye recognized the woman as Yolanda. They had gone to high school together, though Yolanda was a couple of years younger than Skye.

Teenage twins Elvira and Elvis were seated at the kitchen table, along with a woman who looked older than Stonehenge. The Formica tabletop was littered with playing cards and piles of toothpicks. Cletus and Bambi were sitting on the floor, racing toy cars over the dirty linoleum.

Earl's semitoothless mouth flapped as he yelled, "I was not cheating!"

Yolanda screamed back, "There are only four aces in a deck of cards. You had the fifth one up your sleeve."

Skye tensed. Even though Earl was as thin as a blade of grass, except for a modest beer belly that hung over the elastic waist of his sweatpants, she feared what would happen if Yolanda pushed her brother too far. Everyone in Scumble River knew you didn't accuse a Doozier of cheating at cards, at least not to his or her face. Obviously, the heat of the moment made Yolanda forget.

Earl's face was now redder than the king of diamonds, and he thrust both arms in Yolanda's face. "I ain't wearing no sleeves, you stupid bi—"

Skye cleared her throat. Both combatants swung around to face her.

Junior pushed her forward, saying, "Pa, look, Miz Denison is here. She wants to talk to Auntie Yolanda."

Earl glared and Yolanda frowned.

"Hi," Skye said. "I guess this is a bad time, huh?"

"No, Miz Skye." Earl smiled meanly at his sister. "We're just havin' some old-timey family fun."

She decided to accept Earl's statement at face value. "Well, good, then." She turned to Yolanda. "Hi. You probably don't remember me. I'm Skye Denison. We went to high school together. I'd like to talk to you about Ken Addison, if you have time."

The brunette looked her up and down. "You're Vince's sister, right?"

"Yes." Skye wondered how Yolanda knew her brother. She hoped it was because he cut her hair, and not because he had dated her. Vince's love life tended to be complicated.

"You're the one who solves all the murders." Yolanda's violet eyes were thickly lashed, and her sable-colored hair was intricately curled and artfully arranged on top of her head.

"I've helped the police with a couple of cases."

"Are you working on Ken's murder?"

"Sort of."

"Then I have time. This game is over with." She shot a malevolent glare at her brother.

The twins slunk off without acknowledging Skye, although she knew them both from school. The old woman sat and stared but didn't speak, and no one introduced her. Skye figured she had to be the infamous MeMa, the clan matriarch.

Yolanda said, "Have a seat."

Skye sank into a chair. Interesting. Yolanda spoke without the Dooziers' unique speech pattern.

"So, what did you want to know about Ken?"

"Well, anything you could tell me would be great. But specifically, I'd like to know about him and Dr. Zello, and what's going on in their practice."

Before Yolanda could answer, Glenda Doozier trudged up the steps carrying a huge purple-and-green purse. From her stiletto-heeled silver boots to her Frederick's of Hollywood blond wig, she was the quintessence of Red-Ragger womanhood.

Earl, beaming like the proud owner of a blue ribbon hog, rushed over to her and put an arm around her waist. "Glenda, honey, Miz Skye come here to talk to Yolanda." He turned to Skye. "You remember my lovely wife, Glenda, doncha?"

"Of course." Skye waved. "Hi."

Glenda ignored her and stared at Earl. "What'd you do to your hair?"

Skye noticed for the first time that Earl's greasy brown hair was sticking up in uneven clumps all over his head.

He looked down and mumbled, "I should never've tried to give myself a haircut after drinking a case of beer."

Glenda cuffed him on the side of the head. "Fool." She stormed out of the kitchen, followed by her daughter, Bambi.

Earl didn't seem upset by his wife's assessment. He and the boys pulled chairs up to the table and looked at Skye. "So, you gonna ask Yolanda something, or just sit there with your mouth hanging open catching flies?"

Junior and Cletus giggled.

"Sorry." Skye refocused on the matter at hand. "Let's

start with the medical practice. Have they been losing patients?"

"Lord, yes," Yolanda answered quickly. "I'd say not a day goes by that someone or other stops in and asks for their records to be transferred."

"Any idea why?"

Yolanda snickered. "Those two had what you might call a monopoly on sick people for a long time, and their attitude toward their patients showed it. But about five or six months ago, a couple of lady doctors opened up an office in Clay Center. Tony and Ken were sure people wouldn't drive the ten miles to go see them. They were wrong."

"Attitude? What do you mean?"

"Well, let me give you a for instance." Yolanda pursed her mouth in thought. "If you came in with a cough and Tony didn't know what the problem was, instead of sending you for a chest X ray, he'd prescribe whatever the drug companies were slipping him big bucks to push. It got to be whenever I heard him say, 'This should fix you up,' I'd shudder, knowing he was at it again."

"Did Ken do the same thing?"

"He was worse." Yolanda picked up the playing cards and started to shuffle. "Whenever I heard him say, 'Let me schedule you for some tests,' I knew that translated to 'I have a forty-percent interest in the lab and want to buy a new car.' "

"Boy, I may never go to a doctor again."

"Oh, honey, you don't know the half of what goes on." Yolanda smiled thinly. "Ever since those two started doing research, I wouldn't let them work on my dogs."

"Tell me about this research project," Skye urged, perking up. Joy had mentioned something about that, too.

"It's two projects. That's another part of the problem."

"Oh?"

"At first they worked together, but then Ken had some sort of breakthrough on his part of whatever they were doing, and so the next time they had to apply for a grant, he did it on his own." Yolanda held up her hand. "Don't ask me what it was. I have no idea, and it doesn't matter. The important thing is that it caused Tony and Ken to have a huge fight."

Skye chewed her lip. "So, did Tony get cut out of the loop completely?"

"No. But Ken got the big money and an article in some fancy doctor's magazine." She dealt out a hand of solitaire.

"How did Tony take that?"

"'Bout like you'd expect for someone with an ego the size of a semi truck."

Skye thought that over, then asked, "Did it bother Ken that Tony was upset with him?"

"Nope. Not at all. He said that a couple of more breaks in his research and he could put Scumble River in his rearview mirror for good."

"So, he wasn't happy living here?"

"He hated it. Almost as much as his wife did." Yolanda shook her head. "They only moved here because Tony convinced them that they could make a lot of money, fast."

"They sure seem to have done that." Skye thought of their big house, Barbie's jewelry, and their cars. "So, when Ken died, he and Tony still weren't on very good terms?"

Yolanda snorted. "That's one way of putting it."

"Was old Doc Zello involved?"

"No, that sweet man only comes in a couple of mornings a week. He has no idea what his son and Ken were up to."

Skye hesitated to ask her next question, and tried to ease into the subject. "I've heard that Ken was a bit of a womanizer."

"You are the queen of understatement, aren't you?" Yolanda started to turn over cards. "He would screw anything in skirts."

"Do you know who his most recent mistress was?"

"No. And that was peculiar." Yolanda studied her nails.

They were painted candy-apple red and manicured into perfect ovals. "Usually he liked to rub my nose in his conquests, but this time he kept it hush-hush. Even had me stop answering his private line. I figured this one must have a real jealous husband."

"Maybe somebody jealous enough to kill him?"

Yolanda nodded. "That's what I was thinking."

"I hate to ask, but did you yourself ever, ah . . ." Skye trailed off, not quite knowing how to phrase her question.

"When I first started working for him, we had a brief fling." Yolanda turned over a queen of hearts and put it on top of a king of spades. "But I knew it wasn't ever going anywhere, and I ended it."

Skye's expression was skeptical.

"Look, that man's idea of honesty in a relationship was to tell you his real name."

"So everyone says. I wonder how he ever got women to go to bed with him, considering his reputation."

"They were blinded by his prestige and money. And they were able to convince themselves that they were special. That they were the one who would change him."

Earl had been silent while the women talked, but now he scratched his crotch and said, "The only woman who knows where her husband is every night is a widow."

Glenda charged into the kitchen and whacked Earl on the head with a hairbrush. "You best remember, I'd better know where you are every night, mister, or I *will* be a widow."

Earl mumbled, "Geez, I was just bein' funny."

Glenda grabbed his ear and pulled him from the room. "I keep telling you, you ain't that amusin'."

With that insightful observation, Skye stood up. "Thanks for taking the time to talk to me. Sure wish I knew more about his latest affair."

"Well, you could always ask his ex–cleaning lady, Dorothy Snyder." Yolanda didn't look up from her card game. "You might want to ask her about why she was fired, too."

As Junior walked Skye out to her car, she mulled over Yolanda's last comment. Her mom and Dorothy had been good friends since grade school. May would probably smack her the same way Glenda had hit Earl if she tried to question Dorothy. So how could she get the information she wanted without ticking off her mother? Junior's tug on her sleeve interrupted her thoughts.

He gestured for her to lean down and confided, "Did you know that if you spray dust bunnies with hair spray and then run over them with Rollerblades, they catch on fire?"

"No, I didn't." Skye opened her car door. "It sounds sort of dangerous."

"Nah, it's fun."

"Have you tried it?"

He nodded and grinned. "The basement has a cement floor, and it's real good for skating. We took all the dust bunnies from under the beds and put them in a laundry basket and brought them there. It was sorta like fireworks."

"What did your parents think of that?"

"Mom was mad that we used up all of her Final Net, but Dad said it was cool and he'd buy us our own can."

# CHAPTER 11

*The wheel that squeaks the loudest . . . gets the
grease.*

—Josh Billings

"What time are you leaving?" It was late Saturday afternoon, and Bunny was on Skye's bed grilling her about her evening plans.

Skye stood in front of her closet. Some days it felt like she spent more time figuring out what to wear than wearing it.

Bingo was sitting on Bunny's lap purring loudly as she brushed him. The feline and the redhead had become fast friends.

"Simon's picking me up at six. We're going to dinner, then to the GUMB dance." Skye tensed, sure Bunny would beg to come along, and she'd have to tell her no. Skye hated being in the middle between mother and son.

"What're you going to wear? How about the short black number?"

"This?" Skye reached into the back of the closet and withdrew a black silk sheath with a beaded V neckline and a lace hem. When Bunny nodded, Skye asked, "How did you know I had this dress?"

"Every woman has a black dress," Bunny said smoothly with no hesitation.

Skye narrowed her eyes. "Have you been going through my things while I've been away?"

"Of course not." Bunny maintained eye contact and an innocent expression.

She was either telling the truth or a very good liar. Skye would wager it was the latter. "Have you checked with Charlie today?"

Bunny went rigid. "What do you mean? Why would I talk with Charlie?"

"About renting a cabin at his motor court." Skye wondered about Bunny's reaction. What had happened between her and Charlie after they left the bowling alley last night? "What else could I mean?"

"Renting a room. Right. I should go call him now. Last night he said some people might check out today." Bunny lifted Bingo from her lap to the floor, stood, and backed out of the bedroom.

Bunny was acting odd. Skye shrugged. There was nothing she could do about it—short of interrogating the older woman—and she wasn't quite ready to do that. Turning back to her closet, she pondered the age-old question: What to wear?

The flared skirt on the bronze velvet dress swirled around Skye's knees as she twirled in front of the full-length mirror attached to the back of the bathroom door. Since this was the Thanksgiving Dance, it was a little more formal than usual. She just hoped this outfit was right. Most of the other women attending this function had rich husbands and could afford to purchase their clothing from stores at which Skye could only window-shop.

The doorbell rang while she was fastening citrine studs to

her ears, and she yelled, "Bunny, could you get that, please?" Did she need a necklace? No. The lace insert that veed down the bodice was enough. A swipe of cinnamon lipstick, a spray of Chanel, and she was ready.

When she opened the bedroom door, she found Bunny and Simon sitting on the sofa. Bunny was saying, "You remember what fun we used to have? Remember that day you ran naked through Grant Park, and skinny-dipped in Buckingham Fountain? You were three and the cutest little boy ever."

Simon's expression softened for a second, then iced over. "I remember you left the next morning."

Bunny sagged. "Me and my big mouth. I guess I shouldn't have mentioned that."

"Time to go." Skye walked over to Simon and pulled him from the couch. Over her shoulder to Bunny she said, "When you get hungry, there's a couple of TV dinners in the freezer."

The exterior of the GUMB Assembly Hall looked different at night. Shadows softened the shabbiness, and hinted at what the building had looked like when it was brand-new. A golden cone of light spilled from the fixture above the front door.

Although shoveled clean, the sidewalk had glazed over with newly fallen sleet. Simon steadied Skye as her foot slid. "What I don't understand is why Bunny is still staying with you," he said. "Surely Charlie has an opening by now. Some people must have left this morning."

"She called him while I was getting dressed this afternoon, and he's still full. I think as soon as one batch of stranded travelers leaves, the weather gets bad again, and another group checks in. Besides, he has only twelve cabins, and they're usually full of hunters and ice fishermen." Skye shed her coat, and handed it to Simon to hang up.

Simon guided Skye to the ballroom. They stopped at the

entrance and looked around. It had been dramatically altered since Thursday night's meeting. Chairs were now positioned along the sidelines, and the wooden dance floor gleamed under twinkling lights strung from the ceiling. Evergreens and flowers had been strategically placed around the periphery.

Simon frowned, clearly fighting the urge to stay on the subject of Bunny, but took a deep breath instead. Finally he smiled. "Have I told you how beautiful you look tonight?"

"No. I'm fairly sure I'd remember that. You look extremely handsome yourself."

He ran a hand down her back. "Your clothes always feel so good."

"Thank you. I like to be comfortable as well as look nice." Skye fingered his burnished gold shirt. "This is a great color on you. It matches your eyes."

"If you two are through admiring each other, maybe you could get the hell out of the way so someone else could get in."

"I'm so sorry. We wouldn't want to keep you from anything important," Simon apologized and moved aside. He murmured to Skye as Nate Turner pushed his way past, dragging a barely dressed woman in his wake, "Like an appointment with Miss Manners."

"Is that his wife he's towing behind him like a bass boat?" Skye asked.

"That's Polly, and, yes, she is a little dinghy."

Skye snickered at Simon's joke, then said, "I feel sorry for her. He's the most obnoxious man I've run into in a long time." She described his behavior at the grocery store on Wednesday. "Why did they nominate him for head honcho?"

"Assmosis. He kissed up to the movers and shakers."

It took Skye a second to get it, but then she giggled. "Simon Reid, I can't believe you said that."

"I'm chock-full of surprises."

"You know, despite everything, you and your mother do have some traits in common."

"Yeah, we breathe." Simon took her hand. "So, do you want to dance, or talk about Bunny?"

"Dance." Skye had never enjoyed dancing until she met Simon. She had no sense of rhythm, but his natural grace and casual expertise made her feel like Ginger Rogers.

They entered the dance floor and were immediately swept into the crowd. Skye recognized most of the couples on the floor. Everyone from Thursday's business meeting was there, but many of those men seemed to be doing more talking than dancing. Several of the wives sat on chairs lined up against the wall and looked bored.

When the band took a break, Skye said, "Let's go say hi to Vince." Her brother was the drummer in the group.

"Sure." Simon cupped her elbow and they moved toward the stage.

At the front of the room, Vince was already leaning against a wall and swigging from a can of Mountain Dew. His long butterscotch-blond hair was tied in a ponytail, and beads of sweat shone above his emerald-green eyes. He was dressed in black jeans and a black suede vest, with no shirt. His perfect tan and sculpted muscles seemed out of place in the dead of winter.

He hugged Skye and shook hands with Simon. "I didn't see you guys arrive. How long have you been here?"

"About a half hour," Skye answered. "The band sounds wonderful." The group had only been together for six months. She was surprised at how much they improved with every performance.

"Thanks. Big crowd tonight. I thought between the snow and the murders, no one would come." Vince crushed the soda can. "I hear you and Dad found the bodies. You okay? Mom says Dad's been real quiet."

"Dad's always quiet. I'm fine, but it was an awful experience."

Simon put an arm around her. "Skye's had a rough few days."

"So I hear. A surprise houseguest, a bad cold, and a couple of dead bodies. Not your run-of-the-mill week in Scumble River."

"True. Thank goodness." Skye moved closer to Vince. "You always know all the gossip. Who was Ken Addison's latest lover?"

"Funny you should ask. That's been quite a topic of conversation at the shop." When he wasn't drumming, Vince owned and operated the Great Expectations Hair Salon.

"And?"

"And no one seems to know." Vince smirked. "Man, that guy was a sleaze. He must have screwed half the women in town, and a good percentage of those in the surrounding area."

"You haven't exactly been a monk yourself," Skye said. "Shall I start naming names?"

"Hey, I'm not like him. According to what I hear, sex was more addicting than heroin to that guy." Vince looked at his watch. "Time to get back on stage. See you later."

"What do you make of that?" Skye asked Simon as they headed toward the back of the room.

"If Addison was the sex junkie Vince thinks he was, it's odd that all of a sudden he started being discreet about his love life." They had reached the bar. "Do you want something?"

"A diet Coke." Skye nodded toward the rest rooms. "Try and find an empty table. I need to use the facilities."

As usual, there was a line in front of the ladies' room. Skye leaned against the wall and concentrated—she had waited too long and now she really had to go. A familiar voice penetrated her meditation. It couldn't be, could it?

"My philosophy is never pass up an opportunity to pee,"

Bunny confided in a loud voice to the woman standing behind her, before disappearing into the rest room.

How had Bunny gotten to the dance? Skye had a bad feeling she was about to find out. It was her turn to go in the bathroom next.

The ladies' room was tiny. Two aqua metal cubicles took up half the space; a sink with a mirror and a folding chair occupied the rest. The walls had been painted a hideous stomach-medicine pink.

Bunny stopped primping and waved when Skye came into view. Skye fluttered her fingers in acknowledgment as she hurriedly entered the stall. She hoped Bunny would be gone by the time she finished using the toilet, but the older woman was still there when she came out.

Bunny made room for her at the sink. "I bet you didn't expect to see me here."

"You'd win that bet. How'd you get here?"

"Your sweet Uncle Charlie was kind enough to escort me."

"He called and asked you out?" Skye would need to have a talk with that man.

"Actually"—Bunny applied mascara to lashes that already were already black and gooey—"I asked him. At first he said he was too old for this kind of nonsense. But I told him that once you're over the hill, you're supposed to pick up speed, not slow down."

"Oh." Skye washed her hands and reached for a paper towel.

Bunny put away her makeup bag, then swung a leg up on the chair's seat to adjust her nylons. "You know, men and pantyhose have a lot in common."

"They do?"

Bunny said with a straight face, "Yeah, they both either droop, run, or don't fit in the crotch." Skye burst out laughing, and Bunny slung an arm around her. "Let's go find the boys."

The "boys" had found each other. Simon and Charlie were sitting at a table for four. Skye noticed Simon was drinking a glass of wine. Since he usually stuck to diet soda, he probably already knew about Bunny's presence.

As Skye and Bunny approached the men, Nate Turner barreled in front of them, trailed by his wife, who wore a short see-through lace dress and stiletto sandals.

Bunny frowned, and Skye could almost hear her thoughts. Compared to Polly's flashy outfit, Bunny's red spandex tube dress and leather bolero jacket looked tame.

Turner ignored Simon and the women, and concentrated his wrath on Charlie. "Patukas, what's this crap about you running for Imperial Brahma Bull?"

Charlie pushed back his chair. "You got a problem with that, Turner?"

"Yeah, I do." Turner poked Charlie in the chest with his index finger. "You're going to split the vote and let that horse's ass Ginardi win."

"Funny." Charlie rose to his full six feet, towering over Turner, who was broad but not tall. "That's what he said about you."

Simon got up and stood beside Charlie.

"You better watch it, Patukas." Turner continued to jab his finger into Charlie. "You're not the big shot you used to be."

"And you never were." Charlie took Turner's finger and bent it back. Sweat popped out on the other man's already flushed face, and he tried to back away. Charlie growled, "Never, ever touch me again." Suddenly Charlie released Turner's finger, and Turner staggered.

Polly rushed up and took her husband's arm. He shook her off like a dog getting rid of a flea and stomped away. She tottered after him at a prudent distance.

Charlie turned toward Skye and Bunny as if nothing had happened. "Ladies, just in time. You both look gorgeous."

Simon shot Bunny a hard look. "I was surprised when Charlie told me you were here."

"You know I hate to miss a good time." Bunny moved closer to Charlie and hugged his arm.

"Even if it means ruining someone else's." Simon walked to the opposite side of the table.

The four of them stood there, an awkward quartet. Skye searched for something to say. Nothing came to mind.

Bunny didn't seem to have the same problem. "So, who was The Blob, and why was he threatening Charlie?"

While Charlie explained the situation to Bunny, Skye quietly said to Simon, "You know, it's possible that Turner killed the Addisons over this grand pooh-bah thing. And if that's true, Charlie could be in danger."

"Turner does seem to be a loose cannon. But do you really think being elected the head of a small-town organization would be enough motive for murder?"

"Who knows? I wonder if he had any other reason to dislike Dr. Addison."

"Hey, you two, did you come here to talk or to dance?" Not waiting for an answer, Bunny pulled Charlie away from the table and danced him away.

"If she doesn't leave town soon, I'll be the one committing murder," Simon said, gritting his teeth as he and Skye sat down.

"Just be patient. You said yourself that she never stays long. All you have to do is wait her out." Skye had decided not to mention that Bunny was hunting for a job in town. "You know, maybe you should give her another chance. For your sake, if not hers."

"No. Dad and I gave her a hundred chances to straighten out. She blew every one of them."

"Well, maybe instead of wanting her to 'straighten out,' you could just accept her as she is, and have a relationship based on that."

"Why should I?" Simon's expression was stubborn, like that of a disappointed four-year-old.

"In my experience, getting rid of emotional baggage is always a good thing."

Before he could respond, Polly Turner sidled up to their table and said to Simon, "Would you dance with me?"

He threw Skye a quizzical look, and she nodded. "Sure. It would be my pleasure," he said.

Skye tapped her fingers on the table. That was odd. Nate Turner did not impress Skye as the type of man who would allow his wife to dance with other men. Something was up. A shadow loomed over her, and she sucked in a loud breath.

"I want to talk to you," Nate Turner demanded.

Ah, so that was it. Polly had been sent to lure Simon away, and leave Skye sitting alone. "So talk."

Instead, he stared at her chest.

Skye waited a second or two then said, "Are these your eyeballs? I found them in my cleavage."

His eyes snapped to her face. "What're you talking about? I was just thinking," he blustered. "You dames are all alike."

"Right, and the same could be said for you jacka . . . gentlemen." Skye raised an eyebrow. "Now that we have that settled, what did you want?"

He pulled out a chair and plopped down. "People say you're pretty good at figuring things out."

"Things?" Skye asked.

"Murders. I hear you solved more cases than Perry Mason before he turned into Ironside."

Skye tried to follow the man's train of thought, but she was afraid it had derailed. "I wouldn't say that. But, yes, I helped the police out a couple of times."

Garlic and beer fumes washed over her as he leaned closer. "I want you to figure out who killed Ken Addison."

She scooted away. Barbie's death was obviously not important to this cretin. "Why do you care?"

"He was a good friend of mine, a fellow GUMB, and I want justice."

"Say I believe that, even for a second. What makes you think the police won't find the killer?"

"The police in this town don't know their ass from a hole in the ground."

"Chief Boyd and all the other officers are extremely competent."

"It sure doesn't look that way since a girl has to solve all their really hard crimes for them."

*Girl!* Skye couldn't remember meeting a more odious person than Nate Turner. He seemed to hate everyone and everything. He treated people like toilet paper, to be used and flushed away. She was beginning to really hope that he was the murderer, and she was the one who pinned it on him. "I appreciate your confidence in me. I'll do what I can to find out who killed Ken *and* Barbie Addison."

"Good. Let me know what you find out."

Skye stared at him and thought, *Yeah, I'll report to you the day you vote for a woman to be president.* She chewed her lip. Another faction heard from. First Tony Zello and Bob Ginardi, and now this clown. The GUMBs must have some mighty big secrets they didn't want brought to the public's attention.

A few minutes later Simon and Polly returned to the table. Polly looked at her husband like a dog who has been kicked in the past looks at its master, like she knows she'll be kicked again. "Did you have a nice talk with Skye?" she asked.

"We came to a mutually satisfactory conclusion," her husband answered, and clomped away. Polly followed.

"What was that all about?" Simon asked.

Skye explained, then said, "That man has made me realize why people get divorced even though it's so expensive."

"Why?" Simon seemed puzzled by the swerve in the conversation.

"Because if you were married to someone like him, it'd be worth it."

# CHAPTER 12

*Be to her virtues very kind;*
*Be to her faults a little blind.*

—Prior

Who would have guessed that Bunny would want to go to church? Skye scrutinized the redhead sitting next to her on the wooden pew. What was Bunny up to now? For Sunday morning services she had chosen a fairly modest pantsuit. Granted, it was made out of cranberry stretch velour with metallic threads, but at least the neckline's V was not plunging, and the top and pants met in the middle so her belly button didn't show.

They had made it through Mass without incident, but Skye couldn't relax. She still had to get Bunny out of the building without any close encounters of the embarrassing kind. Could she slip her past Father Burns's watchful eye? Who knew what totally inappropriate comment Bunny might make to the priest.

The choir started the closing hymn and Bunny joined in, her confident alto surprisingly sweet. Skye exited the pew, stepping back so Bunny would be in front of her. They were shuffling down the aisle with the crowd, and the door was in sight, when Bunny veered to the left, stopped dead in front of the priest, and stuck out her hand.

Father Burns took it and asked, "Are you new to our parish?"

He was a tall, ascetic-looking man who had been the priest at St. Francis for as long as Skye could remember.

"I'm here visiting my son. He's Simon Reid. He owns the funeral home."

"Yes. I know Simon well. A fine young man. He was at the eight o'clock mass." The priest smiled. "You don't look old enough to be his mother. But then, they say life starts at fifty."

"Too bad it starts to show then, too."

Father Burns patted her hand. "In the end, looks won't matter. We'll be judged on how we lived our lives."

Bunny frowned at his comment, and hurriedly changed the subject. "I'm staying with Simon's fiancée, Skye Denison."

The priest looked at Skye. "I didn't know you two were engaged."

Skye had stood silently, hoping the priest wouldn't notice her, but now she felt herself flush. "We're not. Wishful thinking on our parents' parts."

His dark, serious eyes studied her for a long moment, but he didn't pursue the matter. Instead he said, "I understand you and your father were the ones to discover those unfortunate people's bodies on Wednesday."

"Yes, it was awful."

"Does Chief Boyd have any idea who committed the crime?"

"I don't think so." Skye wondered why the priest was so interested. The Addisons were Episcopalians, not members of his congregation. "Have you heard anything?"

"Dr. Addison had many enemies. Several people blamed

him for their loved ones' deaths. They say his treatment plans were not always in the best interest of the patient."

"Did they have any grounds for their accusations?" Skye asked. She remembered what Yolanda had said yesterday about the poor medical treatment Ken Addison provided to his patients and was curious to know how many people in town knew what he had been up to.

The priest shrugged. "The first few people who complained, I chalked up to grief, but there have been several in the past year—more than you'd expect about one doctor."

Skye nodded. So his patients, or at least their families, were beginning to figure things out.

Bunny danced from one foot to the other and sighed loudly, clearly bored with the conversation. When there was a pause, she jumped in, steering the attention back to herself. "Hey, Father, I just thought of something I've always wanted to ask a priest."

Skye flinched, and prayed that Bunny's question had nothing to do with sex.

"Yes?" Father Burns turned to the older woman.

"How come no one sat on the other side of the table at the Last Supper?" When he didn't answer right away, Bunny added, "You know, in all the pictures everybody's facing the camera."

He blinked, then said with a straight face, "I'll need to look into that."

"Okay, but you let me know when you figure it out."

Skye breathed a sigh of relief as Bunny moved away from the priest. That hadn't been too bad.

Father Burns patted Skye's arm with a cool dry hand. "This too shall pass."

"I know God won't give me more than I can handle," Skye said over her shoulder as she followed Bunny. "I just wish he didn't trust me so much."

A smile played around the corners of the priest's mouth, but he didn't comment.

Bunny had walked down the stairs and was nearing the door when suddenly she stopped, and started back up.

Skye made a grab for her and missed, then hurried after her, demanding, "Where are you going?"

"I want a bulletin."

"Why?"

Bunny shrugged. "It's like a receipt for attending Mass. If anyone asks, you can prove you were there."

Skye wondered how many times proof of church attendance was required.

As soon as Bunny grabbed a newsletter from a pile on a side table, Skye took her arm and steered her outside, breathing a sigh of relief as they reached the parking lot. It was snowing again as they got into the Bel Air. Skye started the engine and was grateful when warm air came rushing out of the vents. With such an old car, it was always possible that the heater wouldn't work or the convertible top would fall down.

An aqua 1957 Chevy Bel Air was not exactly the vehicle of Skye's dreams, but her dad and Charlie had restored it for her, and there was no way she could turn down their gift. Besides, for some reason the cars she drove tended not to have long lives—which was not her fault—and she figured there was a fifty-fifty chance this one would be totaled before spring.

Skye turned on the radio and the announcer said, "Now for the weather and road reports. Snow is predicted on and off the rest of today, and the highways remain impassible due to the high winds and ice."

So far the local road crew had been able to keep the streets clear in Scumble River, and Jed had kept their families' driveways plowed, but they were pretty much cut off from the next town. Skye was stuck with Bunny for at least one more day.

When they got home, Skye surveyed her refrigerator. Normally she would have had dinner with her parents and

Vince, but May had not asked her this Sunday. Skye suspected her houseguest's presence might have something to do with her mother's lack of hospitality.

"What's for lunch?" Bunny leaned against the kitchen door while she filed her nails.

"We have our choice between cereal, tomato soup, and peanut butter. There's no milk or bread, but I did manage to snag a box of crackers from one of the stores we stopped at, and I have some hamburger buns in the freezer."

Bunny had polished off most of what Skye had been able pick up on Thursday. Skye had stopped before church at both of Scumble River's groceries, but hadn't been able to buy much. Due to the weather, the supply trucks weren't making it through with any regularity.

"Do you think Sonny would bring us something?"

Skye shook her head. "No, probably not." The woman was clueless. Simon was more likely to bring her rat poison than a hot meal.

"Why don't you call and ask him?"

Skye thought briefly of telling Bunny that Simon wanted her gone, but instead settled for a partial truth, realizing that the older woman wasn't ready to hear the rest. "Simon has some work to do this morning, and a town council meeting to attend this afternoon. Although we haven't received a check yet, Scumble River is supposed to be getting a donation of a hundred thousand dollars soon. The council is meeting to talk about what the money should be spent on."

"How about after the meeting?" Bunny pressed.

Skye gave up. "Sorry. He's not coming over today at all."

"Did you two have a fight?" Bunny put her hands on her hips. "I hope you didn't get him mad at you and ruin my chances to talk to him."

Skye bit her tongue. Lord, this would be a long Sunday.

# CHAPTER 13

*A sadder and a wiser man,*
*He rose the morrow morn.*

—S. T. Coleridge

Monday morning, Skye arrived at the elementary school, relieved to be back at work and vowing that, no matter what, Bunny would move out that afternoon. Sunday in the cottage with her had been endless.

Skye signed in at the main office, and grabbed a stack of messages from her box. Flipping through them, she edged past the counter and into the back room to use the telephone. She punched in the nonemergency number for the police department, and the dispatcher answered on the first ring.

Skye identified herself and asked to speak to Wally. When he came on the line she said, "Can we get together for lunch to talk about the murders?"

"Sure. What time?"

"How about twelve-thirty at McDonald's?" Skye had only a thirty-minute lunch hour, but since she'd be going between schools, she wouldn't have to count her travel time.

"Okay. Have you heard something interesting?"

"I had a few fascinating conversations at bowling Friday night, with the Dooziers Saturday morning, and at the dance on Saturday. Even my priest had something to say after Mass." Skye twisted the cord on the phone. "Gossip really *is* the lifeblood of this town."

"Men don't gossip."

"Then how do they keep track of who's 'easy'?" she asked, and hung up before he could answer.

Skye greeted several teachers as she made her way out of the main office and down the hall toward her room. There was a pleasant buzz in the air that she attributed to the short week and the upcoming Thanksgiving holiday.

Her office at this school was even tinier than the one at the junior high. It was hardly bigger than a Porta Potti, and outside the door was the milk cooler that had occupied the space before it had been assigned to Skye. The refrigerator made strange gasping and squawking noises that often scared the kids she was working with.

Still, it was her own private room—except on Tuesday and Thursday mornings when the speech therapist used it. Skye hung her coat behind the door, placed her WISC-III kit on the floor by the desk, and tucked her purse in the drawer. This morning she planned to write a psychological report and evaluate a student suspected of having a learning disability.

It was close to ten o'clock by the time Skye finished her report, set up the material for the first test, and went to fetch the fifth-grader. The girl's class was just returning from recess—a perfect time to take a child for testing.

The teacher introduced Skye by saying, "Audrey, this is Ms. Denison. You're going to go work with her this morning, but she'll have you back in time for lunch with your friends."

Skye walked the girl down the hall, making small talk until they were in her office. After settling the child on a chair opposite her own seat with a folding tray table containing the test material between them, Skye said, "Audrey, do you know why you're here?"

She nodded. "My parents told me you were going to see why learning is so hard for me."

"That's exactly right." Skye smiled at the girl, glad her parents had explained things so well. "The tests I'm going to give you are nothing like the tests you take in school. There's no grade. I want you to do the best you can, but it's all right to say, 'I don't know.' These tests are given to kids who are as old as sixteen, so I don't expect you to know all the answers."

Audrey looked interested.

The black canvas case holding the Wechsler Intelligence Scale for Children–Third Edition sat next to Skye's chair. She took a spiral-bound booklet from the case, and opened it to a few pages from the front. "What's missing from this picture?"

Audrey breezed through the first subtest, getting all but five of the answers correct. She did well on the first few questions of the second subtest, too.

Then Skye asked, "How is dew formed?"

Audrey hesitated before answering, "The sun shines down on the leaves and makes them sweat."

Skye's expression remained neutral, but she had to fight a smile as she asked the next question. "What is a planet?"

Audrey was more confident this time. "A body of earth surrounded by sky."

"What is a fibula?" Skye was curious what the girl would come up with. So far she had shown a lot of creativity.

Audrey wrinkled her brow. "A small lie."

A knock interrupted them. Fern Otte, the school secretary, poked her head in the door. "Sorry to bother you, but there's a problem, and Mrs. Greer would like you to come to the office immediately."

"Sure." Skye stood up, curious. Caroline Greer, the elementary school principal, rarely asked for help. "Could you escort Audrey back to her classroom?"

Fern nodded and left with the girl. Caroline and Theresa Dugan were sitting silently in the principal's office when Skye arrived.

Caroline waved Skye to a chair. "We had an incident in our first grade this morning that I'm not quite sure how to handle, and I'd like your opinion."

"Okay."

"Theresa, tell Skye what happened."

"About a half hour into class, I noticed that Mack Craughwell was squirming around, scratching his crotch, and not paying attention to the lesson. I went over to see what was going on. He whispered to me that he'd had stitches 'down there' over the weekend and they were itchy." Theresa looked at Skye. "I was afraid to ask him why he would need stitches in that area, so I sent him to the health room."

Skye nodded and glanced at Caroline. The principal's expression gave nothing away.

Theresa continued, "The nurse wasn't here, so Fern had Mack call his mom and ask what he should do."

"That sounds like a good decision." Skye studied Theresa, who looked flushed.

"Right. So he called her and returned to class. I didn't want to embarrass him any further, so I didn't ask what his mother had said."

Skye nodded again, agreeing that was appropriate.

Theresa's face went from dusky rose to ruby red as she finished the story. "I had just started a new lesson when suddenly there was a ruckus in Mack's part of the room. I went over to investigate, and found him sitting at his desk with his you-know-what hanging out."

Skye's eyebrows rose. "Oh, my. What did you do?"

"I had him zip up and marched him down to the office."

Which should have been the end of it, but obviously wasn't. "Then what?"

"When we got here, I asked him why he'd done that."

"What was his answer?"

"He said that his mom told him that if he could stick it out until noon, she'd come pick him up from school."

There was a moment of silence, then Skye snickered. "So, what do you want my opinion about?"

Caroline leaned forward. "Do we believe him? Was it a misunderstanding, or is he playing us all for fools?"

Skye considered what she knew about child development and asked, "Did his mom really say that?"

Caroline nodded.

"Then I'd believe he was telling the truth and let him off the hook." Skye blew out a long breath. "Let's face it, this is not a matter we really want to have to investigate, right?"

Caroline and Theresa both nodded.

As Theresa and Skye left the office, Theresa gave Skye a sly glance and said, "Gee, I wonder if this is how Ken Addison got murdered."

Skye looked puzzled.

An amused twinkle lit her eyes. "You know, maybe Ken stuck his weenie out when he should have kept it zipped in his pants."

Skye laughed, then sobered quickly. "Speaking of that, how did Barbie take his fooling around on her?"

"She never gave the slightest indication that she was aware of his affairs." Theresa shrugged. "But she should have expected it. Hilary told me he was engaged to someone else when he met Barbie."

The comforting thing about McDonald's was that it never changed. Sure, they occasionally added or deleted menu items, and sometimes even redecorated, but the essential experience of eating there remained the same.

Skye turned into the restaurant's parking area at exactly

twelve-twenty-five. The absence of Wally's cruiser indicated that he hadn't arrived yet.

The asphalt was currently clear of snow, but an eight-foot mountain of the white stuff was heaped in the center of the lot around a light pole. At the rate they were going, the pile would still be there in April.

She maneuvered the Bel Air between two yellow lines. The huge car made parking a challenge, especially if another car took up more than its allotted space. And backing out could be a nightmare if the vehicles behind her were sticking out too far.

Skye turned off the engine and flipped the rearview mirror toward her. Her hair still looked good. She had taken the time that morning to use hot rollers, and with the low humidity, her normal curls had been tamed into hanging in a long curve over her shoulders. A couple of quick strokes of blush, a coat of lip gloss, and she was good to go.

The temperature was dropping, and Skye tightened her green paisley scarf as she carefully picked her way across the slick blacktop. She did not want to perform a pratfall for the lunch crowd.

When she neared the door, someone reached around her and swept it open. She turned, and Wally's warm brown eyes met hers. He smiled, put his free hand on her back, and guided her inside.

Skye moved away from his touch and walked toward the counter. "Brrr. Sure has gotten cold again."

"Weather Channel is saying we might get below zero tonight." Wally followed her. "I can't remember the last time we had a November this bad."

"Hi, may I take your order?" The woman at the counter interrupted their small talk, glancing pointedly to the line that had formed behind them.

"Sure, sorry. I'll have a cheeseburger Happy Meal with a diet Coke," Skye said.

Wally stared at her. "A Happy Meal?"

"Yes." Skye stared back. "I want a cheeseburger, small fries, and a soft drink, which is exactly what a Happy Meal is. It's cheaper than the adult version, plus I get the toy, which I'll use as a reward for one of the kids."

"I see you have it all figured out." Wally turned to the counter woman. "Give me a Quarter Pounder with cheese, large fries, and coffee." He laid a twenty on the counter and pointed to Skye. "This is for hers and mine."

"I'll pay for my own lunch," Skye objected.

The woman behind the counter handed Wally his change, and he said to Skye, "Too late."

Sweeping a glance across the dining area, Skye headed for a table in the rear corner. She liked having her back to the wall and face toward the action. That way she could observe without being in the spotlight herself.

Skye and Wally put their trays down and took off their coats before sliding into opposite benches. Wally's face was drawn and his eyes were bloodshot.

Skye asked, "Are you still having trouble sleeping?"

"Some." He started to add something, then stopped.

"What?"

"I was just going to say that between the murders and Darleen, missing a little sleep is the least of my worries."

"I'm sorry to hear that." Skye didn't encourage him to go on. She didn't really want to get into the topic of Wally's ex-wife.

Wally didn't take the hint. "I told you she started calling me at the end of last summer."

Skye nodded politely.

"At first it was just to talk. She felt bad about the way she had left me. But now, she's admitted that she and the new guy aren't getting along, and since I'm not dating anyone, she's convinced I want her back—"

"That's a tricky situation, but I'm sure you'll figure things out," Skye cut him off. "Sorry to rush you, but I have to get back to school soon and I wanted to ask for a rundown on the Addison case." Skye gave him a sidelong glance. "I figured since you had asked me to be your spy at GUMB activities, you'd be willing to share information."

"Sure." An easy smile played at the corner of his mouth. "Though, I don't have much to report."

"Has the time of death been determined yet?"

"Generally bodies lose heat at about one and a half degrees per hour. One of the problems with this case is that whoever killed them turned up the thermostat before he or she left, then one of our officers turned it down, so we don't know the true temperature inside the house from the time of death to when they were discovered. The best the medical examiner can say is that they died between thirty minutes and three hours before you found them at ten-thirty."

Skye had taken the legal pad with her questions out of her purse. She jotted down Wally's answer, then asked, "Did they find any evidence at the scene that pointed to the killer?"

"There were hundreds of fingerprints all over the inside of the house and garage, but none matched anything in our computer system. The techs are coming back this afternoon and processing the Addisons' vehicles to see if we can come up with something."

"Why?"

"Both cars were sitting in the driveway. Maybe one of the victims gave the killer a ride to the house." Wally shrugged. "We just want to make sure we cover all the bases."

Skye glanced around. No one was paying any attention to them. "So, do you think the murderer was looking for something?"

"We can't rule out robbery completely, but even though the house was trashed, the TV, jewelry, and quite a bit of cash were all there." He leaned forward, his forearms on the table. "My guess is that whoever did it was in a rage. Maybe they were looking for something, or maybe they just wanted to destroy everything the Addisons stood for."

"Do you have any suspects?"

A line formed between Wally's brows. "Addison was a real piece of work. His little black book was in three volumes, he had a slew of unhappy patients, and he had made a lot of enemies during his presidency of the GUMBs."

"Imperial Brahma Bull."

"What?"

"That's the correct title for the head of the GUMBs," Skye answered distractedly as she shredded a napkin. "So you haven't narrowed down the suspects at all?"

The chief wadded up the trash from his lunch and stuffed it into his empty coffee cup. "Nope. Half the town is on the list."

"Any alibis?"

He shook his head. "Not really. Some have witnesses for a part of the time in question, but not the full three hours."

"Did you find out anything about their financial situation? Why Barbie was selling Instant Gourmet rather than playing tennis at the country club?"

"Everything indicates that they had plenty of cash and assets. They had a big mortgage and huge credit card bills, but they never missed a payment, and there was more money coming in each month than going out." Wally shrugged. "Maybe she just enjoyed having all those other women working for her."

"She might have liked the feeling of power and control." Skye twirled her straw. "I guess because I hate selling things to people, I think everyone does." She took a sip of her diet Coke. "Thanks for telling me all this."

Wally put Skye's trash on his tray and stacked them together. "You know I trust you."

She felt a rush of pleasure. She had lost his trust for a while some months back, and it was good to have regained it. "By the way, at the GUMB bowling league Friday night, Tony Zello and Bob Ginardi asked me to investigate the murders. And Saturday night at the dance, Nate Turner asked me to do the same thing."

"I wonder what those three are up to."

"I'm pretty sure it's something to do with GUMB secrets. I'll let you know if I find out anything."

Wally nodded.

"As I mentioned earlier, I visited Yolanda Doozier, Addison and Zello's office manager, Saturday morning."

"What did she have to say?"

"Did you question her?" Skye asked.

"Briefly. She wasn't too talkative."

Skye smiled. This was an advantage she had over the police, and one reason Wally appreciated her help—people who wouldn't talk to the cops would often talk to her. "She told me quite a bit about Ken's womanizing, but she doesn't know who his latest fling was."

"Nothing new there."

"Right. The part I found interesting was about Ken and Tony's relationship." Skye leaned forward and told Wally what Yolanda had said about the research money. She ended with "So it seems to me that Tony had a real grudge against Ken, and might even benefit from Ken being out of the picture. Maybe now Tony can take over that lucrative grant Ken stole out from under his nose."

"Not bad. I'll check and see if Zello is in line to pick up Addison's research project now that he's dead. Did Yolanda know what type of research the good doctors were doing?"

"No." They were silent until Skye said, "Oh, I almost forgot. Father Burns mentioned Addison's unhappy patients after Mass yesterday."

"Yeah, we're trying to get the court's permission to let us look through his medical files. But doctor/patient confidentiality is a bear to get around."

Skye slid out of the booth. "Well, I'd better get going."

He deposited their trash in the bin, and they walked outside. Skye unlocked her car and slid inside.

Wally stood in the open door and stared into her eyes. "I'm glad for your help with this case, but be careful. There's a lot of violence in this killer."

"I won't take any chances." She crossed her fingers and added under her breath, "That I absolutely don't have to."

# CHAPTER 14

*O, what a tangled web we weave . . .*

—Sir Walter Scott

During the rest of the afternoon, Skye thought about what she had learned at lunch. It hadn't occurred to her until she talked things over with Wally that there were really two motives stemming from Ken Addison's medical practice— Tony Zello's anger over losing the grant, and the patients who felt they had been mistreated.

When the teachers' dismissal bell rang at three-thirty, Skye stuffed her appointment book into her purse, grabbed her coat, and hurried out of the building, anxious to get home and oust her unwanted houseguest.

Five minutes later, Skye was home. She fed Bingo, then went into the guest bath to clean his litter. *Shit!* Her breath caught in her throat. She knew Bunny was a slob, but this was too much. Used towels and dirty washcloths were everywhere, the floor was sticky with what Skye could only hope was hair spray, and red nail polish had dripped on the pale gray marble counter.

"Bunny." Skye waited a second. No response. She tried

again, louder. "Bunny." No answer. That did it. Bunny had crossed the line. If Skye had wanted to raise someone with this type of behavior, she would have adopted a teenager. "Bunny! Get in here right now!"

"What?" Bunny yelled back. "I'm on the phone."

"Hang up and get in here right now."

"It's a real important call."

"Now!"

Bunny darted into the bathroom. "That was about a job. I need to call them right back. Can't this wait?"

"No." Skye swept the small room with her arm. "Look at this mess."

"Yeah. I was wondering when your cleaning lady comes."

A picture of May with a bottle of Windex briefly flitted across Skye's mind, but she firmly thrust it away. "You're looking at her."

"Oh." Bunny played with the zipper of her warm-up jacket. "Ah, so I guess I should clean this up. I'll do it as soon as I call back about that job."

"Do it now." Skye glared. "Cleaning supplies and rags are in the utility room."

"Really." Bunny backed up. "I'll do it later, as soon as I finish with that call."

That was it. Skye had had enough. "There is no later for you. At least not in this cottage." She grabbed the redhead's hand and led her into the great room. "Start packing."

"Don't be like that." Bunny shook herself free and sat on the couch. "I'll clean the bathroom, but I need to find a job."

"That's not the point. The point is you showed up six days ago saying you needed a place to spend the night, and I reluctantly let you stay here." Skye located her house-guest's suitcase, flipped open the lid, and started stuffing Bunny's belongings inside. "You said you wanted a chance to get to know your son again, and I've tried to help you. But so far you've made no effort toward that goal. In fact, you seem to be doing everything in your power to alienate him further. All you've done is put me in the middle."

Bunny jumped off the sofa and tried to take out what Skye was putting into the suitcase. "I just need a little more time to figure out how to convince Sonny I'm sorry."

"You need to start by acting sorry." Skye continued to pack.

"I know I've been a lousy mother." A single tear ran down Bunny's cheek. "But it wasn't all my fault. Sonny's father and I had different dreams. He wanted a white picket fence and a nine-to-five job. I wanted a chance to see if my dancing could take me somewhere other than Scumble River, Illinois. Haven't you ever wanted to see if there was some other kind of life out there for you?"

Skye paused in her packing, remembering how badly she had wanted to leave Scumble River, and how hard it had been to admit her failure and return.

Bunny pleaded, "I've made mistakes, but is another chance too much to ask for?"

Skye flashed back to her valedictorian speech over fourteen years ago when she had said that Scumble River was filled with small-minded people with even smaller intellects. When she moved back, the citizens had given her a second chance. They hadn't made it easy, but they'd given it to her. Maybe Bunny deserved a second chance, too.

"I'll do whatever I can to persuade Simon to spend some time with you, but that's all I can do. And no matter what, you can't stay with me any longer. My mom told me Charlie has an empty cabin now."

Bunny froze. "But . . . ah . . . I mean . . ."

Skye had never seen Bunny at a loss for words. Why was moving into the Up A Lazy River Motor Court so upsetting? Charlie must have been right about her money problems. Well, that didn't matter. If worse came to worst, Skye would pay for Bunny's room. "I'll give you an hour to make your call, pack, and clean up your mess, then I'm driving you over to the motel."

Bunny burst into tears and collapsed on the couch.

Skye turned her back on the sobbing woman, forcing herself to harden her heart and not give in. She walked into her bedroom and leaned against the closed door, her heart pounding. Phew! That had been a lot more difficult than she thought. She wasn't used to talking to people like that. It was exhausting.

After slipping off her clothes, she stretched out across her bed wearing only her panties and bra. Her fingertips idly traced the stitching on the quilt. It had deep rose-colored diamonds and ivory rings on a cranberry background, and had been on every bed she'd owned since her Grandma Leofanti made it for her when she turned sixteen.

To take her mind off her escalating domestic issues, she turned her thoughts to something even more disturbing—the Addisons' murders. Too bad she hadn't been able to find out the identity of Ken's latest mistress. Was she losing her touch as a sleuth?

No. Bunny's presence had been a huge distraction. Once she was gone and Skye had her cottage back to herself, she'd be able to concentrate. She began making a mental list of people to talk to. Tony Zello, Dorothy Snyder . . .

The repeated ringing of the doorbell merged into Skye's dream, and she woke up disoriented. It finally occurred to her that Bunny should be answering the door.

She jumped out of bed and grabbed her robe from the hook in the bathroom. What was going on? Why did whoever it was keep ringing and ringing? If no one came to the door, most people just went away.

Smoothing her hair and hoping her face wasn't creased from her unexpected nap, Skye ran through the great room and into the foyer. She peered out the side window and saw Wally and Roy Quirk on the step. Both were in uniform. Uh-oh. What now? She doubted they were bringing news that she had won the Publishers Clearing House Sweepstakes.

She flung open the door, but before she could invite them in, Wally said, "Is Bunny Reid staying with you?"

"Yes, for the moment. Why?"

"We'd like to talk to her." Wally had on his official face, and Skye knew now was not the time to get any information from him.

"Sure. Come on in. Excuse me while I put on some jeans. I was . . . ah . . . just changing from my school clothes." Skye was not about to admit they had caught her sleeping.

Come to think about it, where was Bunny? She hadn't been in the great room when Skye walked through. A quick glance to her left confirmed she wasn't in the guest bath, although it had been cleaned. The kitchen was empty, too.

The men were watching her, waiting. Skye chewed her lip. Aha! She remembered the last time Bunny had disappeared. Skye went through the kitchen. Wally and Quirk followed her. She slid open the pocket door to the utility room. Bingo raced out between their legs, startling Quirk, whose hand went to his gun.

The small room was empty. A washer and dryer took up one entire wall and a built-in table took up a second. Shelves above the appliances held detergent, softener, stain remover, and a laundry basket. The only other items in view were an ironing board and a hamper.

"Where is she?" Wally asked.

"Her things are still here, and she doesn't have a car. She has to be around somewhere."

They searched the cottage. No Bunny. Skye didn't have a garage or a shed. There was no place to hide outside.

"Could someone have picked her up while you were sle . . . changing clothes?" Quirk asked.

"I guess so, but she doesn't know many people in town." Skye hesitated. "At least I don't think she does."

"Could she be with Simon?" Wally asked.

"Oh, I really doubt that." Skye didn't explain why. She was sure Simon wouldn't want everyone to know his business. "Maybe she's with Charlie. But I was going to drive her over there, so why would she have him pick her up?"

Wally shrugged. "I'll call Simon and Charlie while you put on some clothes."

When she came out of the bedroom, Quirk was gone and Wally was on the sofa flipping through one of Bunny's fashion magazines. He seemed bemused by the contents. He pointed to a girl with orange hair sticking straight up all over her head and asked, "Is she dressed up to go trick-or-treating?"

"No, that's the latest style."

He shook his head and threw the periodical on the coffee table. "Not in Scumble River."

Skye didn't comment, but instead asked, "Any luck?"

"Nope. Simon and Charlie both say they haven't seen or heard from her today."

"Where'd Quirk go?"

"I sent him back to the station. No use both of us wasting our time."

"So, why do you want to talk to Bunny?" Skye had waited as long as she could stand to ask the question.

"I can't talk about it," Wally said, then added, "I promise I'll tell you all about it after we find her."

"Not that I mind the company, but are you just going to sit here and hope she shows up?"

"No, you can call me if she comes back." Wally got up and moved toward the door. Bingo rubbed against his legs, and he reached down to pet him.

Skye stared at the cat. "How did Bingo get locked in the utility room?"

"Huh?"

"He was out here when I got home from work. I rarely close the door between the laundry and kitchen, so how did the door get closed and the cat get on the other side?"

"Oh." Understanding dawned on Wally's face. He put a finger to his lips and beckoned Skye to follow him.

They walked quietly through the kitchen and silently surveyed the utility room. Skye poked Wally in the arm and pointed to the hamper. It was about three feet high and two feet deep.

He nodded, stepped up to it, and threw back the lid. Bunny squealed, then popped up as if she were jumping out of a cake at a bachelor party. One of Skye's bras was draped over her head, and a pair of slacks hung from her shoulders like a cape.

Wally moved back and held out his hand. "Mrs. Reid, I presume?"

Bunny shook off the dirty clothes and accepted his help as she climbed out of the hamper. She fluffed her curls, batted her lashes, and said, "Call me Bunny."

"Okay, Bunny, you need to come with me to the police station. I have some questions I want to ask you about—"

Bunny interrupted him, nodding at Skye. "Let's wait until we're alone to do this."

Skye sat on the familiar vinyl couch in the police department waiting area. She couldn't count the number of times she had been forced to spend hours and hours with the sofa's old springs poking her in the derrière. Bunny's bravado had quickly faded, and she had begged Skye to come with her. Wally hadn't objected, so here she was. Too bad neither Wally nor Bunny wanted her in the interrogation room.

In the meantime, she had phoned Simon. He was in the middle of a wake, but said he'd call to see what was happening when it was over. He hadn't been shocked or even particularly upset to learn of his mother's interrogation. If anything, he seemed resigned.

It was nearly seven-thirty. A matron from the county had arrived a few minutes ago, which meant they could finally begin questioning. Skye wasn't sure whether it was a state

law or a Wally law that a woman had to be present when a
female suspect was interrogated.

Either way, they'd had to wait for more than forty-five
minutes while the matron drove over from Laurel. Scumble
River needed to hire a female deputy.

Skye's thoughts skittered in another direction. Maybe she
should call Loretta. Loretta Steiner was one of the best criminal attorneys in Illinois, and she and Skye were both alumni
of Alpha Sigma Alpha sorority. They had lost touch after
college, but a couple of years ago, when Skye's brother had
been charged with murder, Skye had called her. Since then
Skye had provided the lawyer with three other Scumble
River clients. Should Bunny be the fourth?

No. Bunny was an adult, and she had been clear that she
didn't want Skye to call a lawyer. Skye would just have to
curb her natural instinct to help.

Bunny hadn't wanted Skye to call Simon either, but that
was different. No way was she keeping something like that
from him. That had to be one of the top ten ways to get your
lover to leave you.

Skye's stomach growled. She looked at her watch. Eight
o'clock. She never did get any supper. What was taking
them so long? Why did the police want to talk to Bunny?
Was it about the Addison murders? What could she have to
do with that?

Finally the door between the waiting area and the rest of
the station opened.

Bunny trotted through, followed by Wally, who said,
"Now remember, you promised not to leave Scumble
River."

She made an exaggerated X across her chest. "I
promise."

Skye stood up. "What's going on?"

Wally looked at Bunny. "Okay?"

"If you have to." The older woman stuck out her lower
lip and pouted.

"You agreed it would be best," Wally reminded her.

The redhead heaved another big sigh. "I said go ahead."

"Bunny's compact was found in Ken Addison's car."

"What? How did it get there?" Skye looked at Bunny. "You knew Dr. Addison?"

"He was at the motor court when I tried to get a room. He drove me over to your place."

"Why was he at the motor court?"

Bunny shrugged. "It looked like he was checking out."

Skye glanced over at Wally. "How interesting. Did Charlie mention that Addison had rented a cottage?"

"Originally we never thought to question him," Wally said. "After all, Addison lived right in town. But when I called just now, he confirmed Bunny's story. Said Addison was a frequent flyer."

Bunny headed toward the door. "If you all are through, I'm starving."

Skye started to follow but stopped. "Wait a minute. How did you know it was Bunny's compact?"

"By her fingerprints," Wally answered.

"How did your fingerprints get into the police computer?" Skye asked the older woman.

Bunny licked her lips. "Ah, I had a teensy little problem, and I'm on court supervision."

"What did you do?"

"They claim I forged a prescription for some pain medicine, but that's not true," Bunny huffed. "My doctor told me to take those pills whenever my back was bothering me. I ran out, and I was just trying to get some more. I was following doctor's orders."

"I thought you couldn't leave the state if you were on court supervision." Skye had a lot of other questions, but that one seemed the most pressing. Was Bunny a fugitive, running from the Nevada police?

Wally answered, "She hasn't. She was arrested in Chicago."

"But you said you came from Las Vegas."

"That's true. Only I thought Sonny still lived in Chicago, so I stopped there before coming here." Bunny folded her arms. "Can we get something to eat now?"

Skye considered making Bunny explain things more fully, but decided Simon really needed to be present at that discussion. "I'd better get her some dinner before she gets cranky," Skye said to Wally. "Do you want to come to the Feed Bag with us?"

"No, I'm heading home. I've been on duty since seven this morning."

"Okay. Get some rest." Skye ushered Bunny out the door.

Bunny was uncharacteristically quiet as they drove to the restaurant, were seated, and placed their orders. Skye slipped away and called Simon. The wake had ended at eight-thirty, and he was just cleaning up and making sure things were set for the funeral the next day. He'd meet them at Skye's. When she tried to fill him in on what she had found out since their last phone call, he told her to wait until they were face to face.

Skye had just taken a sip of her hot chocolate when Bunny said, "I hope you're not two-timing my son with that police chief."

Skye snorted the hot liquid. After she mopped her face and recovered, she asked, "Why would you say that?"

Bunny snapped her fingers, no small trick considering her nails were an inch-long with tiny rhinestones glued to the tips. "It's obvious he has the hots for you."

Simon's Lexus was parked in Skye's driveway when she and Bunny returned from the Feed Bag. Even though she was expecting him, the meal she had just eaten formed into a lump in her stomach. This showdown wouldn't be pretty.

Bunny and Skye got out of the car and went up the sidewalk. Simon met them at the front door holding Bingo.

Skye walked in, kicked off her boots, and hung up her coat. "Have you been here long?"

"About fifteen minutes."

"How'd the wake go?"

"It was Mrs. Jeffries. She was ninety-two, so people were sad but not distraught." He answered aloud, then muttered under his breath, "I've helped hundreds of families say good-bye to their loved ones, and I can handle that. But here I am with a mother I thought I had buried long ago, who pops up and insists on exhuming the past, and I don't know what to do."

During this exchange, Bunny had tried to sneak past Simon and into the bathroom. He grabbed her by the hood of her fuchsia fake fur jacket. "Let's hear it."

"Hear what?" Bunny attempted to shrug out of the coat and escape.

"For starters, why the police wanted to question you." Simon put Bingo on the floor, steered his mother into the great room, and sat her down on one of the director's chairs.

"I need to use the little girls' room first." Bunny rocked from cheek to cheek.

"Fine, but don't think you can stay in there until I give up and leave."

She scurried away without responding.

Skye put an arm around him. "Want some tea, coffee, a stiff drink?"

"There isn't enough alcohol in the world to make that drink stiff enough." Simon hugged her. "Why did she have to come back?"

"So you two could get straight with each other?" Skye guessed.

He sighed and buried his face in Skye's neck. "She's not going away, is she?"

"Not for a while. Wally wants her to stay in town until the Addison murders are solved."

He became rigid. "She's involved with that?"

"I am not," Bunny said, returning from the bathroom and plopping down on the sofa.

"Glad to hear it." Simon moved in front of her, and stood looking down. "Then why is the chief of police telling you not to leave town?"

"Well." Bunny twisted a red curl. "You see . . ." With some prodding from Simon, Bunny ran through the whole story and finished by saying, "So, he gave me a ride, and my compact must have fallen out of my purse."

Simon zeroed in on the part his mother had skimmed over. "But you are on court supervision for forging a prescription."

"I explained all that. It was just a silly misunderstanding."

"You seem to get involved in a lot of misunderstandings." Simon refused to let her look away. "And they all seem to involve you trying to get something that you're not entitled to—like Dad's money."

"Now, don't be like that." Bunny tried to take his hand, but he shook her off. "That's not how it happened at all."

"No?" Simon raised a brow. "Funny, I remember it clearly, almost as if it had been videotaped."

"I loved your father." Bunny played with her hair. "But he and I wanted different kinds of lives."

"You loved him so much you went to his bank, withdrew ten thousand from his savings, and left." Simon stared at his mother. "What am I missing?"

"He told me I could have the money. He understood I had to give my dancing one last chance." Black mascara trails forged their way down Bunny's cheeks. "A friend called me and said that a new hotel was going up in Las Vegas, and a friend of a friend was in charge of putting together the show. But I had to get there right away so I could audition. And if I got a spot, I'd need enough money to live on while we rehearsed. It was my last chance to be a star."

"And how'd that work out for you?" Sarcasm dripped from his voice.

Skye frowned and opened her mouth, but quickly closed it. This was not the time to interfere.

"Not too bad." Bunny spoke into her chest. "It was good for a while."

Simon's expression softened, but then he shook his head and his mouth took on an unpleasant twist.

Neither mother nor son seemed to know what to say next. Bunny's makeup had long since dissolved, and the years of bad decisions were a road map on her face. Simon's shoulders drooped. Skye could feel her neck and head throbbing with tension. They all needed a time-out and some rest.

Skye moved over to Simon and whispered in his ear, "It's too late to take her to the motor court. She can stay here one more night, then we'll get her settled over there tomorrow after school. Okay?"

He nodded and Skye relayed the message to Bunny.

"Yeah, we girls gotta get our beauty rest." Bunny yawned and stretched.

Simon frowned at his mother and whispered to Skye, "It seems like forever since we were alone together."

"You two don't have to keep whispering." Bunny moved toward the bathroom. "I'll go take a shower and give you some privacy."

Skye scooped up Bingo and led Simon into her bedroom. She closed the door, wanting to make sure her houseguest couldn't hear them.

Skye had met Simon when she returned to Scumble River a little more than two and a half years ago. They had dated for ten months, broken up over Skye's unwillingness to take their relationship to the next level, and then started seeing each other again six months ago.

In September they had finally taken the big step and spent the night together. Since then, they'd been trying to find a way to continue the intimate side of their relationship without the whole town finding out that they were sleeping together. This had been harder than they expected.

Scumble River was a small town, and both of their jobs put them in the public eye. In addition, each drove extremely distinctive cars, and Skye's mother worked as a police dispatcher. The result was no privacy and a lot of frustration.

As soon as the door closed, Simon pulled her into his arms. She buried her face against his chest. They stood like that for a long moment. She could feel him trying to let go of his negative emotions.

He brushed a gentle kiss to her temple and put his hand under her chin, urging her to look up. His lips slowly descended to meet hers. She shivered at the tenderness of his kiss. There was a well of sweetness in him that he didn't often let anyone see.

Raising his mouth from hers, he said softly, "I needed that."

"Me, too." Skye caressed his cheek with her hand. "Why do we let so many things get in the way of this, of us?"

"It's who we are." He kissed her palm. "We realize that our actions affect others. Both of us have seen what happens when people forget that point, and only care about themselves."

Skye thought of the problems she dealt with at school. Simon was right. She started to move away, but his lips recaptured hers, more demanding this time. She let the heady sensation wash over her and parted her lips.

Gently he eased her down on the bed. He had the first two buttons on her blouse undone when the television in the next room blared into life. Skye went rigid, then quickly slid out from beneath him. She knew she was being a prude, but the thought of Bunny on the other side of the wall drained all the desire out of her.

Simon sat up and scrubbed a hand over his face. His expression was grim, but he shrugged in mock resignation. "Bunny strikes again."

"I'm sorry, it's . . ." Skye struggled to explain, without

sounding like she had just been transported from Victorian England.

"Sit down." He scooted over so he could lean against the headboard and patted the bed. "I understand. Bunny in the next room is a definite mood breaker."

Skye was grateful he wasn't angry. She snuggled against his side.

"Guess I should go home." He looked at the clock. "It's nearly midnight."

Neither made any movement to get up.

"You know what?" Skye said suddenly.

"What?"

"Bunny was right. Sex is a lot like air. It's no big deal unless you're not getting any."

Simon's eyebrows disappeared into his hairline. "You've really hit rock bottom when you start quoting Bunny."

"Very funny." Skye made a face.

"I need to figure out what to do about her. Clearly she's here for a reason and until I figure it out, she's going to stick around. It makes me feel . . ." Simon trailed off, at a loss for words.

"Sort of like when you're sitting on a chair and you lean back so you're perched on only two legs, then you lean back even farther and you almost fall over, but at the last second you catch yourself?"

"Yeah, that's it exactly. Off balance."

"I'm used to it." Skye squeezed his arm. "I feel like that most of the time."

"Well, I don't want to get used to it. I want things to get back to normal."

"I know," Skye said soothingly, but thought, *There is no such thing as normal.* They were silent for a while, then Skye said, "Hey, did I mention Bunny went to Mass with me Sunday? And it was her idea."

Simon rolled his eyes. "Going to church doesn't make you a good person any more than moving to the country makes you a farmer. But thanks for trying." He hugged her. "Time for me to go."

They walked out of the bedroom and to the front door. Bunny was asleep on the couch, pink curlers in her hair and green cold cream on her face.

Skye stood on tiptoe and kissed him. "Night."

"Call me when you leave school tomorrow." Simon put on his coat. "I'll come over and help you move Bunny to the motor court."

"Sounds like a plan."

# CHAPTER 15

*'Tis strange but true; for truth is always strange,—*
*Stranger than fiction.*

—Byron

Skye spent Tuesday morning at the junior high school, meeting with Joy Kessler and the sixth-grade team. They came up with a behavior plan to help Alex be more successful at school. Some of the teachers were skeptical, but everyone agreed it was worth a try.

After lunch Skye drove to the high school. She stopped to empty her mailbox, then went on to her office, by far the nicest of the three in the district. Originally, the guidance counselor had used it, but when the board made that a part-time position and assigned one of the coaches to those duties, Skye had successfully argued that he already had an office near the gym and didn't need this one, too.

Now that they had moved out the metal filing cabinets that contained the guidance records, the room was spacious. It even had a window. Granted, the old metal blinds needed replacing, but considering what she had at the other schools, this was the Taj Mahal.

Skye hung up her jacket on the coat tree she had brought in, a garage sale bargain at two dollars, and sat behind the big wooden desk. The comfy old leather chair welcomed her bottom, and she smiled in contentment before she started to write yet another psychological report.

In the three months they'd been in school this year, she'd already tested twenty-nine kids, and had at least that many coming due for reevaluation. Heaven only knew how many new referrals the year would bring. And they would all need reports written about them. She suffered from permanent writer's cramp, and longed for a computer.

Skye had finished one report and started on another when there was a knock on her door. She looked at the clock. The afternoon had flown by. The dismissal bell must have rung a few minutes ago without her noticing.

She quickly closed the files she had spread out over her desk, turned her legal pad over, and checked that her visitor could see nothing confidential. Only then did she call out, "Come in."

Frannie Ryan, followed closely by Justin Boward, swept through the door and flopped into the visitor chairs facing her desk.

As usual, Frannie spoke first. "We've got to tell you something."

Justin sat forward. "We heard some kids talking, and it could be a clue to the murders."

Skye asked, "What did they say?"

Frannie looked at Justin. "You go first."

"Bert Ginardi was talking to some of his buddies in the locker room while I was changing for PE."

"Is he Bob Ginardi's son?"

Justin said, "Yes. He's always bragging about how rich and successful his old man is."

"Go on."

"Anyway, as usual Bert was me-deep in conversation and didn't notice me." Justin checked to see that Skye had caught his witticism. She smiled and he continued, "He said that his mom and dad were in this group that did some kinky kinds of sex stuff."

"Mmm." Skye wasn't sure how to respond to that, but since both teens were looking at her, she tried to seem interested without being *too* interested.

"What got my attention was when they said that the Addisons had been in the group, too."

"Did they mention any other names?" Skye asked.

"No. They were headed in one direction, and I had to get to class in the other." Suddenly Justin pounded his knee with his fist. "I think talking about your parents that way should be a smiting offense."

"It feels like a betrayal, huh?" Skye knew from Justin's home situation that the subject of parents was a touchy one for him. His father had a chronic illness, and his mother was clinically depressed.

Frannie didn't wait for Justin to respond. "And I heard a girl talking to her friends about this party her parents were having tomorrow at nine o'clock. She was saying it was too bad her folks were making her stay at her grandma's house, or she could get some really incriminating pictures of the town's leading citizens." Frannie twirled her hair. "By the way they were giggling, and the stuff they were saying, it's got to be the same group as the one Justin heard the boys talking about. How many sex perverts can there be in Scumble River?"

That was a question Skye didn't want to think about, let alone discuss with a sixteen-year-old. "But tomorrow's the night before Thanksgiving," she said. "That's an odd time to hold that kind of get-together."

"No," Justin chimed in, "don't you see? That's the perfect time to hold a sex party. Everyone's so busy, and lots of people are coming and going and visiting."

Skye nodded. He was right. No one would notice anything funny going on, because they'd all be occupied with the holiday. Another thought occurred to her, and she asked, "Who was the girl?"

Frannie shot Justin a calculating glance. "Bitsy Kessler."

He frowned. "Why didn't you tell me that?"

"I'd explain it to you, but your brain would explode," Frannie taunted, the look of hurt on her face contradicting her tone.

*Uh-oh, trouble in paradise. Frannie might actually have to admit she likes Justin as more than a friend, or she'll lose him to Bitsy.*

"Well, you two sure have come up with some interesting information," Skye said, "but the more I think about it, the more I'm convinced this isn't something we can write about in our school paper. Anyway, this probably has nothing to do with the murder."

Justin stood up so suddenly his chair wobbled. "That's bogus!" He stalked out of the office.

He was right, and Skye felt like a phony saying it, but she had to keep these two from investigating and stumbling into a dangerous situation.

Frannie stayed seated. "You know this is important." She gave Skye an evaluating look. "You just don't want us involved. You think we're babies."

"I don't know how to say this without sounding preachy, but you really have no idea what you might be getting yourselves into." Skye tried to make the girl understand. "Even if it weren't dangerous, and it is, the whole situation is just so sleazy . . ."

"I hear what you're saying, but *you* don't realize how much sleaze teenagers are exposed to every day. Ever watch one of the popular music videos?" Frannie got up and started to leave. She paused with her hand on the knob. "Hey, I got a different question."

"Okay."

Frannie didn't look at Skye. "What do you do when your boyfriend walks out on you?"

This was not what Skye had been expecting, although considering the Bitsy issue, she should have been prepared for it. "There's not much you can do." She searched her mind for good advice. "The only thing is to make really, really sure he's gone before you close that door."

"Why can't I stay with Skye?" Bunny whined from the backseat of Simon's Lexus. "It's not like she's home much anyway."

Simon kept his eyes on the road, and didn't respond to his mother's complaints.

Skye bit her lip to stop herself from explaining just why she had rarely been in her cottage since Bunny's arrival. Recalling the older woman's histrionics while they were packing her up and getting her into the car, Skye decided silence wasn't just golden, it was platinum, at least in this situation.

When Simon turned left on Basin, Skye noticed that the main street had lost its snow-induced shine and had begun to look shabby again. At six o'clock, most of the businesses were closed, and the only lights came from the restaurant, the bowling alley, and the four taverns.

When the traffic signal on Basin changed to green, Simon turned left again. The buildings on Kinsman were dark, too, until they neared the bridge. The Up A Lazy River Motor Court glowed brightly on the left side, and the Brown Bag's neon signs shone on the right. Skye briefly wondered how the new owner of the liquor store was doing. That had to be a tough business to run.

Simon pulled into an empty parking spot in front of the motor court's office, and cut the engine.

Bunny started to cry. "Sonny Boy, how can you be so cruel to your mama?"

Simon ground out through clenched teeth, "Don't call me Sonny Boy." If Bunny didn't leave soon, he'd end up at the dentist with TMJ.

He got out of the car and Skye met him at the office door.

She glanced at Bunny, who remained in the Lexus, hunched over and crying. "What should we do about her?"

"Let's get her checked in, then worry about it." Simon's tone was grim.

The cowbell over the door clanged as they entered. Moments later, Charlie appeared from the back living quarters, wiping his hands on a red-and-white-striped dishtowel.

His frown turned to a sly grin when he saw Simon and Skye. "Do you two need a room?"

Skye felt her face flush. Pretty soon someone would start a pool as to when they would get married, or pregnant, or both.

Simon arched an eyebrow and said, "As a matter of fact, we do."

"Ah, huh?" It was Charlie's turn to look chagrined. "I mean, what's going on?"

Skye took pity on her godfather. "We're checking Bunny in. Mom told me yesterday you had a vacancy." It hit her that they should have called and told him to hold the cabin for them. "You still have it, don't you?"

"Sure." Charlie went behind the counter. "May had me reserve it for Bunny."

"How does she do that? I don't remember telling her we were moving Bunny tonight," Skye muttered.

"Who knows?" Charlie shrugged. "May has her sources. You might have mentioned it to Wally, who talked about it at the police station. Or Simon could have said something to someone who told May in passing." Charlie took out the sign-in book and handed Simon a pen. "Shall we make this official?"

While Charlie and Simon took care of the business end of things, Skye shed her coat and rested her bottom against the registration desk. She scanned the small office.

A couple of months ago, she had talked Charlie into redecorating. The drab brown walls had been painted a lighter cocoa and hung with oak-framed hunting and fishing prints.

Taupe Berber carpeting had replaced the old flooring, and a new ceiling fan had been installed.

Over massive protests, Skye had convinced her godfather to refinish the wooden top of the check-in counter, and now it gleamed in the overhead light. He had balked at replacing his desk chair, so she'd had the seat padded and the wood refinished.

Charlie grumbled at the waste of money, but she had caught him beaming when people complimented the motor court's new look. Next, she would have to see what she could do about getting him to update the guest cabins' interiors.

The telephone rang, and as Charlie answered, he handed Simon a key attached to an oval plastic holder. It had the number three printed in white on one side, and lettering on the other that advised anyone finding it to drop it in the nearest mailbox and postage would be paid by the addressee.

Skye waited in the office while Simon went outside. She had no desire to accompany him as he attempted to pry Bunny from the backseat of his car.

While Charlie was occupied by the phone call, Skye noticed how much better his color looked than in recent months when summer and various aggravations had made his blood pressure soar. Now he seemed more like his usual self. His doctor—thank goodness neither Zello nor Addison—had prescribed a new medicine, change in diet, increased exercise, and decreased stress. Even though Charlie had ignored most of the advice, his last appointment showed his blood pressure was back within a safer range.

In order to distract herself, and fight the temptation to see how Simon and Bunny were faring, Skye dug into her purse until she found her makeup case. She added a little eye shadow, brushed her lashes with mascara, and put on a new coat of lipstick before returning the small black bag to her tote.

Charlie unwrapped a cigar and put it between his teeth. She tapped her fingernails on the counter to get his attention, and shook her head when he looked up. He was not supposed to smoke.

He covered the mouthpiece on the receiver and snapped, "For crying out loud, I'm not lighting it." Charlie banged down the phone. "You're as bad as your mother." He heaved himself out of the protesting chair and hugged her. "Anything going on at school I should know about?" Charlie was the president of the school board.

He always squeezed too tight. She hugged him back and said, breathlessly, "I don't think so. But we really need a social worker. Any luck in hiring one?"

Releasing her, he headed toward the connecting door. "We've been trying. The few who apply and are qualified say we aren't offering enough money for all the problems they'd have to deal with."

Skye frowned. "Then raise the salary."

Charlie ignored her statement. "What's happening on the Addison murders?"

"Not much. So Ken stayed here a lot?"

"He'd check in for a couple or three hours, once or twice a week."

"Who was his latest companion on these little rendezvous?"

Charlie walked over to her and shook his finger in her face. "You know I don't kiss and tell. I'm kind of like a priest or a doctor."

"Sure," Skye wheedled. "But this is different. She could be the killer."

"Really, I don't know. Ken's last lady friend never came into the office, and she was real careful to make sure no one saw her coming or going."

"I thought you told me when I first moved back here that

there wasn't a person in Scumble River who didn't know every last detail of their neighbor's business," Skye said. Her voice took on a cajoling tone. "There must be something. Some little thing you noticed."

Charlie started to shake his head, then stopped. "Well, once, I did find one of those fake nails among the dirty towels from their cabin."

"Did you save it?"

"Nah. I tossed it in the trash."

Skye sagged. "Shoot."

"Hey, I remember it had something special about it. But what?" Charlie stroked his chin. "Ah, I know. There was a tiny parrot painted in the center."

"Interesting." Skye considered the suspects. Who wore false nails done up that fancy? Yolanda and Bunny came to mind, but Bunny had just arrived in town, and Yolanda claimed her fling with Addison was long over. Besides, Yolanda wasn't married; she'd have no reason to keep her affair a secret. Skye'd have to keep an eye out for anyone else.

Charlie interrupted her thoughts. "So, who do you think the murderer is?"

"Nate Turner." Skye moved toward the door. "Not that I have any reason to single him out, but if I could choose, he'd be my favorite candidate for a life sentence."

"He's an ass, alright." Charlie helped her into her coat. "He sure wouldn't have any problem killing someone who got in his way. And he's strong as an ox, so he is certainly capable of strangling them both to death."

"Good point." Skye's smile turned sickly. She had blocked out of her mind how the Addisons had been murdered. "I'd better see if Simon and Bunny are okay."

Skye was surprised to see mother and son still sitting in the Lexus. Simon seemed to be staring out the windshield. Bunny was talking. Simon got out of the car as soon as he saw Skye. Bunny rolled down her window. Clearly, she didn't want to miss any of the conversation.

"What's going on?" Skye asked Simon.

"She refuses to get out of the car."

"I'll bet I know why." She moved Simon away from Bunny's earshot and whispered in his ear.

Bunny popped out of the car. "What? What?" She trotted back and forth between the two of them like a puppy that had to pee.

Simon held her still by placing a hand on each of her arms. "I'll pay for your stay at the motor court if you promise not to contact me, and if you leave as soon as the police say it's okay."

Bunny started to sob. "Why are you treating me like this? All I want is to spend some time with my only son."

"If you don't agree, Skye and I are getting into my car and driving away, and you'll have to pay for your own room or spend the night outdoors."

"Okay. You win." Bunny's shoulders slumped. "Which cabin is mine?"

"Number three."

She turned to Skye. "If anyone calls for me, about a job or anything, you'll give them this number, right?"

Skye felt a tug at her heart. "Sure."

Simon's expression was hard to read as he retrieved Bunny's suitcase from the trunk. Bunny trailed him as he walked to cabin three. He opened the door, put the bag inside, and handed his mother the key. He let her hug him, then said, "Good-bye."

Silently Simon returned to the car, and he and Skye climbed inside. He started the engine and turned left out of the parking lot. "How about dinner at the Shaft in Clay Center?" he suggested.

Clearly Simon did not want to talk about what had just transpired. Skye decided to go along with him. "My mouth is watering for that chicken already."

They were silent as the miles clicked by. Finally Skye couldn't stand it. "Maybe I should have let her stay with me."

"No." He sighed. "This is my problem. You need her out of your hair."

Skye opened her mouth to protest his statement, but closed it without speaking. He was right. It was a relief to think of having her cottage to herself. And Simon would need to work out his relationship with Bunny himself. There wasn't anything Skye could do to help.

# CHAPTER 16

*I do not love thee, Dr. Fell.*

—Thomas Brown

Skye spent most of Wednesday with a smile on her lips and a song in her heart. For some reason a tune kept playing in her head. It went something like "Ding, dong, the Bunny's gone."

By the afternoon it was clear nothing much would be accomplished at school that day. Everyone's thoughts were on the upcoming long holiday weekend. Skye gave up trying to see students or consult with teachers, and instead sat in her office at the high school writing reports. She was nearly caught up and would start testing again on Monday morning.

As soon as the bell rang, she locked away her files and checked her appointment book to see what was on her schedule for Monday. Since she would be starting the day at the high school, she didn't need to take anything home with her except the student newspaper story ideas.

She shoved those in her tote bag, put on her coat, and walked out to her car. The parking lot was already nearly empty. As Skye got into the Bel Air and turned on the engine, she considered her mental To Do list.

Both Zello and Turner had called her that morning to see if she was making any progress with the investigation. Neither man was happy with her answer, but she had assured them she was still working on it.

With Bunny moved into the motor court, she could finally concentrate on the murders. The question was: Who did she want to talk to first? And the winner was—Tony Zello. Darn. She should have set something up during their phone conversation that morning. Now she didn't know where to reach him.

He wouldn't be at his medical office. No doctor worth his prescription pad worked on Wednesdays. But it was obviously too cold to be golfing. Where would he be?

From what the Bettes said, he wasn't the type to spend much time at home with the wife and kiddies. He was much more likely to be somewhere with the "boys." But where?

Okay, she'd move along to number two on her list—checking in with Wally. She wanted to share what she had learned from her talk with Charlie and see if he had found out anything about Addison's medical research. When she had tried to telephone earlier, the new dispatcher didn't seem to know how to use the radio to find the chief. In fact, she didn't seem real sure of who the chief was. Skye wasn't even positive the woman had known she was in the town of Scumble River.

The police department parking lot was almost as empty as the school's. Her mother's white Oldsmobile, a beat up Ford pickup, and a lime-green Gremlin were the only cars there when Skye pulled in.

She didn't recognize the truck, but she knew the Gremlin was the librarian's. That poor woman worked twelve hours a day for six hours' worth of pay, and the board still tried to cut her salary every year. She'd probably be driving the Gremlin until it rusted out around her.

May spotted Skye as soon as she entered the station and buzzed her back behind the counter. "What's up?"

"I just wanted to talk to Wally for a second. Is he still here?"

"He's in his office." May wheeled her dispatcher's chair away from the computer. "He hardly ever leaves anymore. Seems like he's afraid to go home." She faced Skye. "You know any reason for that?"

Skye shrugged, not about to tell her mother about Wally's problem with his ex-wife calling him. She was a little surprised that May didn't know. Darleen must not phone him at the station. Skye changed the subject. "How's Dad?"

"He's spending a lot of time in the garage with that dog of his." May wrinkled her brow. "I think finding those poor people like that, and then having you in danger, got him real upset. But you know your father, he won't talk about it—at least not to a human."

"True. The Denison men are definitely the strong silent type. They don't yack about a problem—they fix it," Skye said. "And this is something he can't stick a little duct tape on and make it all better."

"Good thing Vince takes after my side of the family. The Leofantis enjoy a good talk. Your dad can be downright aggravating with his silence."

Skye and her mother nodded together in a rare moment of perfect mother-daughter rapport.

After a second, May asked, "Are we still going Christmas shopping Friday?"

"Definitely. You don't have to work, do you?"

"No, I'm off for the next two days. I took the weekend shifts instead." May opened a drawer and pulled out a pad of paper. "I've been making my list. Do you know what you want to get?"

"I'll think about it tonight."

The radio blared, and May turned back to work. Skye waved at her mother and went to find Wally.

As Skye stood in his open office door waiting for him to look up, the faint smell of cigarettes drifted over her. Although Wally had never smoked, the ever-present odor was a gift from his predecessor, along with the faded linoleum and battered metal desk.

Wally finished what he was writing, and spotted Skye as he turned to put the file in his drawer. "Well, hi. I wasn't expecting you."

"I tried to call around lunchtime, but the daytime dispatcher seemed . . ." Skye searched for a kind word to describe the woman's behavior.

"Stupid?" Wally asked.

"I was going to say new."

"Yeah, new to this planet."

"That's not a very gentlemanly thing to say."

"I don't do impressions." Wally leaned back and crossed his arms behind his head. "Remember, Simon is the gentleman. I'm just a cop."

Skye let that comment pass and took a seat. "So, did you learn anything about Addison's research?"

"Yep." A slow smile spread across Wally's face. "Zello wouldn't tell me anything, and the judge wouldn't give me permission to go into the records, but it occurred to me that someone had to be typing his papers. Yolanda said it wasn't anyone in the medical clinic, and I didn't think it would be the good doctor or his yuppie wife, so I put the word out that I was looking for the typist."

"So who was it?" Skye's smile matched Wally's. There was nothing like the grapevine in a small town if you really wanted to find out something.

"The biology teacher at the high school."

"Makes sense. What did he tell you?"

"He showed me the article Addison had gotten published in the *Midwestern Medical Review*. Basically, it boils down to rashes. It turns out that a lot of Midwestern towns located along small rivers have been reporting a high incidence of unspecific skin inflammation among their population. A pharmaceutical company that manufactures dermatological creams is funding a study among doctors who practice in these towns. Addison found a connection between the change of seasons and the rashes."

"How much money did he get for it?"

"The teacher didn't know exactly, but thought it was probably in the neighborhood of six figures."

Skye whistled. "Nice neighborhood." She shook her head. Could someone really have been murdered over a skin rash? She refocused. "Sounds like you've been busy. Oh, before I forget, I wanted to tell you what Charlie told me last night."

"Something he conveniently forgot to tell me?"

"I don't think he was purposely concealing it. It probably never even occurred to him that it was important." Skye crossed her legs. "I was trying to get him to remember something about Addison's latest mistress, and he suddenly thought of a false fingernail he had found among the used towels."

"Did he keep it?" Wally asked sharply.

"No. But he did recall that it had a parrot painted on it." Skye leaned forward. "How many women in town have nails that fancy?"

"Good point. I'll get Quirk to question the local manicurists." Wally rocked back in his chair and stared at the ceiling. "Anything else?"

Skye chewed her lip. Should she tell Wally about the sex party supposedly going on tonight? Quentin Kessler was one of the police commissioners, and Wally had to work closely with him. How would this information affect that relationship? She decided not to mention it and said, "No, nothing right now." Some stones were best left unturned, because if you disturbed them, some really slimy things might crawl out.

As she left the building, she poked her head into the dispatch room and asked her mother, "Any idea where I'd find young Dr. Zello this afternoon?"

May answered without stopping what she was doing on the computer. "Sure. He has a standing appointment with Vince every Wednesday at five o'clock."

Her mother's uncanny knowledge of the Scumble River citizenry truly amazed Skye. It was quarter after five, so if she hurried, Vince would be just finishing Tony's haircut when she arrived.

The gravel parking lot of the Great Expectations Hair Salon had been turned to a frozen concoction that resembled gray peanut brittle—slick and lumpy. Skye was getting really tired of trying to walk across slippery surfaces, and wondered if there were some kind of cleats she could attach to the smooth soles of her boots.

She tugged at the door of the salon, and nearly fell when it abruptly opened. Vince needed to have that repaired. Maybe she'd mention it to her father. It would give Jed something to do, and help take his mind off discovering the bodies. Her dad liked nothing better than a fix-it project.

Only one customer sat in the waiting area. The lone woman looked up as Skye entered, and the cold wind ruffled the pages of her magazine. She was seated on an upholstered white wicker chair, a large black handbag on the glass table in front of her. The garden print of the cushions along with the mauve walls gave the room a spring look. The waiting customer nodded to Skye and went back to reading *People*.

The styling area was located through a lattice archway. This time of year, May had it decorated in the oranges, rusts, and browns of fall, but come next week, the Christmas garland, red ribbon, and shiny gold ornaments would be brought out.

Tony Zello sat talking in an elevated chair, shrouded in a

mulberry colored nylon cape. Vince had on his the-customer-is-always-right face. Once again, May's people-locating radar had been right on the money. If May worked for the FBI, the Ten Most Wanted list would quickly become the We Gotcha list.

Skye sized up the situation. Vince was using an electric razor to trim the back of Zello's neck, which meant he was nearly finished with the haircut. He glanced up from his work and waved at Skye.

She hung her jacket up on the coat rack and walked through the arch, stopping in front of the two men. Vince gave her a quick hug. "Need a trim?"

"No. I'm fine. Thanks." Skye turned to the man in the chair. "Hi, Tony. I realized after I spoke with you this morning that I needed to ask you a few questions, so I was wondering, after you finish here, would you have time to discuss something with me?"

He looked put-upon and glanced at his Rolex. "I've only got a few minutes."

"Well, I'm not going to make much progress on that matter you wanted me to look into until I talk to you."

"If it's that important." Tony looked at his watch again.

Skye took the hint. "Maybe we could talk right here." She turned to her brother, who had finished with Tony and was busy sweeping strands of hair from the floor. "Vince, is the tanning room occupied?"

"No."

"All right if we use it for a few minutes?"

"Sure."

Tony stood up, leaned close to the mirror, and inspected his haircut. He gave himself a little smile, then got out his wallet and handed Vince a twenty, saying, "Keep the change."

Skye stole a quick glance at her brother. That had been a six-dollar tip. Tony was clearly a big spender, at least by Scumble River standards.

"Thanks, Tony." Vince walked over to the cash register and put the bill inside. "Same time next week?"

"Right. Got to keep up the old image."

To Tony Skye said, "The tanning room is this way." She headed for a door that led off the short hallway going back to the shampoo bowls.

After they settled themselves, Tony looked at his watch for the third time. "What's so important?"

"I've talked to some people and a couple of questions have come up."

"Oh?" His mouth tightened. "About me?"

In her best counselor mode, Skye leaned forward with her hands held loosely on her lap. "About Ken and his dealings with people."

"I don't like speaking ill of the dead, and I'll deny I said this, but he wasn't always the most upright citizen." For all his protests, Tony seemed anxious for Skye to know that Ken wasn't one of the good guys.

"I've heard quite a bit about his womanizing. Do you know the identity of his latest conquest?"

His squirming caused the vinyl seat of his chair to squeak loudly. "No, we didn't talk about that."

She looked at him skeptically. They saw each other every day, were partners in a medical practice, and they didn't talk about their personal lives? Maybe men really were aliens from Mars. "But you knew he had affairs?"

"Well, yes. Everyone knew that."

"Did you know who his other women were?"

Tony ran a finger around the inside of his collar, found a stray hair, and flicked it from his fingers. "Most of the time."

Boy, someone needed to talk to this guy about maintaining a poker face. If she and Simon ever got to play bridge against him again, she'd have to remember to tell Simon how transparent he was. "Is it true he and your office manager had a fling?" Might as well check Yolanda's story. It never hurt to confirm the credibility of your sources.

"A long time ago." His grin was sour. "She saw through him pretty quickly."

"Who else did he sleep with?"

"I couldn't even begin to list them all."

"I heard it was almost every woman in the Bettes," Skye prodded.

"Probably," Tony mumbled.

Skye raised her eyebrow. "Including your wife?"

Tony's mouth snapped shut. "That's an offensive question. I'm not going to dignify it with an answer."

In other words, yes. Skye tucked that bit of info away. "Let's change the subject."

"Let's." He slumped back in his chair, clearly relieved that Skye had given up so easily.

"Okay. Let's talk about skin rashes." She watched his reaction carefully as she spoke.

His face froze. "What do rashes have to do with anything?"

Skye tsked. "Please. I'm not stupid. I know Dr. Addison and you were both doing research on skin rashes, and when you began to get close to a solution, he stole the valuable part of your study and turned in the report without your name on it."

Tony shot out of the chair. "How did you find out about that?"

Skye smiled. A direct hit. "I have my sources."

"It's none of your business. It has nothing to do with the murder."

"The fact that he double-crossed you, stole hundreds of thousands of dollars from you, and got his name rather than yours in the medical journals doesn't make you a prime suspect?" Skye asked, deliberately goading him.

"No, of course not." His gaze bounced from wall to wall. "I wouldn't kill someone over that."

"Money and betrayal—seems like a strong enough motive to me."

"Look." Tony sat back down and finally made eye contact. "Would I have asked you to look into the murder if I was the killer?"

"You're a smart man. It would be a clever way to get me on your side."

Tony's face flushed a dull red, and his fists clenched. Skye was glad she was seated nearest the door. How long would it take him to strangle her? Could she summon her brother, or would she be unable to make a sound? An image of the Addisons' bodies floated through her mind and she shuddered.

A few seconds passed and Tony took a deep breath, then reached into his pocket. Not waiting to see what he was grabbing for, Skye popped out of her seat and backed toward the door. No way was she ending up like Barbie Addison.

He waved a small, leather-bound pad with an attached pen at her, and smiled meanly. "Not as imperturbable as you try to appear, are you?"

It was her turn to blush. She couldn't think of anything to say to that.

"And speechless, too. How refreshing." He took the pen from the loop that held it to the notepad and wrote something down. "Sorry to scare you, but you reminded me of something I want to take care of, and I didn't want to forget it. Hope you're okay."

"Guess I had too much coffee today." Skye's heart had returned to its normal rhythm, and she was itching to find out what he had written on that paper. "Maybe I'd better switch to herbal tea."

"That would probably be a good idea. Calm you down some. Help you be less impulsive." His concerned tone was as false as Grandma Denison's teeth.

She frowned. Was he insulting her or threatening her?

She didn't like either possibility. "I prefer to think of it as being alert and spontaneous."

He didn't quite snort, but said, "I need to get going. Was there anything else you wanted to discuss with me?" He moved toward her.

This time she refused to let his actions alarm her. "One last thing. Do you think, with Ken gone, you'll win back some of the patients who have taken their business over to those two women doctors in Clay Center?"

His chest heaved, but that was the only sign he gave that she had hit another nerve. "Some might come back, but it's no big deal. There are invariably more sick people than our practice can handle. Doctors never have to worry about job security."

Skye wasn't sure she believed that, but she let it go. "I've always found it sort of scary that doctors call what they do *practice*." She opened the door and stepped aside to let him through.

At first she didn't think he would respond to her verbal jab, but as he passed her, he stopped and said, "The more I think about it, the more you may be right. Maybe the murderer was some disgruntled patient, or one of their family." Zello made a show of scratching his chin and narrowing his eyes as if deep in thought. "I've seen it happen time and time again. Relatives come in and want to talk to you about the loss of their loved one, but we have a whole roomful of live patients to take care of and we can't drop everything to listen to them. Besides, how do you bill an insurance company for the time you wasted listening to them whine?" Tony shook his head, clearly disgusted with anyone who would stand in the way of his making money.

Skye stared at him, thinking how nice it must be to be the center of the universe—or believe you are.

He shook his head again and went on, "Most people need to learn that no matter how bad they feel, the world doesn't stop for their grief. At least not my world."

Skye tried to quell the slow boil rising inside her. She could feel her hands curling into fists and the blood rushing to her head. If she didn't gain control within the next few seconds, she would punch this coldhearted, unsympathetic son of an ATM machine in the nose.

He must have sensed the danger because he said, "Well, just something for you to think about while investigating poor Ken's murder." He took off at a trot, adding over his shoulder, "Got to run."

Skye found that Vince had finished with his last customer and was getting ready to lock up.

"So, what's going on between you and Zello?" he asked.

"He and his buddy Ginardi asked me to look into the Addisons' murders. They want the killer found before GUMB secrets get out."

"Ah, that makes sense." Vince took the money drawer out of the cash register and started to stack the bills. "Both of them have egos bigger than a beauty queen's hair."

"Have you heard anything new about the murders?"

"No. Everyone's talking about them, but no one is saying much, if you get my drift."

Skye nodded. "Are you bringing anyone to Thanksgiving dinner tomorrow?"

"Nope. Can't single out one lady. It makes the others jealous."

Skye knew her brother rarely dated more than one woman at a time. She tilted her head and looked at him. What, or better yet who, was he hiding from the family?

Vince secured the cash with a rubber band and put it into a small vinyl bag with a zipper. Stamped on the front of the pouch was SCUMBLE RIVER FIRST NATIONAL BANK and the bank's hours. "You bringing Simon?"

"Yes."

Vince put his coat on and helped Skye with hers. As they walked out to their separate cars, he asked, "How about Simon's mother? Are you bringing her, too?"

"Shoot. I forgot about her. I guess we can't leave her sitting all by herself at the motor court on Thanksgiving." Skye felt a headache start to form. Neither Simon nor May would be happy with the idea of Bunny joining them.

# CHAPTER 17

*There is but one step from the sublime to the
ridiculous.*

—Napoleon

After saying good-bye to Vince, Skye drove to her cottage. It was nice coming home to an empty house.
Bingo was all the company she wanted at the moment. He
rubbed against her ankles and purred as she put food into his
bowl, then promptly forgot her existence as he got down to
the serious business of eating. She briefly wondered if
Bingo missed Bunny and vice versa. The redhead truly
loved him and had spent a lot of time petting and grooming
him.

Skye pushed that thought away. Bunny's move to the
motor court was for the best, and Skye had three current
problems to solve, each with its own degree of urgency and
concern. The most pressing one was figuring out what to
bring as her contribution to Thanksgiving dinner. Breaking
the news to her mom and Simon that Bunny would be joining them came next. But, by far, the sex party Frannie and
Justin had told her about was the most worrisome. What if

the kids decided to investigate even though she had told them not to?

First things first. The aunts could bring all the good stuff for family dinners—the pies, the pork sausage dressing, the scalloped corn, and the Parker House rolls. Skye's generation was restricted to the boring things like salads and vegetables. This was a challenge to Skye and her cousins. Each holiday they tried to come up with something new, a dish that would become the next family favorite.

As Skye flipped through her cookbooks, looking for the right recipe, the phone rang. "Hello, sweetheart." Simon's warm voice sent a tingle to her stomach.

"Hi. I was just thinking about you."

"Good. I thought of you all day."

"Ah." Obviously, he was in a good mood. Skye hated to be the one to change it, but it was better to jump in and get it over with. "Before I forget, we'll need to take Bunny with us tomorrow to dinner at Mom's." Silence greeted that statement and Skye hurried to explain. "We can't leave her alone on Thanksgiving."

"She never seemed to mind leaving Dad and me alone on the holidays."

"But that's different. You had each other. You weren't really alone."

Another silence, then Simon said, "You're right. Just don't expect me to talk to her."

"Well, I could ask Uncle Charlie to bring her. That way you wouldn't have to be in the same car with her."

"That's a good idea." Simon sounded happier. "Considering the huge size of your family, I might not even see her there."

*One down, one to go.* "That's right. The women and the men don't even sit together for the meal."

"True. Maybe it won't be too bad." Simon said good-bye after telling her he had a wake that evening and he had to go set up the viewing area. "I'll pick you up tomorrow at eleven-forty-five."

Without even bothering to hang up the receiver, Skye dialed her mother. May wasn't any more thrilled than Simon had been, but admitted that Bunny couldn't be left by herself on a holiday.

Charlie was Skye's next call, and the only one who was happy to hear her suggestion. He said he'd invite Bunny and drive her to Skye's folks'.

Skye picked up a cookbook and resumed her search. Nothing appealed to her. Where was that recipe her friend Sally had sent her for that wonderful chicken liver pâté? It would be a risk. Many of her relatives would turn their noses up at the thought of eating something foreign, but she hoped at least a few of the younger ones would try it. And Simon loved it.

On the down side, she didn't have all the ingredients, which meant a run to the grocery store. The good news was the delivery trucks had finally made it into town, so food would be available. The bad news was every Thomasina, Dixie, and Harriet would be at Walter's picking up last-minute items for tomorrow's big feast. The place would be a madhouse.

As Skye drove to the supermarket, she thought about Frannie and Justin and the sex party that was supposedly scheduled for that night. How could she stop them if they decided to investigate?

The grocery store was as crowded as Skye had been afraid it would be, but at least this time there were carts and no one was fighting in the aisles over food. She grabbed a cart and headed toward the meat department to get the chicken livers.

As Skye rounded the corner, she caught a glimpse of a woman with long blond hair. She was slender, and at her throat she wore an apricot scarf tied in a big bow.

Skye froze and flashed to an image of Barbie Addison

lying in the freezer with the peach ribbon knotted around her neck. The fluorescent lights hummed overhead and the waxed linoleum squeaked underfoot.

Suddenly, Skye felt removed from her surroundings, almost as if she were shrouded in cling wrap. She could see the people around her, but they seemed blurry, as if she were looking through a lens smeared with Vaseline. Too much had happened in too short a time. A sense of dread enveloped her. She couldn't seem to break through the plastic.

Finally, someone brushed against her and everything came back into focus. Skye leaned against her cart and closed her eyes until her head stopped spinning. She looked around. No one seemed to have noticed.

That had been weird. Had she just had a panic attack? Was she experiencing the first signs of post-traumatic stress disorder? No, she refused to believe that. It was just low blood sugar—she'd had only a small salad from the cafeteria for lunch. Or exhaustion—she hadn't gotten much sleep last night. A candy bar and a nap would fix her right up.

Still, she needed to get home. Skye made a hasty circuit of the store, grabbing the ingredients for the pâté and a baguette of French bread to serve it on, then heading toward the checkout.

She joined the ten-items-or-less line and scanned the nearby shoppers. Joy Kessler stood in the next lane, her cart full of chips, dips, and other party munchies. When Skye waved, Joy flushed and turned her head away. That was odd. They had parted on good terms yesterday. Something was up.

Skye felt her heart sink. Frannie and Justin were probably right about the Kesslers hosting a sex party. Now she really would have to do something about the teens' plan to investigate.

It was nearly seven by the time Skye got back to the cottage. After a quick supper, she started making the pâté. Her first challenge was finding a small saucepan. Bunny hadn't put things back where they belonged.

While Skye worked, she considered what to do about the Kesslers' alleged party. An idea came to her as she was putting the completed dish in the refrigerator. At nine o'clock she would call Justin and Frannie. If they were home, she would make up some question about the school newspaper. If not . . . well, then it looked like she might be attending her first orgy.

Neither teenager was home. Justin's mother said he was over at Frannie's studying. Frannie's father said she was over at Justin's watching a video. Skye didn't mention to either parent that the only thing their kids were likely to be looking at was X-rated.

Skye slammed the telephone receiver onto the hook. Crap! There were four aspects of investigating a murder that Skye hated, and now it looked like Frannie and Justin would force her to do most, if not all, of them in one night.

She disliked sneaking around, she detested spying on people's private lives, and she despised having to lie. And more than anything, she hated getting caught. She hoped she could at least avoid the last one.

No matter how many times she told herself that a girl had to do what a girl had to do, whenever she was compelled to sneak, spy, or lie, she felt ashamed.

Fortunately, like most other people, Skye was good at rationalization, and her justification for tonight's foray into the wild side was twofold—she had to make sure Frannie and Justin were safe, and it might help her find out who killed the Addisons.

She pushed the consequences of her last illegal search out of her mind. Getting trapped in a coffin months ago hadn't really been *that* scary. At least that's what she told herself as she put on her black jeans, sweatshirt, and rubber boots. After tucking her hair underneath a dark ski cap, she rummaged in the kitchen junk drawer for her heavy-duty flashlight, a pair of latex gloves, and her Swiss Army knife.

In her car, she headed south of town. As Skye passed the Addisons' driveway, she could see both the Zello and Ginardi houses, and the Kesslers' was just around the corner. They all lived within walking distance of one another.

This was the expensive part of Scumble River, where each of the houses was situated on several acres of land. It was ironic that they all backed up to an old graveyard. The homeowners had fought long and hard to have the bodies moved, but had lost the fight.

At the time, Skye had wondered why they had built their houses there to begin with, if they didn't like living next to a cemetery. It wasn't as if the tombstones had popped up overnight and surprised them.

Tonight Skye was glad of the cemetery's location. Previously the Bel Air's distinctiveness had proved to be a problem in her sleuthing, but the graveyard was the perfect place to stash the Chevy while she was on her spy mission. No one would notice her car parked there at nine-thirty at night.

Skye turned into the cemetery's entrance and stopped. She hadn't considered all the snow they'd had in the past week. Only a narrow pathway was plowed, and none of the normal parking pull-offs were open. Now what should she do?

To her right was a maintenance shed, the area in front of it cleared of snow. Skye pulled in and cut the motor. Surely no one would be doing yard work in the dead of night.

Unfortunately, this put her at the opposite end of the cemetery from where the Kesslers' house was situated, which meant a brisk hike among the gravestones. She wrapped a wool scarf around her throat, tugged her hat down over her ears, and pulled on her mittens before getting out of the car.

Yikes! It was freezing out. Skye much preferred her environment to have a controlled temperature of seventy-six degrees with low humidity. Tromping through a winter won-derland was not her idea of a good time.

She was nearing her destination when she heard rustling. It wasn't the wind—there was no wind—so what or who was in the cemetery with her? As she broke into a jog, she tried to pinpoint where the noise was coming from, and whether it was getting any closer.

It was off to her left and, yes, it was gaining on her. She prayed, *Please, please let it be a nice, friendly dog and not a mean, hungry zombie.* She really had to quit reading Stephen King novels, or maybe just stop going into funeral homes and graveyards after dark.

In the moonlight, the Kesslers' backyard glowed brightly about a hundred yards ahead. Once there, she could at least see what was chasing her. She didn't want to use her flash-light and give away her location.

As Skye cleared the boundary between the cemetery and the yard, she kept running until she reached the side of the house and leaned against the rough brick. Taking huge gulps of air, she waited to see if whatever had been trailing her would follow her into the open area.

Nothing emerged from the cemetery. Could the whole thing have been her imagination? When her breathing got back to normal, she examined her surroundings. The win-dows were dark. At first she thought no one was home, but then she heard music and realized that all the drapes were tightly drawn.

To her left, a vapor light brightly illuminated the area in front of the garage. Skye kept to the building's shadow as she crept toward it. She took a small notepad and pencil from her hip pocket and noted the license plate numbers of all the cars parked on the concrete apron.

She checked all around the house's perimeter and throughout the yard, but there was no sign of Frannie or Justin. Maybe she had been mistaken, and they hadn't come after all. But then, why had they lied to their parents?

With the drapes closed, there didn't seem to be any way to see what was going on inside the house, which meant there was no use sticking around. She decided to take the long way back to her car: down the road, onto the next, and into the front of the cemetery. Somehow, going back among the tombstones did not seem like a good idea.

As she passed the side entrance to the garage, she saw that the door was ajar. She was fairly sure it had been closed the first time she checked. What was going on? She pulled off her mittens and shoved them in her pocket, then tugged on the latex gloves.

The last time she had entered an unlocked garage, it had turned out badly. She hoped this would not be a repeat performance. The sound of a teenage girl's giggle spurred her forward. Frannie!

Before she could take more than a few steps inside, a hand descended on her shoulder. She let out a scream, but another hand quickly covered her mouth, muffling the sound. Slowly she was turned around and came face-to-face with her captor. A light was shined on his face from somewhere to his left, and he put his finger to his lips. When she nodded, he let her go.

Justin Boward stood in front of her, a smirk on his face and Frannie by his side. He pointed to a plain wooden stairway leading to a second-floor entrance and said in a low voice, "The door up there's not locked."

She pulled him and Frannie close and whispered, "How nice. Now let's get out of here."

He shook his head. "They're all in the big room at the back of the house, and you should see what they're doing."

"No. We have to leave right now." What *were* they doing in there? She didn't want to know. Probably best not to get that mental picture stuck in her head.

Justin shrugged and looked at Frannie. The girl said, "Why? We've been inside twice and no one's noticed."

"Try being arrested for breaking and entering, that's

why." Skye was getting frantic. How would she make these kids leave if they didn't want to?

Justin whispered something to Frannie, and she nodded. He turned back to Skye, "We'll leave if you take a look inside first."

"Why?" Both teens shrugged, their expressions impossible to read. Skye knew she would regret this, but she said, "Okay. A quick peek. But you two stay here."

She walked up the stairway, eased open the door at the top, and stepped inside. A burst of laughter greeted her, and for a heart stopping moment she thought she had been discovered. She quickly realized she was standing in a loft area with a balcony that overlooked the living room below. On the other side of the loft was a large playroom with its own set of stairs leading into what she guessed would be the kitchen.

As Skye crept forward, the sound of music and voices got louder. She crouched down by the bottom of the balcony rails and stuck her face close to the opening.

A quick scan of the room confirmed that the gang was indeed all there. It was amazing how many people didn't look good with their clothes off. Skye sat back on her heels and watched in open-mouth disbelief. She might not learn anything about the murders, but she was certainly being taught a lesson in deviant sexual behavior.

Polly Turner, wearing a black satin corset with a matching G-string, was lying on a long, cream leather sofa next to Tony Zello, who had on some sort of black rubber suit that squeaked whenever he moved. Judging from the expressions on their faces, neither seemed to be having a very good time.

Joy Kessler, dressed in an abbreviated French maid's costume, was sitting on the lap of a man Skye had seen at various GUMB functions but never met. They were doing things with whipped cream, chocolate sauce, and maraschino cherries that made Skye vow that she would never again eat a hot fudge sundae.

Hilary Zello had on some wire contraption that looked like a half bra and thong hooked together. Another GUMB member Skye couldn't put a name to was kneeling in front of her as she ground her white stiletto into his backside. He was making the same sound Bingo made when Skye scratched the cat under his chin, but he wasn't nearly as cute.

The more Skye watched, the more it seemed that the partygoers weren't actually *doing* anything. It looked like they were all dressed up for their wildest fantasies, but more pretending to sin than actually sinning.

Still, Skye's skin crawled. Seeing people she knew behave like this was profoundly repulsive.

Tony Zello tottered to his feet and grabbed a martini glass. "May I have your attention, please?"

Skye blinked. The way he was speaking, he seemed to think he had on a tuxedo rather than a rubber suit. What was he supposed to be, a condom?

Tony waited for everyone to stop what they were doing, then continued, "Let's all raise our glasses to the late Ken Addison. The man who talked us into trying these kinds of parties by playing on our fears that we would seem too unsophisticated and 'small town' if we refused." The guests complied and Tony added, "The biggest asshole that ever lived."

Skye noticed that everyone toasted except Polly Turner, who surreptitiously wiped away a tear. Skye squinted. Were there parrots painted on Polly's nails? She couldn't tell for sure from this distance, but it made sense. Parrots were often named Polly, as in "Polly want a cracker?" Charlie had said that the fake nail he found had a picture of a parrot. Could Polly have been Ken's last mistress?

Joy Kessler struggled to stand, and was finally assisted

by a shove on the derrière from her partner. "And to Barbie Addison, runner-up in the contest for chief asshole."

A couple of the men looked puzzled, but everyone raised his or her glass.

Skye rocked back on her heels, and her stomach churned. A small voice inside her warned that it was time to leave. She got to her feet and backed away from the balcony. As she turned around, she smacked into what felt like a padded wall. A moist and smelly padded wall.

Her gaze flew upward. It was Nate Turner. He looked like Bigfoot in a tank top. Rolls of flesh covered with a dense overlay of oily brown hair oozed out of the armholes and from underneath the hem.

He and Skye stared at each other. She thanked God he was wearing boxer shorts. Being exposed to his package would have scarred her for life.

Turner growled, "What the hell are you doing here?"

"Joy asked me to stop by," Skye offered weakly, hoping he might be drunk enough to believe her, even though she was clearly overdressed for this party. "But I must have gotten the date mixed up. This isn't the Instant Gourmet demonstration, is it?"

Turner was blocking her way to the garage stairs, and she didn't think going down the ones leading to the kitchen would be a wise move. She tried to edge past him, but he refused to budge, and she was forced to back up. Coming in contact with that sweaty, disgusting skin again was not something she was prepared to do.

"You nosy bitch. You just couldn't leave it alone, could you?" He lunged for her.

She danced out of his reach. "I was only trying to do what you asked me to—find out who killed Ken Addison. Let me go, and we'll keep this between us."

Turner made another grab for Skye. She stepped farther back and felt the balcony rail dig into her butt. She was trapped. Too bad she wasn't Supergirl. Being able to fly right now would come in mighty handy.

Turner stuck his hand out, and Skye slid to the left. She tried to sound tough. "Did I mention the kick in the groin you'll be receiving if you touch me?"

Before Turner could respond, Quentin Kessler appeared at the top of the playroom stairs, dragging Frannie by the arm. "Look what I found." He smacked his thin lips. "I could go for a sweet young thing right about now."

Skye and Turner both rushed into the playroom.

"I'm not your type." Frannie shook him off and moved over to stand by Skye. "I'm not inflatable."

Quentin grabbed Frannie by the throat, and Skye jumped on his back, clawing at his eyes. "Let her go!"

Turner peeled the three of them apart. "Are you out of your mind, Kessler?" He glared at the other man.

Frannie poked her head around his bulk and taunted Quentin, "What's the matter? Did I step on your poor, little, itty-bitty ego?"

Skye put her hand over the teenager's mouth and hissed, "Shut up."

"You two better keep quiet about this," Turner exclaimed, then added over his shoulder, "I don't want to hear that you've been talking about anything you saw tonight. Now that Ken's out of the way, this will be our last party, and we don't want anyone else knowing they ever took place. Got it?"

Skye nodded vigorously.

"Good. Remember, I know where you live. Now get out of here!"

He didn't have to tell Skye twice. She gave him a quick nod and grabbed Frannie's hand, then they both ran down the stairs and into the garage. "Where's Justin?" Skye paused at the door to the outside.

"He sent me to see if you were okay," Frannie replied. "We unlocked the kitchen patio door when we went inside the first time. The manual says it's important to plan a second escape route."

Skye wondered what instruction booklet the teen had been reading.

Skye thumbed on her flashlight and swept the garage with its beam. No Justin. "Let's look for him outside." She urged Frannie through the door and followed close behind her.

Justin came sprinting around the corner as Skye stepped through the door. He was pale, his expression worried. He panted, "You two okay?"

"Yes, but we have to get out of here right now," Skye said, grabbing hold of his arm.

Frannie took the other arm, and the three hurried down the driveway toward the road.

After they had put some distance between them and the Kessler house, Skye slowed the pace. Once Justin caught his breath, she asked, "What happened?"

"I was about to go in the house when I heard a noise from outside, so I went to check it out. Just as I ran around the garage into the backyard, something disappeared into the trees in the cemetery."

"What?" Skye asked.

"Who?" Frannie chimed in.

Justin shrugged. "All I saw was a flash of white and silver and some weird tracks in the snow."

"Weird, how?" Skye stopped and faced Justin.

"They weren't footprints or pawprints." He paused and thought for a second or two. "They looked sort of like big ovals."

Frannie's eyes widened. "I'll bet it was an alien."

They discussed the possibility of ET arriving in Scumble River as they walked the rest of the way to the cemetery entrance. Frannie had parked her father's pickup just around a bend in the road.

Fifteen minutes later Skye followed Frannie as the girl

dropped Justin off and drove home. It was nearly midnight when Skye pulled into her own driveway. Her cottage was blessedly quiet and empty.

She undressed, adjusted the shower to as hot as she could stand, and stood under its cleansing spray until the water turned cold. After drying off and slipping on her nightgown, Skye crawled into bed.

What had she learned? She ticked the points off in her mind. Ken Addison had been the driving force behind the sex parties. Polly Turner might have been Ken's last mistress. Barbie was as disliked as her husband. And there appeared to be aliens in Scumble River.

As Skye was starting to doze, another thought occurred to her. Unless there truly were zombies living in the cemetery and aliens landing in Scumble River, someone was following her—and it was probably the murderer.

# CHAPTER 18

*Over the river and through the wood . . .*
                                        —Lydia M. Child

Simon pulled his Lexus in between Vince's Jeep and Gillian's minivan, and got out of the car. "Didn't you once tell me that Thanksgiving was your least favorite holiday?" He walked around to Skye's side and opened her door.

Before getting out, she reached into the backseat and retrieved the tray of pâté and bread rounds. "If you recall, my relatives were driving us both crazy when I said that. And since Thanksgiving is the only holiday that both the Denisons and the Leofantis celebrate together, I just meant . . . Heck, I don't know what I meant."

"Whoa, this is slippery. Be careful." Simon did a little tap dance to remain upright. Jed had plowed the driveway, but there wasn't anything he could do about the thin layer of ice. Salt didn't work on gravel.

Skye stopped and pointed. "Isn't that beautiful?" The yard was swathed in a mantle of pure white, with an occasional pawprint decorating its surface.

"I thought you didn't like the snow."

"As long as I don't have to hike through it, shovel it, or scrape it off my windshield, I like it just fine."

"Those trees are certainly magnificent." A windbreak of towering evergreens bordered the property on three sides. "How long ago did your dad plant them?"

"The week my parents moved in." Skye stopped to calculate. "That would have been nearly thirty-four years ago. Vince was three years old, and I hadn't been born yet."

As Skye and Simon stepped up onto the back patio, she noticed her mother's concrete goose dressed in a pilgrim costume, complete with hat, buckle shoes, and a tiny musket resting along its wing. She was extremely relieved to see that May had finally changed it out of the wedding dress it had worn the last couple of months.

She and Simon went into the back door of the redbrick ranch-style house, through the utility room, where they added their coats to those piled across the washer and dryer, and into the large kitchen. Simon waved and said hello to the bustling women but didn't stop to chat. He had learned his lesson the first time Skye brought him for a holiday gathering. The men all sat in the living room while the meal was being prepared.

Skye greeted everyone, then nodded to the tray she was carrying. "Where shall I put this?"

Her mother, standing at the sink draining potatoes in a colander, looked around and said, "Put it on the table under the picture window." May peered suspiciously at the platter. "What is it?"

"Chicken liver pâté." Skye kissed her mother's cheek, and set the dish down.

May tsked. "What happened to the nice Jell-O salad recipe I gave you?"

"Nothing. I just thought this might be something a little different."

"Different is right." May sniffed and turned back to the sink.

Skye's Aunt Kitty was stirring gravy at the stove, and her grandmother, Cora Denison, had the oven door open and was basting the turkey. She kissed both of them and asked her mother, "What do you want me to do?"

"Grab an apron and start wrapping the rolls in foil," May ordered.

Skye wondered why she had even bothered asking. This was the only task they ever trusted her with.

As she started tearing off sheets of Reynolds Wrap, her grandmother asked, "How are things with you and Simon?"

"Good," Skye answered cautiously. Too much enthusiasm and the family would start planning the wedding. Too little and they'd start setting her up on blind dates.

Along a counter bisecting the kitchen from the dinette, her twin cousins, Gillian Tubb and Ginger Allen, sat on stools and rolled silverware into napkins. They were from the Leofanti side of the family.

"What do you think of his mother?" Gillian asked, then smirked at her sister.

Ginger snickered.

Skye could tell they had already heard all about Bunny. "She seems really . . . really . . ."—Skye searched for a word and settled for three—"full of life."

May rolled her eyes. "She's full of something, alright. You'll all get to meet her. Skye invited her to dinner." May paused for effect. "Charlie's bringing her."

A murmur swept through the kitchen, echoing off the celery-colored walls and the freshly waxed linoleum.

Ginger said, "But we heard Simon didn't want to see her. Is that fair to him?"

Skye tore off another piece of foil. "Ginger, all reports are in: life is officially unfair."

That seemed to give the twins something to think about, and they whispered back and forth between themselves for several minutes.

May finished at the sink and moved the bowl of boiled

potatoes to the counter. As she added milk and butter she asked, "Ginger, Gillian, where're your husbands?"

Gillian sighed. "They're defending Scumble River from the threatened invasion of various deer and pheasant."

Skye grinned. *In other words, hunting.*

The outer door slammed, and footsteps sounded from the utility room. Charlie and Bunny had arrived. Bunny entered first, wearing a royal-blue calf-length sheath. Her makeup was subdued, and her red curls were pulled back into a French twist.

For a moment Skye was relieved. Then Bunny moved farther into the kitchen. The slit up the front of her dress opened and the keyhole neckline parted.

Skye's cousins and aunt stared as Charlie made the introductions. Her grandmother nodded pleasantly.

May bared her teeth in a fake smile and said, "Charlie, why don't you take Mrs. Reid into the living room? Dinner will be ready soon."

"Bunny, call me Bunny. Mrs. Reid reminds me of my mother-in-law, may she rest in peace."

Charlie shot May a sharp look—it was obvious he knew that the women stayed in the kitchen—but put his hand on Bunny's back and said, "This way, my dear."

As Charlie and Bunny left, the women started talking. Skye listened as her female relatives proceeded to tear into the subject of Simon's mother.

They stopped abruptly when Bunny reappeared in the doorway. She eyed them all coolly, then grinned. "While I'm always happy to be the only hen in the rooster house, I think the real fun is probably out here." She walked over and linked arms with May. "So, whose reputation are we trashing?"

The men were seated at two long folding tables set end to end in the living room. They filled their plates from the food set out on the counter in the kitchen and then sat down. It was Skye's and her female cousins' jobs to fetch drinks and disburse the hot rolls and butter. She was not happy with her position as serving wench, but fulfilled her duties in order to keep peace in the family.

As Skye poured iced tea into her brother's glass, she whispered in his ear, "Doesn't this archaic double standard bother you?"

"You think of it as a problem?"

Skye hissed, "Yes. I do."

"Funny." Vince grinned. "I think of it as a feature." He held up an empty basket. "Oh, and when you get a chance, we need more rolls."

Skye fought the urge to make Vince wear the breadbasket as a bonnet, and stomped off to the kitchen. When she arrived, the children were going through the food line. They would be seated at card tables in the family room, along with the teens who were supposed to keep an eye on them.

May thrust a pitcher of milk in Skye's hands and said, "Hurry up. What's the matter with you? You're about as quick as a tortoise on Prozac today."

Skye gritted her teeth, and trailed the children to their tables. She had tried to change how things were done several times in the past, but May's silent treatment and the other women's scorn had worn her down. Now she did as she was told, and bit her tongue.

After everyone else had been fed, the women were allowed to eat. They crowded around the dinette table. Skye found herself wedged between her mother and her grandmother, with her back against the wall. Until the people around her left, the only way to get up from the table would be to crawl underneath it.

Skye cut into her turkey and savored the flavor. She had been lucky and nabbed a piece with crispy brown skin. Okay, she had hidden it before anyone else went through the buffet line. She counted this as the one advantage of being chained to the kitchen. The food was wonderful, and she intended to enjoy every bite.

May leaned toward Skye just as she forked sausage stuffing into her mouth. "I thought you were going to try and get into shape."

Skye swallowed, determined not to let her mother ruin this meal. "I am in shape. Round is a shape."

May pursed her lips and turned to talk to her sister, Minnie Overby.

Skye looked around. The twins were chatting with her cousin Kevin's wife. Skye turned to her grandmother and asked, "Do you think it bothers Ginger and Gillian that their husbands never attend any of the family get-togethers? Flip and Irvin always seem to be either hunting or fishing. The only time they show up is for funerals."

"Irvin and Flip may not be the sharpest hooks in the tackle box, but they're hardworking and loyal," Cora replied, buttering a roll. "For a lot of women, that's enough."

"It wouldn't be for me."

"Me either."

Skye knew she shouldn't ask, but she couldn't resist. "What do you think of Simon's mother?"

"There's a lot of hurting going on behind those false eyelashes and that flashy dress." Cora took a sip from her coffee cup. "It'd be best all around if you could help Simon and her make their peace."

"I know. But he doesn't want to hear that."

"You've just got to convince him that living well is the best revenge." Cora's wrinkled face took on a faraway expression. "You tell him that being miserable because of something bad someone did to him in the past just might mean the other person was in the right all along."

Skye pondered her grandmother's words, not sure she was willing to repeat them to Simon, and not even sure she knew what her grandmother meant.

Bunny's voice rose above the others, talking to one of the

Leofanti relatives. "Honey, women may not admit their age, but men don't act it."

Skye fought a grin. Bunny's view of life was certainly unique.

After dinner, the women cleaned up and did the dishes, while the men watched football on TV, played cards, and napped.

The afternoon drifted by. Little groups would form, chat, then drift into other clusters. Skye noticed her cousins were eating the pâté she had brought, but her aunts and uncles never touched it. Next year, she'd stick to Jell-O salad and save the pâté for romantic evenings with Simon.

Once Charlie and Bunny left, Skye felt it was safe for her and Simon to leave. She liberated him from her Uncle Dante, who was extolling the virtues of John Deere versus International Harvester tractors, and they said their good-byes.

As they were driving to Skye's cottage, Simon said, "Well, that wasn't too bad. Bunny didn't do anything too embarrassing."

"She was fine. Grandma Denison gave me some advice about her."

Simon didn't ask what. Instead he said, "I guess I'm just not used to so many relatives. There really was just Dad and me most of the time."

"Families are like fudge," Skye said with a smile. "Mostly sweet, with a few nuts."

# CHAPTER 19

*Rumour is a pipe*
*Blown by surmises, jealousies, conjectures.*
                                                    —Shakespeare

The next morning, Skye eased the Bel Air to a stop next to her parents' house. Before she could unfasten her seat belt, May zipped out the back door, hopped in the car, and said, "You're late. I thought you'd had an accident."

Skye checked her watch. "Sorry, I hit the red light at Basin and Kinsman." There was no use debating the issue. She had said she'd pick May up around eight and it was a minute after. To her mother, anything other than a quarter hour early was late and cause for alarm.

May nodded, accepting the apology as her due. "Where are we going?"

"Wherever you want." Skye was busy backing the huge vehicle out the narrow lane. Her father would never forgive her if she hit either of the white posts at the end of the driveway.

"Well, a lot of stores opened at six A.M. today, but you didn't want to go that early." May pouted.

"Right." Skye refused to feel guilty. No way was she getting up at four in the morning in order to shop. "So where do you want to go?"

"I can't decide between Joliet and Kankakee."

"Your friend, Dorothy Snyder, lives on the way to Kankakee, doesn't she?" Skye had been trying to figure out a way to talk to the Addisons' ex–cleaning lady ever since Yolanda had brought up her name.

"Yes. Why?"

"Then let's go to Kankakee." As Skye headed the car in that direction, she told May about Dorothy's connection to the investigation. She concluded with "I thought on our way back, we could stop by her house for a few minutes and see what she knows."

"But you don't suspect her, right?"

Skye mentally crossed her fingers. "No. I just want an insider's view of the Addison household."

The hour drive went quickly as Skye and May chatted, and before either woman realized it they were at the entrance to the mall. Even though it was barely nine o'clock, the parking lot was packed. Skye left her coat in the car and made a dash for the entrance. May kept on her jacket, but matched Skye's pace.

"Where shall we start?" Skye asked, adjusting her fanny pack and making sure she tucked her keys in one of the zippered compartments.

"I need to get a dress for the police department Christmas party."

Skye was not surprised. No matter what she and her mother started out shopping for, they usually ended up looking for clothes for May.

"What are you wearing?" May asked, leading Skye toward Carson's.

"I'm not going. Remember, I don't work there."

"Oh, right." May shrugged out of her coat and draped it over her arm. "You know, they should put you on the payroll, considering all the cases you've helped Wally figure out."

As they entered the store, an overwhelming mixture of perfumes greeted them. Skye immediately sneezed, and they walked briskly through the cosmetics department toward the misses petite sizes, trying to distance themselves from the overpowering scents.

Shopping for clothing for May was tricky. She wanted an outfit to make her look ten years younger, ten pounds slimmer, and ten times more beautiful. Skye held up a red dress for her inspection.

"You know I don't look good in red."

"Sorry." Skye felt her eye start to twitch. "Give me a hint. What should I be looking for?"

May ticked off the requirements on her fingers. "Nothing fancy. It should be casual, but in a dressy way. No black. Not long, but not short either."

"Okay." Skye's head was spinning with the conflicting descriptions. "That should be easy to find."

"And I don't want to pay a lot of money for it."

It would be a long day. Skye held up another dress, this one a navy blue with a straight skirt and a tailored bodice.

"No. That's too fitted. It would show all my rolls of fat."

Skye bit the inside of her cheek. Her mother wore a size six or eight, and the only bulges were in her imagination.

May finally found a couple of dresses to try on and Skye perched on a bench outside the dressing room, waiting for her mother's command to bring her a different size or color.

The white louvered doors burst open. May strode to the three-way mirror and turned from side to side. "What do you think?"

Before Skye could answer, her mother declared, "It doesn't do anything for me, does it?"

The dress hung loosely on May's small frame. "It's too big." Skye tilted her head. "Why don't I get an eight?" May had insisted on trying on a twelve.

"Then it would be too tight." May's expression was stubborn. "Let me try on the other one and see if I like it."

"Go ahead. I'll be right here." Skye resumed her seat.

The second dress fit a lot better—but May concluded the neckline was too low. Skye's suggestion of a scarf was vetoed, and May decided they should go on to the next store.

As they neared an escalator, Skye spotted Polly Turner descending. Grabbing her mom's arm, she said, "I need to talk to someone. I'll meet you at Penney's."

"Why can't I go with you?"

"You'd be bored." Skye strained to keep Polly in sight. "I'll meet you in the petite dress section in ten minutes."

May muttered, but took off down the corridor.

Skye hurried to catch Polly as she stepped off the escalator. She linked her arm with the older woman's and said, "Polly, what a nice surprise."

"Well, hi. I think all of Scumble River is here today."

"It wouldn't surprise me." Skye maneuvered Polly to a bench, and they sat down. "I know you're probably in a hurry, but I wanted to ask you something."

"Oh?" Polly turned to Skye, a bright note of query in her eyes. "What?"

"I was admiring the artwork on your nails." Skye took the other woman's hand and held it up. "I love those cute little parrots. I've never seen anyone else with those."

Polly puffed out her chest. "And you won't. Those are my original design. I drive all the way to Joliet to have them done."

"Really? Do you always have parrots painted on your nails, or do you have other things, too?"

"Only parrots. They're my trademark. Because of my name."

Skye nodded her understanding. "That's actually very interesting, because Charlie Patukas told me he found one of those nails in a cabin he had rented to Ken Addison for a couple of hours."

Polly's face stiffened. "You must be mistaken."

"No. Uncle Charlie said that normally Dr. Addison was very careful to remove any trace of who he'd shared the cabin with, but this time there was a nail caught in one of the towels."

"That doesn't prove anything."

"I think it proves that before he died, you were Dr. Addison's mistress."

Polly gripped Skye's arm, her nails biting into the flesh. "Please, you can't tell anyone. If Nate found out, he'd kill me."

Skye freed her arm, her response automatic. "Are you sure he doesn't already know? Maybe he's the one who murdered the Addisons."

"No," Polly whispered. "Nate has a terrible temper, but he would never . . ." She trailed off, perhaps realizing that indeed he might.

"I'm sorry"—Skye stood up and scanned the mall, looking for a phone to call Wally and let him know this latest development—"but I have to tell the police."

After making the call to Wally, and helping May try on several more dresses at JCPenney's, Skye and her mother continued their way around the mall. May stopped to look in the window of the Petite Sophisticate shop.

"What do you think of that?" May pointed to a forest-green coatdress.

Skye leaned in to take a closer look, and a reflection of the person standing a few feet behind her caught her attention. What was Lu Ginardi doing staring at them? Skye turned around, and their eyes locked. Skye took a step toward her, and Lu pivoted and walked away.

"Who was that?" May asked.

"Lu Ginardi." Skye stared at the retreating figure. Lu had lost weight since Barbie's Instant Gourmet party.

"Isn't she the one who teased you so bad in high school?" May asked.

Skye nodded absently, still thinking of how gaunt Lu looked. May took Skye's arm, and as they moved toward the next store said, "She flushed your bra down the toilet during PE, right?"

Skye nodded again. "And that was one of her milder forms of harassment." She chewed her lip. Lu looked gray and haggard. Was she sick, or did she have a guilty conscience?

Skye pulled in her chair and looked around the restaurant where she and May had decided to have lunch. "How late did everyone stay after we left yesterday?" Skye asked.

"They were all gone by seven." May straightened the salt and pepper shakers.

"It was a nice Thanksgiving."

"Yes." May flipped the pages of the menu back and forth. "How long is Simon's mother staying in town?"

Skye wasn't sure if May knew that Wally had questioned Bunny about the Addisons' murders and ordered her to stick around, so she answered cautiously. "I don't think she's made up her mind yet." Then, in an attempt to change the subject, she asked, "What are you having?"

Before May could answer, the waitress approached. "Hi. My name's Tara and I'll be serving you today. Are you ready to order?"

They both asked for a diet Coke and a cup of the cheese broccoli soup. May ordered chicken strips with honey mustard dipping sauce, and Skye decided on the Cobb salad.

When the server left, Skye asked, "How long did Dorothy work for the Addisons?"

"Mmm, quite a while." May took a sip of ice water. "I think she started when her oldest went to college."

When their waitress finished serving their drinks and first course, Skye asked, "Did she like working for them?"

"She didn't talk about it much."

"Was that unusual for her?"

"A little." May spread honey butter a roll. "But I think I remember someone saying that the Addisons had fired the cleaning lady before Dorothy for gossiping about them."

"Sounds a little mean."

"I have a notion they weren't the easiest people to work for." May moved her hands out of the way, allowing the server to put the plate of chicken strips in front of her. "I know it had to stick in her craw to have Miss Barbie ordering her around and acting so superior."

After serving Skye's Cobb salad, the waitress asked, "Anything else I can get for you ladies?"

They both said no.

"Why did she stay with it so long?" Skye speared a piece of lettuce and a black olive.

"At the time, there weren't a lot of jobs within driving distance, and she needed the money after her husband passed away."

"Did she clean for other people, too?"

May shook her head. "No. She worked at the Addisons' house two days a week, and at the medical office the other three."

"Where's Dorothy working now?"

"She got hired at the new factory between Kankakee and Brooklyn." May dipped her chicken strip into the sauce.

"Did Dorothy ever say why she was let go?" Skye knew she was entering shaky ground, but wanted a sense of what had gone on before she talked to Dorothy in person.

"She wasn't let go. She quit."

"Oh." Was Yolanda wrong, or didn't Dorothy tell people she was fired? "Did she say why?"

"I don't think she ever answered me when I asked." May wiped her mouth with her napkin. "Maybe she quit working for the Addisons because she found the factory job. It probably pays a lot better than cleaning houses."

\*     \*     \*

By the time May and Skye made stops at Farm and Fleet and K's Merchandise Mart, it was nearly four o'clock.

As they drove past Kankakee State Park, May said, "Dorothy's house is the next one on the left."

Skye turned the Bel Air into a long narrow driveway and parked on a concrete area beside an older model Cadillac. May hopped out, and Skye followed as her mother walked over to the side entrance.

They made their way through a breezeway. Waiting for them in the doorway was a tall, solidly built woman in her late fifties.

"May Denison. How the heck are you?" She swept May into a hug. "I saw the car pull in. Is that the Chevy Jed fixed up for Skye?"

"That's the one." May hugged her back and stepped away. "I'm fine as frog hair, Dorothy Snyder. We were on our way home from the mall, and Skye wanted to stop and say hi."

Dorothy grinned at Skye. "I haven't seen you since you left town. Your ma is sure glad you're back."

Skye smiled. "It's hard to stay away."

May asked, "Are we interrupting anything?"

"I just finished cleaning up after yesterday's party. Come in and have a drink. It must be five o'clock somewhere in the world." Dorothy motioned them into a short hallway, through the kitchen, and into a huge living room that ran nearly the entire length of the front of the house.

The lush white carpet looked like no one ever stepped on it. Skye hoped her shoes were clean. Dorothy led them to a conversation grouping near an enormous picture window overlooking the snow-covered front yard. May and Skye sat on a buttery soft sofa the color of milk.

"What can I get you?" Dorothy stood with her hands on her hips.

"Nothing for me." Skye looked around. She hadn't been

at Dorothy's house in years, and didn't remember it being so lavishly decorated.

"How about a Bloody Mary, May?"

"You twisted my arm. Not too much vodka, though."

"Right. We wouldn't want you cooking supper drunk like that time at the lake last summer." Dorothy turned and went into the kitchen.

Skye raised an eyebrow. "What happened at the lake last summer?"

"Oh, Dorothy inherited a houseboat, and I spent the weekend with her at Lake Shelbyville." May waved away Skye's question.

"And?"

"And we had a couple of beers while we were cooking and burned the steaks." May gave Skye a stern look. "Nothing for you to go repeating to anyone, especially your dad."

"Oh."

Dorothy returned with a silver tray and put it down on the glass-and-chrome coffee table in front of Skye and May. She handed May a tall glass garnished with a celery stalk, and took a similar one for herself.

May took a sip. "How was your Thanksgiving?"

"Great. All the kids came. How about yours?" Dorothy settled into a chair that matched the couch.

"Good. Seems to be more people every year." May took a bite from the celery.

Skye tried to figure out a way to subtly steer the conversation to the Addisons. "I suppose you heard about Ken and Barbie Addison?"

"That was terrible. A body's not safe even in their own home."

"Good thing you weren't working for them anymore," Skye offered, hoping the older woman would add something.

"Yeah. Knowing the missus, she would have somehow managed to blame me."

"Sounds like she was hard to work for."

Dorothy paused and took a deep swallow. "Nothing I ever did was right by that woman."

"I'm surprised you didn't quit sooner."

Dorothy shrugged. "The pay was good, and I just let her harping and complaining roll off my back like water off a duck."

"What finally made you quit?" Skye asked casually, watching her mom's friend closely.

Dorothy turned her head and looked out the window. Snowflakes drifted through the twilight. She finally answered, "It was time to move on."

"No hard feelings?"

May poked Skye in the side. "Dorothy never holds a grudge."

Skye got the message and changed tracks. "I'll bet you saw quite a few interesting things working for that pair."

"Oh, I could tell a story or two."

"Like what?"

"Lots of yelling and screaming coming from the garage. Those lady friends of Mrs. Addison were none too happy about being roped into the Instant Gourmet scam she was running."

"Really?" Skye was surprised. "What do you mean?"

"All I'm saying is she had those women over a barrel." Dorothy shot her a shrewd look. "If you're investigating the murders, it'd be a good idea to take a close look at Mrs. A's business."

"But can't you just tell me?"

"I've said my piece."

Skye and Dorothy stared at each other.

May hurried into the conversation. "How're the grandkids doing?"

They chatted about families for a while, then May excused herself to use the bathroom.

Skye seized the opportunity to ask Dorothy a question

out of May's hearing. "Please don't take this the wrong way, but someone told me you didn't quit your job with the Addisons', you were fired."

"So?" The older woman crossed her arms. "And you want to know why?"

"Yes." Skye felt her stomach tighten. May would blow a gasket if she knew Skye was doing this.

"Just between you and me—I'll deny I ever said this if you tell anyone."

Skye nodded her understanding, but didn't promise anything.

"I found Dr. Addison and his wife's best friend in bed together one afternoon. He was sure I was going to tell, so he threatened me and I quit. He gave me a big check as severance pay. Once I started spending it, he told Mrs. Addison he fired me for stealing and I was using that money for my purchases. I didn't dare tell her otherwise."

"What did he threaten you with?"

"That's none of your business." Dorothy narrowed her eyes. "Let's just say he knew a lot of people's little secrets."

On the way back to Scumble River, Skye felt restless and on edge. It was a good thing that the GUMB Friday night bowling was canceled because of the holiday weekend, and Simon had a wake to oversee, because she was in no mood to socialize. She and Simon had a date for dinner Saturday night, and Skye hoped she'd be in a better humor by then.

She dropped her mother off at home, then drove to her own cottage. Bingo greeted her as she stepped inside. He wound around her ankles purring loudly and demanding food. Skye filled his bowl, put her packages away, and changed into sweatpants and a T-shirt.

There was a message on her machine from Frannie and Justin. They had come over to talk to her that afternoon, and had seen someone trying to get into her cottage. They thought she shouldn't be alone.

Skye called Justin's house and reassured the teens she was fine. She warned them to be careful themselves, and turned down their offer to come over and keep her company. Company was the last thing she wanted.

As she checked her doors and windows, making sure they were locked, she wondered who had been trying to get into her cottage that afternoon. Could it be Nate Turner or Quentin Kessler, still angry about what she had witnessed at that party Wednesday? Or maybe it was Polly, upset that Skye had found out she was Ken Addison's last mistress? Or, and this was the most chilling possibility of all, maybe it was the same person who had followed her through the cemetery Wednesday night.

With that in mind, she called Wally and notified him about the possible intruder. He said he'd have Quirk patrol her street that night and told her to call immediately if she felt the least bit threatened. While she had Wally on the phone, she filled him in on what she had learned from Dorothy— especally Lu and Ken's affair.

Having done all she could to ensure her safety, she turned to a matter she had control over, dinner. Skye made herself a turkey sandwich from Thanksgiving leftovers, carried her plate into the living room, and checked the *TV Guide*. There was nothing interesting on television, so she put on a Patsy Cline CD and settled back on the sofa with a crossword puzzle. Maybe concentrating on something other than the murder would jar loose a clue in her mind.

But her thoughts refused to cooperate, and as she took a bite of her sandwich, she mulled over what she had discovered so far. Number one, Ken Addison was a major creep. He had been involved in numerous extramarital affairs, which meant that a lot of husbands, fathers, and ex-lovers wouldn't mind seeing him dead. And Nate Turner would be at the top of the list, if he knew about Addison's affair with Polly.

Second, Addison had cheated his partner out of a research grant, which cost Zello both money and prestige. Certainly Zello wouldn't have shed any tears when he heard about Ken's demise.

Then there were the GUMBs. Here was an organization with a dark underbelly that was kept carefully concealed from public view. How many of the members knew about the sex parties attended by certain club members? How many of the select group was sorry they had ever decided to cross over into the wilder side? And, more important, how many of those involved would be willing to commit murder to stop it, or at least keep it a secret?

Next, there was Bob Ginardi, who wanted to oust Addison from his position of power as head GUMB. Had Addison threatened to tell all about the inner circle's sexcapades if he wasn't reelected? Would that be enough to make Ginardi want him dead? Dorothy had said she had caught Addison in bed with his wife's best friend, Lu. Did Ginardi know about that?

Frustrated, Skye put aside the crossword puzzle and stretched out on the sofa. Instead of reducing the list of suspects, she was adding to it. Maybe they had all killed Ken, like in that old movie on TV the other night.

No. That was silly. If they had all killed him, they would also have had to turn around and all kill Barbie, too. Skye grabbed a throw pillow and stuffed it under her head. What was she missing?

# CHAPTER 20

*Misery acquaints a [wo]man with strange bed-fellows.*

—Shakespeare

Saturday morning, Skye sat at her kitchen table writing up a grocery list. With Bunny gone and the stores back to normal, she could finally stock up again. Suddenly, she stiffened. That was it! What an idiot! She'd been overlooking it all along. Even when Dorothy told her about it yesterday she hadn't made the connection. So much for her supposedly high IQ and great intuition.

Skye slumped back in her chair and thought about it. Could they all have been looking at the wrong victim? Everyone had been under the assumption that the murderer had been after Ken, that Barbie had been collateral damage.

But what if the reverse was true—what if the killer had intended for Barbie to die all along, and Ken was the innocent bystander? What if the couple's deaths were connected with Barbie's Instant Gourmet business?

Dorothy had said that she frequently heard arguing coming from the garage, and that Barbie's friends hadn't been happy with their involvement in Instant Gourmet. In fact, Dorothy had said that Barbie had had her friends over a barrel regarding that enterprise.

Skye drained her cup of tea, stood up, and put it into the sink. As she dressed, she started to form a plan. The first thing she needed was to see Barbie's business records, and find out which of her friends had been over the biggest barrel.

After stuffing a legal pad and pen into her purse, she hopped in her car and headed toward the police station.

Her mother was sweeping the waiting area when Skye came in. The station was quiet. Saturday morning during a holiday weekend wasn't prime crime time.

May paused in mid-sweep. "I didn't expect to see you here today. Something wrong?"

"No." Skye gave her mom a one-armed hug. "Why do you always think the worst?"

"Because I don't like to be caught off guard." May put her broom aside, picked up a can of Endust and a rag, and said, "So, then, what's up?"

"I had an idea about the Addisons' murders and wanted to ask Wally some questions. Is he around?"

"No. Quirk is working today."

"Darn." She frowned as she watched May wipe down the vinyl sofa and side table. "Why are you doing that? I thought the PD had a cleaning lady."

May tsked. "She doesn't do a very good job, so I touch things up when we aren't busy."

Skye wasn't surprised by her mother's statement. While the other dispatchers might read or do needlepoint or puzzles during the slow time, May would always find some kind of work to do. "When will Wally be back on duty?"

"Monday."

"Crap." Skye chewed her lip. "Hey, maybe I don't need to talk to him after all. Do you know if he took the Addisons' financial records in as evidence?"

May paused in Windexing the glass door. "Everything he collected is out in the garage in the storage area."

"Would it be okay if I took a look?" Skye explained her theory about Barbie's Instant Gourmet business.

"Sure. Makes sense. One of your cousins got involved in selling some cleaning products a while back. Nearly drove her crazy trying to keep up with her quota. Luckily the contract she signed was for only six months; otherwise she'd have gone broke. I'll get the key." May disappeared into the back of the station and returned in seconds with a key attached to a small block of wood. "Here. Put everything back the way you find it and don't remove anything."

"No problem."

The storage area had been created by erecting eight-foot-tall plywood walls in the corner of the garage. It had no roof, and the door swayed in its frame as Skye unlocked it. She slid the key into her jacket pocket and entered. It was dark and dusty. A bare bulb hung from a strip of wood nailed from corner to corner.

Skye had to stretch on tiptoes to reach the string and turn on the light. She gasped in dismay as the space was illuminated. Junk was piled everywhere. How would she find the material from the Addisons' murders among this mess? Maybe she should just wait until she could talk to Wally.

But she didn't want to wait. She wanted to know right now. There had to be a system. She scanned the contents of the area again. Was it as simple as chronology—old material in the back, new in the front? She hurried over to the boxes nearest the door, snatched off the lid, and pulled out a file. Yes. This one was marked INSURANCE and the papers inside all bore the Addisons' names.

An hour later, she wasn't as jubilant. She had been through all the Addisons' cartons and she knew all about their mortgage—it was a big one—their car payments, and what they put on their credit cards, but she hadn't found anything at all pertaining to the Instant Gourmet business.

That alone was suspicious. There had to be records. Skye considered the condition of the house when she discovered the bodies. The killer had been searching for something, and she'd bet he or she had been looking for Barbie's Instant Gourmet account books.

Had the murderer gotten all the papers that had to do with Barbie's business, or had he or she missed something? To be sure, Skye had to search the Addisons' house herself.

After replacing the boxes in their original spots and locking the door behind her, Skye went to find her mother to return the key.

May was in the staff bathroom scrubbing the toilet when Skye located her. May straightened. "Get what you wanted?"

"Not really." Skye caught sight of herself in the mirror above the sink. Her jeans were streaked with dust, her sweater had a dark smudge near the right shoulder, and her hair was escaping its ponytail.

May's glance followed Skye's. "Looks like you've been working in a coal mine."

Skye took a paper towel and dampened it. "Instead of redoing what the cleaning lady does in here, you should clean up that storage room. The dust is thicker than the meringue on Grandma Denison's pies."

"I can't hear the phone or radio out there." May flicked a cobweb off Skye's back.

"Oh." Skye wiped dust from her black jeans with the wet towel. "Do you know if Wally's home?" She would have to call him after all. Skye needed to search the Addisons' house, and she wasn't breaking and entering to do it.

"Said he would be around most of the day."

"May I use the phone?"

"Help yourself."

Skye finished tucking her hair back into place and entered the dispatch area. She dialed Wally.

He picked up on the first ring, and she explained her thinking. He said, "Okay, I'll meet you over there in about twenty minutes. The crime scene techs from the sheriff's office have released the area, so there's no problem with us going inside."

Wally's car wasn't in the driveway when Skye arrived at the Addisons' house, but he swung open the front door as she climbed the steps.

"Where's your cruiser?" she asked.

"Getting an oil change and tune-up. I dropped it off at the garage and the mechanic's assistant gave me a ride over here."

"Want me to drive you back there when we're finished?" she offered, walking into the foyer.

"Yeah. Thanks. By the way, Quirk said there was no suspicious activity by your house last night. Did you see or hear anything more?"

"No. Maybe Frannie and Justin just saw someone knocking at my door, and their imagination took over."

"Maybe." Wally shrugged. "Oh, Nate Turner is in the clear. He has alibis for that whole morning. Before you saw him at the grocery store, he was with his minister and the church building committee."

"Shoot. I really wanted him to be the killer."

"That would have been too easy." Wally gestured to the rest of the house. "Where do you want to start?"

"The garage." Skye had been considering where Barbie would keep her records, and decided she would want them near where she did business. "If there was anything in the house, either the murderer found it or the crime scene guys would have, but I remember that the garage wasn't nearly as torn apart as the inside rooms were."

"Good thinking. With all those boxes of food out there, a search would have been more difficult."

"I keep forgetting to ask. Who is the Addisons' next of kin?" Skye passed through the utility room and entered the garage. "I haven't heard anything about a wake or funeral being scheduled yet."

"That's been a problem. Both Barbie's and Ken's parents are dead and they had no siblings." Wally walked to a stack of cartons and started to examine them.

"So, have you found an heir?" Skye sat at the table Barbie had used as a desk and tried to picture how she would have done business.

"Yes. It's a cousin who lives in California. We've been trying to reach her, but she must be away for the holiday."

Skye studied the tabletop. She could see where the techs had sprinkled their powder looking for fingerprints. There was a telephone and a fancy fax machine to the right, empty in and out baskets to the left, and a CD player off to the side. Everything had a coating of dust. Skye smirked; obviously the Addisons hadn't been able to replace Dorothy.

Wait. There was a clean square in the center, as if something had been sitting there for a long time. "Wally, come here a second, please."

He finished with the box he was going through and came to Skye's side. "Did you find something?"

"Maybe." Skye pointed to the clean area on the desk. "Something's been taken. Do you remember if you or the crime scene techs removed anything from the desktop?"

"I know we didn't take anything. I'll call the county and check with them." Wally reached for the phone. "Any idea what it might be?"

"A computer." Skye shook her head. "I should have realized right away. Barbie would keep her records on a computer. Just because Scumble River is seventy-five years behind the times doesn't mean a few of its citizens haven't made the quantum leap into the twenty-first century."

"Isn't that square too small for a computer? The one the dispatchers use at the PD is at least twice that size." Wally dialed the phone and asked for the crime scene tech.

"I think this one was a laptop, and I'll bet that fax machine doubles as a printer."

Wally nodded and turned back to the phone. "Hey,

Ozzie, this is Chief Boyd. You remember taking any kind of computer from my crime scene last week?" He waited. "Okay, thanks. Bye."

"Nope. Ozzie checked his inventory. No computer of any kind. And he said they would have taken it if there had been one."

Skye hit the tabletop with her fist. "Dang! The killer must have gotten it. Now what do we do?"

They stood in silence for a while, both thinking. Wally scratched his head. "I don't know much about computers, but do laptops use disks like the big ones do?"

"Yes," Skye said excitedly. "And most people who use computers for their records back them up on disks, and keep the disks separate from the hard drive in case of fire or flood or something." Skye looked around. "Where would Barbie have kept her backup disks, and did the killer get those, too?"

They decided to split up so they could cover more ground. Wally went to take a look at the room Ken used for a home office. Skye decided to check out the master bedroom.

She stood in the doorway and looked around. The murderer had pushed the mattress off the box spring and emptied all the drawers. The shelves in the closet had been cleared with what looked like an angry sweep of a hand. Clothes had been torn from their hangers and thrown in a heap in the center of the floor. Obviously, the search had been thorough.

What could both the murderer and the crime scene techs have missed? Skye sat at the dressing table and tapped her fingernail on the glass surface. A memory was trying to break through. What did she know that she couldn't quite recall?

She had seen something the night of the Instant Gourmet party. What was it? It came to her in a flash, the nearly invisible container under the bed. She flew off the stool exclaiming, "Yes! Yes! Yes!" She shoved the mattress out of the way and lay down on her stomach.

As Skye worked her head and upper torso under the bed, she heard the sound of the bedroom door closing, then locking. She tried squirming back out, but hands encased in rubber gloves clamped down on her back and a muffled voice said, "If you don't want to end up like the Addisons, hand me what you're reaching for. And don't turn around."

# CHAPTER 21

*Heav'n has no rage like love to hatred turn'd,*
*Nor hell a fury like a woman scorn'd.*

—Congreve

Skye screamed Wally's name. Immediately she heard footsteps pounding down the hall. Within seconds, the doorknob started to rattle and Wally shouted, "Skye, are you alright?"

The hands holding her down jerked away, but before she could wiggle out from under the bed, something big and extremely heavy was dumped on her back. The breath whooshed out of her, and she fought to inhale. As she struggled to free herself, she vaguely registered the tinkle of breaking glass.

The next sounds she heard were wood splintering and Wally's voice as he removed the object pinning her to the floor. "Skye, what happened? Don't move. I'll call an ambulance."

She scooted out from under the bed and sat up. Gasping, she managed to squeeze out a few words. "I'm fine. No ambulance." She pointed to the shattered French door. "Follow."

Wally hesitated, but Skye pointed again, and he took off running. After he left, she took a deep breath, felt no pain, so presumably had no broken ribs. Maybe having extra padding in that area wasn't such a bad thing after all. It had probably saved her from a serious injury.

She was pacing in front of the smashed bedroom door when Wally returned. "What happened?" she asked.

"I heard a car engine revving up as I came around the house, but since I didn't have the keys to your Chevy I couldn't pursue it."

"Did you see anything?"

"No. How about you? Did you get a look at the guy?"

"No. In fact, I can't swear it was a man. It could have been a woman. He or she disguised their voice, and with my head under the bed I couldn't see anything."

Wally moved closer to her. "Are you sure you're okay? You scared the life out of me when I heard you scream."

"Really, I'm fine. I just had my breath knocked out. What was on top of me?"

"The king-size mattress." Wally pointed to the offending object, now leaning against a wall. "What were you doing under the bed?"

"Oh, in all the excitement I almost forgot! There's a container under there. Can you get it?" No way was she going down there again.

Wally reached into his pocket and pulled on a pair of rubber gloves. He shoved the huge four-poster bed out of the way as if it were weightless, retrieved the box, and set it on the dressing table.

Skye held her breath as he flipped open the hinged lid. Yes! It was full of small black plastic squares—the missing disks had been found.

Wally closed the box. "I'll dust this for fingerprints, then turn it over to the county computer experts to look at."

Skye frowned. "That could take weeks. How about after you fingerprint it, we ask Simon to see if he can't open the files on his computer at the funeral home? I know the ones at school and the PD are too old, but he just got a new system this summer."

"Okay, we'll see if he thinks he can do it without harming the disks. Otherwise, we'll just have to wait for the sheriff's department to get to it."

Skye nodded her agreement.

As she was driving Wally to the mechanic's to pick up his squad car, she asked, "How do you think that person knew we were at the Addisons'?"

"I don't think he or she knew *we* were at the Addisons'. I think you were being followed, and your attacker was unpleasantly surprised to find out I was here, too."

"That makes sense. Your car wasn't parked out front. So, if they followed me, he or she would have no idea you were here."

"It was probably the same person Frannie and Justin saw trying to break into your cottage yesterday." Wally took out his pad and jotted down a note. "Do you know if they got a good look at the person?"

Skye shook her head. "They said they couldn't tell if it was a man or a woman because the person had on a bulky coat and a knit cap."

"Too bad."

Skye paused, considering, then said, "What if I had gone to the Addisons' alone?"

"You might be dead right now."

"Don't say that to Mom or Simon."

Wally snorted. "Do you seriously think they won't figure it out for themselves?"

Skye pursed her lips. He was right. Well, this would be a good test for Simon. He claimed he had changed, that he didn't mind anymore when she got involved in investigations. Now was his chance to prove it.

After dropping Wally off, Skye drove home. The plan was for Wally to pick up his cruiser, take the box to the police station and dust it for prints, then call Skye. Meanwhile, she was supposed to get in touch with Simon, and see if he thought he could get the disks to work in his computer.

Skye took a quick shower when she got home. While she waited for her hair to dry, she called Simon. He thought he could open the files on the disks and had an hour between appointments at three o'clock. Skye looked at her watch. I was close to two-thirty already. She hoped Wally would be finished looking for prints by then.

The phone rang while Skye was reapplying her makeup Wally was ready. He'd meet her at the funeral home.

Simon was already at the computer when she arrived Wally standing over his shoulder peering intently at the monitor. Neither man turned when Skye walked in.

"Have you found anything?" She nudged Wally over so she could see what was on the screen.

"Hard to say." Simon shrugged. "These are definitely Barbie's Instant Gourmet records." He pointed to the printer on his desk. "I'll make printouts so you and Wally can start going over them."

Wally and Skye moved from behind the desk and sat in the visitors' chairs. They grabbed the pages and scanned them as the printer started to spit them out. The sheets were still being churned out at a steady rate a half hour later when Simon had to leave for his meeting.

When the printer finally stopped, Skye sat back and rubbed her eyes. At first the words and numbers had made no sense, but gradually she began to understand. "A couple of these women really mortgaged their souls to Barbie and Instant Gourmet. Once they realized what they had done, I could see how they might want her dead."

"What a scheme. Barbie gets these women to sign contracts agreeing to purchase anywhere from a hundred to a thousand dollars' worth of merchandise every month, and then it's their problem to sell it to other people." Wally stood up and stretched. "If you couldn't find anyone who wanted to buy the stuff, the cost could add up real fast."

"Did you notice that beside the initial investment, there were things like shipping charges, advertising fees, and territory restriction tariffs?"

Wally nodded. "Yeah. They were out a pretty penny before they even had a chance to try to sell the product."

"I've read about scams like this, and always wondered how people got sucked into them." Skye started to sort the pages into piles.

"Everyone wants to get rich quick," Wally said, and then asked, "What are you doing with those?"

"Arranging them according to the amount of money involved and length of contract. This group on the left spent the least and signed up for the shortest period of time allowed, six months. The middle stack spent less than ten thousand dollars and had single-year contracts. The bunch on the right committed themselves to five years, and I need a degree in higher mathematics to figure out just how much money they owed Barbie."

"Smart." Wally patted Skye on the back. "Our suspects no doubt come from the last group."

"That would be my guess."

"Then let's make a list."

Skye rummaged in her purse until she found her calculator, then she picked up the pile of papers she and Wally were interested in and started to assess which of the women Barbie had snookered the worst.

She and Wally had just finished adding up the columns of figures when Simon returned.

"Hi." Skye looked at her watch. It was past six o'clock. "Sorry, it looks like we're going to have to miss our dinner date." She would have to change clothes and the restaurant was forty-five minutes away. No way could they make their seven o'clock reservation.

"I kind of thought that might be the case, so I canceled it." Simon kissed her on the cheek and took a seat behind his desk. "How's it going?"

Wally tapped the notes in front of him. "We're finally making some progress on this case." He explained to Simon what they had found in Barbie's records and concluded, "We have it narrowed down to Joy Kessler, Lu Ginardi, and Hilary Zello. Over the last couple of years, they've paid Barbie and Instant Gourmet between twenty-five and thirty thousand dollars each, and they still have three years left on their contracts."

Simon whistled. "I know all three of those women have wealthy husbands, but that's a lot of money to come up with."

Skye had been silent as Wally and Simon talked, but now she said, "And don't forget they each had other reasons for hating Barbie and Ken Addison."

"What reasons?"

"Joy and Hilary are involved in some kinky sex fantasy club, and from what I overheard, it seems that Ken was the one who seduced the group into having those types of parties. He didn't exactly make them participate, but he played on their fear of being uncool and 'small town' if they refused to take part."

Wally's eyebrows shot into his hairline. "How did you find out about this?"

Simon said, half to himself, "These people are amazing. I would never have guessed."

Skye told the story of her discovery, explaining about Frannie and Justin, and why she had had to follow them. While she was owning up, she threw in the fact that Nate Turner and Quentin Kessler had caught her and Frannie, and threatened them.

"And when were you going to mention this to me?" Wally demanded.

"I wasn't." Skye looked him in the eye, daring him to make a fuss. "There was no reason to ruin peoples' reputations unless it turned out to be relevant to the murder. Since it now seems relevant, I told you."

"You shouldn't have gone to the house alone," Wally grumbled.

"Maybe." Skye shrugged. "At the time, it seemed the right thing to do. I couldn't let Frannie and Justin go by themselves. It wasn't a police matter, so I didn't feel right about involving you, and Simon was busy with a wake. Who did you want me to call? May, Charlie, or—hey, I know, Bunny!"

Skye waited for Simon to chime in on Wally's side, but he was smart enough to keep his mouth shut.

Wally let the matter drop. "How about Lu Ginardi? Weren't she and Barbie best friends?"

"That's the point. Besides the money, Barbie hurt her on a personal level. How would you feel if your best friend cheated you out of thirty thousand dollars?" Skye paused, reflecting on what she knew about Lu. "You know, the more I think about it, the more I think Lu should be our prime suspect. I've been out of high school for more than fourteen years, and she still hates me for something that happened when I was a freshman. She's clearly someone who can hold a grudge for a long, long time. And don't forget she had an affair with Ken, which might have been her first attempt to get back at Barbie for swindling her."

Simon looked surprised at this bit of news, then said, "Still, you can't rule out the other women."

"No, but look how the Addisons were murdered. Lu is by far the strongest of the three women. She was quite an athlete in high school."

"Joy and Hilary are no weaklings," Wally offered. "They both belong to the health club. I see them nearly every morning when I work out."

"If only we had a better idea of the time of death," Skye said. "Between thirty minutes and three hours is such a long period. If we could narrow it down, we might be able to do better with eliminating some alibis."

"I'll go pull the file and see where Joy, Hilary, and Lu

claimed to be during that time." Wally stood and picked up the box of disks. "I'll give you a call and let you know who was where."

Simon and Skye waved him away.

Skye took a deep breath. "Before I forget, I've got something to tell you."

Simon eased back into his chair. "Yes?"

She explained about her close call at the Addisons' earlier that day, and about the person Justin and Frannie had seen at her cottage the day before, concluding with, "So it looks like I might have made someone uncomfortable."

Simon's left eye gave a single twitch, then not a muscle moved in his face. Finally he said, "You'll have to be extra careful."

She nodded, relieved he had taken the news so well. After a moment she stood and asked, "Want me to make an omelet or something for dinner?"

"That won't be necessary." He came around the desk and put his hand on her waist, guiding her out of the funeral home and toward his house across the street. "I've made other arrangements."

He unlocked the front door and stepped back so she could enter first. There was a trail of rose petals leading from the foyer into the dining room. The table was set with delicate china, sparkling crystal, and sterling flatware. Candles stood in silver holders on a crisp white linen tablecloth.

Skye exhaled a long sigh of amazement, then turned, and asked, "When? How? What?"

"I'm glad you like it." A laugh rumbled deep in his chest. "Let's see. When—as soon as I saw how much paperwork you and Wally would have to wade through. How—I called someone I know who's trying to get a catering company started. And what—a nice romantic dinner for two—"

She threw her arms around his neck and her lips smothered his last words.

A few seconds later, a sudden noise from the kitchen

caused her to jump. "What was that?" Skye's heart was pounding. She wasn't sure if it was from passion or fright.

"The dishwasher shutting off. The caterers must have put a load in just before they left."

Skye produced a faint smile. "Phew. I am definitely wound up too tight when an appliance scares me." Something flitted near the edge of her memory, and she frowned, trying to focus in on the thought, but Simon's hands burrowing under her sweater distracted her.

He reclaimed her lips and, after that, his slow, drugging kisses drove all other thoughts from her mind.

# CHAPTER 22

*But there is no joy in Mudville—mighty Casey has
struck out.*

—E. L. Thayer

The next morning Skye snuggled against Simon's side,
tracing patterns with her fingertips on his bare chest as
they both slowly came awake. Abruptly, she sat up and
swung her legs off the bed. "Oh, shoot! I forgot about my
car. It's been sitting in the funeral home parking lot all night.
People will talk."

"It's taken care of." He pulled her back to his side and
smoothed the hair from her eyes. "I got up last night after
you fell asleep, and put it in the funeral home's garage. The
hearse spent the night outside."

"Ah." She relaxed back in his arms, enjoying his smooth
skin and firm muscles, only to pop up again a few minutes
later. "Wally."

Simon swore, and this time he sat up, too. "You certainly
know how to ruin a moment."

"Oh, I didn't mean . . ." Skye trailed off, realizing that
calling out one man's name in another man's bed was tacky,

to say the least. She hurried to explain. "It's just that I remembered that Wal . . . ah, Chief Boyd said he'd call me about the suspects' alibis."

"So?" Simon's back was rigid as he got up and walked into the adjoining bathroom. "There's nothing you could have done about it last night."

"That's not the point." She followed him and watched as he adjusted the shower. His stance emphasized the strength of his thighs and the slimness of his hips. He was truly a sexy-looking man, especially naked. "What if he kept calling when he couldn't reach me? After what happened yesterday, he'd be worried." Skye thought, *Or know I spent the night with you.*

As if reading her mind, Simon said, "We're all adults. Don't you think he'd figure out you were probably with me?"

"Yeah." Her face grew warm. Skye was far from comfortable with anyone, especially Wally, knowing that she and Simon were sleeping together. "I guess I'm being silly, but . . ."

"I understand. Small towns are awkward that way." Simon took her hand and tugged her after him into the shower. "Let's pretend we're someplace where no one knows us."

Skye allowed herself to be drawn under the pleasantly hot water, and as Simon started to soap her back she said, "Someplace with no phones, no jobs, and no murder."

It was getting close to ten when Skye finally retrieved her car from the funeral home garage and drove home. Simon followed in his Lexus. She unlocked her front door and was met by an angry black cat. Although there was plenty of dry food and water, Bingo made it clear that nearly twenty-four hours without any Fancy Feast was unacceptable.

Simon tried to pet the furious feline while Skye cleaned his litter, but the cat hissed, backing away with narrowed eyes. "I think Bingo knows it's my fault you weren't home last night to attend to his needs."

Skye glanced at her pet, whose tail was fluffed to twice its normal size, and said, "True. And he's not in a forgiving mood."

"He'll get over it once he's eaten."

Skye raised an eyebrow but didn't comment. Simon had obviously never been on the receiving end of a cat snit before. Skye went into the kitchen, saying over her shoulder, "Would you mind feeding him while I check my messages?"

"Not at all." Simon opened a cupboard and took out a small can with a salmon-colored label. "Should I give him the whole thing?"

Skye nodded distractedly. The light on her answering machine was flashing rapidly; she'd had several calls, all from Wally.

His final message took up most of the remaining tape: "It's almost midnight. Quirk said he saw your car at the funeral home a few minutes ago, so I'm guessing you're safe—at least from the murderer. Here's what I have regarding the suspects' alibis: Hilary was alone from seven-thirty to nine-thirty, but then with a neighbor having coffee for the next hour. Joy was seen at the grocery store at nine-fifteen and her cash register receipt shows she checked out at two minutes after ten. But like Hilary, she has no one to vouch for her during the two hours before nine-fifteen. Lu, on the other hand, was on the telephone with an insurance agent from about eight-forty to nearly nine-thirty, but she has no alibi for the hour or so right before the bodies were discovered."

Skye grabbed a legal pad and replayed the message, taking careful notes of the times. When she was finished, she told Simon, "If we knew exactly when the Addisons died, we could probably name the killer with this information."

"Time of death is hard for the medical examiner to pin

down, unless there's a witness or the victim's watch is smashed or something."

"It seems like for every piece of information we get, we can't figure out two others." Skye sighed.

"Let's go somewhere for brunch. It'll take your mind off the murders for a while."

"Might as well," Skye agreed. "Right now I can't think of what else to do to find out who killed the Addisons."

"I've got to do laundry," Skye said over her shoulder as she and Simon walked into her cottage. It was a little after noon and they had just gotten back from the restaurant. "Seems like I went through a lot of clothes this week."

"I'll stick around."

"To protect me?" Skye shrugged out of her jacket. "Or do you have something else in mind?"

"How about both?" His golden-hazel eyes took on a luminous glow.

"Then make yourself comfortable while I get the first load started."

Simon had put on a Tony Bennett CD and was sitting on the sofa when Skye joined him. A half hour later, as she rested in the cradle of his arms, the washing machine clicked off and she stiffened. That was what she had been trying to remember.

She turned to face Simon. "I know who did it!"

"Who? How?" Simon asked, a puzzled expression on his face.

She jumped off the couch, ran to get her notes on the suspects' alibis, and thrust it into his hand. "Look. It's all right here." She pointed to the suspects and the times they couldn't account for. "It finally came to me. When I first discovered Ken and Barbie's bodies, their washing machine was just shutting off. Remember last night when your dishwasher clicked off? That's what it reminded me of, but I couldn't quite put my finger on the memory. Just now, when my washing machine shut down, it came to me."

"Explain."

"Barbie and I have the same model washing machine." Skye's eyes sparkled. "My machine takes exactly thirty minutes to complete a wash cycle."

"Go on."

"If the killer started the machine just as she left, the time of death had to be within half an hour of when I arrived."

"Why would the killer start the machine?" Simon asked.

"Good point." Skye chewed her lip. "Barbie must have started the machine and then she was killed soon afterward. The Addisons had to be alive before ten o'clock because I got there about ten-thirty and it took me less than five minutes to discover the bodies."

"So, who doesn't have an alibi from, say, nine-forty-five to ten-thirty?"

"Lu Ginardi. She's the only one of the women who were indebted to Barbie because of the Instant Gourmet scheme and can't account for her time during that forty-five minutes."

Simon paced the length of the great room and back. "There's still no hard evidence against her. Yes, she was into Barbie for a great deal of money, and she's the only one of the women without an alibi, but—"

"You're right. There's only one thing to do. Get her to confess."

"That's not what I meant."

"Well, we can't let her get away with it, and as you pointed out, there's no real proof. So, we have to get a confession."

"How do you plan to do that?" Simon's expression was skeptical.

"Lu is impulsive, has an extremely short fuse, and she really, really dislikes me. If I prod her enough, she'll blurt it out."

"Or attack you," Simon snapped. "She may be the one who's been following you."

"Yes. I bet she is." Skye thought for a minute. "Okay. I'll call Wally and tell him what we've figured out, and see if he's willing to bring her in to the police station for questioning."

"You think she'll say something in front of Wally?"

"Of course not. But what if he steps out of the room and I step in?" Skye explained. "I'll make sure the door isn't closed all the way, and Wally can eavesdrop."

"Is that legal?"

"They let cell mates in prison elicit confessions and testify against each other," Skye pointed out. "I think as long as she doesn't ask for a lawyer, it's okay."

"Then you'd better call Wally right now." Simon checked his watch. "It's nearly one o'clock. If he can pick her up immediately, Bob won't be home and insist on going with her to the station as her lawyer."

"How do you know that?"

"There's a GUMB meeting that starts at one. They're voting for Imperial Brahma Bull. Bob will probably be tied up until at least three o'clock."

Skye raised an eyebrow. "I'm surprised you aren't attending."

"I'm thinking of dropping out of the GUMBs. It hasn't turned out to be exactly what I expected."

"Won't Lu be there to support her husband?"

"Women are prohibited from attending an election." Simon's expression was a bit sheepish. "Another reason I've been thinking of quitting. The GUMBs are a lot more chauvinistic than I was led to believe."

"Glad you realized that, because I plan to resign from the Bettes Monday morning." Skye headed for the phone. "I hope Wally's available."

Wally agreed to Skye's plan. He would pick up Lu and meet Skye and Simon at the police station in half an hour.

*   *   *

Wally was already in the interrogation room with Lu when Skye and Simon arrived at the police station.

After nearly half an hour Wally walked into his office where Skye and Simon had been waiting. He plopped into his desk chair and said, "That's one tough woman. She won't budge. Insists she's innocent."

"Let's see if I can rattle her a little." Skye left the office, trailed by the two men.

Lu frowned when Skye entered the interrogation room. "What are you doing here?"

Good question. Skye hadn't thought of how to start things off. She improvised. "You know my mom's the police dispatcher, right?"

Lu nodded, a confused look on her face.

"Well, I was here visiting her, and I saw Wally bring you in. Then when he stepped away a few minutes ago, I realized this was a good time to talk to you." Skye paused for dramatic effect. "About Barbie's Instant Gourmet business."

Lu stiffened. "What about it?"

Skye pulled out a chair, noting as she had Friday at the mall that Lu's polished looks had lost their shine. Her blond hair hung limply, and strands of gray were evident. Her skin seemed dull, and a baggy jogging suit hung on her tall, sinewy frame. Skye watched Lu squirm for a few minutes, then said, "I know about the Instant Gourmet contract you signed with Barbie."

The woman glared. "So?"

"She really duped you, didn't she?"

"I knew what I was doing."

Skye caught a glimpse of Wally by the slightly open door. It was time to stir things up before Lu noticed him, too. Skye leaned across the table. "Hardly. That contract was so one-sided it was insulting, and your husband's a lawyer, too. How stupid could you be?"

"It's finally out in the open, isn't it, Miss Honor Roll

Straight-A Student?" Lu rocketed upright. "I knew from the first day I met you in high school that you thought I was dumb. But who married the star football player and lives in the big house, and who's an old maid?"

Skye was shocked. Lu had hated her all these years because she got good grades in high school? Well, she couldn't think about that now. Lu was close to blowing up, and it was time for Skye to light her fuse.

"Admit it. Barbie took advantage of you. She must have thought you were a real idiot to sign that contract. So you slept with her husband for revenge, but that wasn't enough. You killed her because she betrayed you."

Lu's head snapped up. "Why would you say that?"

"Because you owed her the most money. You were supposed to be her best friend. And you're the one without an alibi."

Suddenly Lu let out a loud peal of laughter, and flopped back down in her chair. "Miss Smarty-Pants is finally wrong. You and your high IQ added up two and two and got five."

Could that be true? If Lu wasn't the murderer, then who was? No, she had to be the killer. Skye decided to push a little harder. "Like I'd believe what you had to say. You've hounded me since I was a freshman. And now I find out the only thing you had against me was that I got better grades than you."

"Believe what you want." Lu picked at a ragged nail.

Skye frowned. Lu seemed relieved, as if being accused of murder wasn't the thing she dreaded hearing from Skye. What *was* she afraid Skye knew? But if Lu wasn't the killer, then who was? Shoot. They were back at square one.

Lu stared off into space, and Skye could think of nothing else to say. It was time to leave.

Simon and Wally joined her in the hall. Skye said, "Did you hear?" The men nodded. "I couldn't budge her."

"Do you still think she's the killer?" Wally asked.

"I'm not sure anymore." Skye shrugged. "But who else could it be? The other women have alibis." Silently, she examined her previous reasoning for flaws. *The washing machine clicked off five minutes after I got to the Addisons, which means twenty-five minutes earlier they had to be alive. No flaws there. If Barbie was the intended victim, it had to be due to her Instant Gourmet racket. So what am I missing? Unless Ken really was the prime target after all.*

# CHAPTER 23

*If at first you don't succeed,*
*Try, try, try again.*

—W. E. Hickson

"Ms. Denison, phone call, line two." The elementary school's PA announcement startled Skye into spilling a can of diet Coke over the papers she had spread on her desk.

After brooding all Sunday night about the fiasco with Lu Ginardi, Skye had somehow managed to sleep through her alarm Monday morning, thus starting one of those days where the smart move would have been to crawl back under the covers and wait for the next sunrise. Now, at two-fifty-nine, with school letting out at three o'clock, a phone call could not mean good news.

As she hurried down the hall to the main office, visions of angry parents, irate superintendents, and litigious lawyers danced in her head.

Skye lifted the receiver and identified herself.

"Skye, honey, this is Bunny. I'm so relieved I found you."

Skye stifled a groan and forced a pleasant tone. "Hi, Bunny. What's the problem?"

"I had a gentleman caller this afternoon that I thought you should know about."

"Who came to see you?" And why did Bunny want to share this information with Skye?

"Bob Ginardi."

Uh-oh. "What did he want?" Had he figured out that Skye and Simon were behind Lu's being questioned by Wally yesterday? Was he using Bunny in his retaliation?

"Well, when I first got to town, I contacted him about my little problem with the law. I had, ah, gotten rid of some papers about my court supervision and then I found out I needed them, so I asked him if he could help me."

"And did he?" Skye pulled up a chair and sat down. This was obviously going to be a long conversation.

"I didn't have enough money for his fee—so, no. But today when he stopped by, he suggested something I could trade for his help." Bunny paused dramatically, then stage-whispered, "He wanted me to pump you for information and report back to him."

"What? Why?"

"He's apprehensive that you've ascertained some unsavory information about the GUMBs, and since he was elected Imperial Brahma Bull yesterday, he wants me to find out exactly what you know." It was clear from the terminology she was using that Bunny was quoting Ginardi word for word.

Skye was surprised to hear that Ginardi had beat Charlie out of becoming the grand pooh-bah, but she refocused on what Bunny was saying. "I see. And did you agree?"

"I told him that I'd think about it and get back to him. That's why I called you to see what you wanted me to do."

Skye twisted the phone cord around her finger. What was Ginardi up to? "Listen, Bunny, I'll go over and clear this up with him as soon as I finish up a couple of things here at school. You stay away from him."

"Sure. I figured that's what you'd want to do." Bunny paused again. "Ah, say, ah, let me know what happens, okay?"

"I'll do that," Skye promised, then added, "I have a friend who's an attorney. I'll ask her to call you and see about getting copies of those papers you need. Her name is Loretta Steiner."

"Gee. Thanks. That's really sweet of you."

"Thanks for letting me know about Ginardi. Take care. Bye."

It was close to four when Skye parked in front of Ginardi's law office. She'd had to attend a last-minute meeting at school and then decided she'd better call Loretta about Bunny's legal problems before she forgot. As she closed her car door, she spotted Simon sitting in his Lexus two spaces over. He saw her at about the same time and got out of his car. They met on the sidewalk in front of the building.

"What are you doing here?" Skye asked.

"I was out of the office for a while, and when I got back there was a message from Bunny on my machine telling me about Ginardi's visit to her and your plan to speak to him this afternoon." Simon opened the front door and gestured for Skye to go inside. "I didn't think you should talk to him alone."

"You're probably right. It's always good to have a witness when you have a discussion with a lawyer other than your own." Skye looked around the small waiting room. It was empty; even the secretary's chair was vacant. "Maybe he's not here."

Simon walked over to the closed office door and knocked.

A voice yelled, "Come in." Ginardi was sitting at his desk. He looked from Skye to Simon and said, "What a surprise. Come in. Have a seat. Did you two come by to draw up a prenuptial agreement?"

"No," Skye answered. "I understand you're concerned about what I might have figured out about the GUMBs."

"Well, since I'm now Imperial Brahma Bull, it is my duty . . ."

While Ginardi was speaking, Skye noticed a silver and white snowsuit hanging from the back of the coat tree in the corner. She swallowed a gasp as the answer to everything hit her dead-on. Now she knew where she had gone wrong in her previous attempt to figure out who had committed the murders.

Bob Ginardi was the "alien" Justin had spotted at the Kesslers' the night of the sex party. He must have been wearing the snowsuit and a pair of oval snowshoes when he was following her through the cemetery.

She had been so stupid. Why hadn't she noticed that the Ginardis weren't among the partyers? Ginardi's son had been the one Justin overheard talking about the party. The Ginardis should have been there.

And if Bob Ginardi was the one following her that night . . . Damn! She had checked the alibis for the women Barbie was bleeding dry, but not the women's husbands. They would have had as much motive as their wives. She had overlooked the obvious, and now she and Simon were sitting in a deserted building with the murderer.

Skye nodded as Ginardi finally finished his speech about protecting the GUMB reputation. "I completely agree with you," Skye said. "That's why I came by, to reassure you that I would keep that information completely confidential." She stood and tugged Simon to his feet, pulling him toward the door. "We have to go now."

"No need to rush off." Ginardi smiled. "How about a drink to celebrate my victory?"

Something in Skye's expression must have tipped him off that she had figured out he was the killer because she could see a sudden dawning of understanding on his face. In the blink of an eye he turned from genial host to stone-cold killer.

When he reached into his desk drawer, Skye looked at Simon. He had caught the transformation, too, and was shoving her out into the reception area and toward the outside. But they were too slow. Ginardi caught up with them before they got to the door.

He pointed a gun at Skye. "I see our town sleuth has finally fumbled her way into figuring things out."

Skye tried playing dumb. After her misjudgment of Lu yesterday, it wasn't much of a stretch of her acting abilities. "I told you I wouldn't say anything about the GUMBs."

"No. You won't." He gestured toward a storage cabinet located behind the secretary's desk. "Both of you get over there." Once they had complied, he followed and reached inside. "Here." He handed Skye a roll of duct tape and pointed at Simon. "Tape his hands behind his back and put a piece over his mouth."

Skye looked at Simon, who nodded slightly. After she had finished, Ginardi checked her work, adding a couple of extra loops to tighten the tape. "Now, we're all going for a ride."

He grabbed Skye by the arm, pushing the gun into her side and dragging her outside toward the Lincoln Navigator parked at the curb. "Skye, you get to drive. Simon, sorry, you'll have to ride in back. And if you try anything, your snoopy girlfriend gets a bullet in the head."

They all climbed inside. Skye desperately searched the street for someone to help them, but there was no one in sight.

Ginardi prodded her with the gun. "Drive east, as if you were going to Kankakee."

She slowly backed the massive vehicle onto the street and started down the road.

When they were out of the city limits, Ginardi said, "I

thought you were really off course when you went and spied on the Kesslers' little orgy."

"I guess I was," Skye acknowledged. "So why did you ask Bunny to get information from me?"

"I got worried when you went over to the Addisons' house Saturday. It was quite an unpleasant surprise to find Chief Boyd there, too." Ginardi frowned, as if just remembering something. "What did you find there?"

"Nothing." Skye pasted a disappointed expression on her face. "It was a big waste of time. The chief was really annoyed at me." Wanting to get his mind off that topic, she said, "What I don't understand is why you asked me to investigate."

"I didn't. Tony Zello did. He was hellbent on you finding the murderer and saving the club's reputation. He would have thought it strange if I didn't go along with him."

"Oh." Come to think of it, Tony had been the more insistent of the two. Skye bit her lip. She had really missed a lot of clues, like Lu's reaction at the police station yesterday. Lu must have known her husband was the killer, and that's why she was relieved when Skye accused her rather than Bob.

"Turn left here," Bob Ginardi ordered.

Skye glanced at the side mirror before stomping on the brakes and cranking the steering wheel. She swung the huge SUV onto the gravel road he had indicated. Had the truck behind them seemed familiar? Probably just wishful thinking, but just in case, she'd make sure Ginardi didn't notice. "For a fifty-thousand dollar vehicle, this Navigator drives worse than my dad's old pickup."

Ginardi's eyes narrowed slightly, but then he smiled. "You should watch that smart mouth." He patted a rifle case next to him. "It'll get you into trouble someday."

Skye wouldn't play his game. She wanted to rile him up, keep his eyes off the road behind them and on her. "Your ridiculous little opinion has been noted."

"Is that the best you can do? You're not very good at inflicting pain, are you?" Ginardi reached over and slapped her with such force that her head snapped back. "I, on the other hand, in my practice as an attorney, have made an art of it."

The SUV swerved, but she wrestled it back into the right lane. Skye looked in the rearview mirror. Simon was struggling wildly to free his hands, and the truck she thought she had seen had disappeared.

She ignored the throbbing in her head and forced her voice to sound undisturbed as she asked, "Is that why you killed the Addisons, because you enjoy causing pain?"

Ginardi ignored her comment and pointed to a dirt path. "Take a right here."

"Where're we going?" They had been driving for nearly an hour, mostly down gravel and dirt roads. She knew they had originally headed south out of Scumble River, but after the first couple of turns, she had become completely lost.

"Camping."

"Huh?"

"A client of mine has a hunting cabin down here, which, due to an unfortunate incarceration, he won't be using for the next ten to twenty years." Ginardi smiled as his own wit. "By the time he's free to go camping again, I'm afraid you and Reid will be just a pile of bones."

"Oh." This wasn't looking good. She glanced at Simon again in the mirror. He was still trying to get his hands loose.

"Stop." Ginardi pointed to a spot by the side of the road. "Park here. We have to hike the rest of the way in."

The path was overgrown and hard to follow. Ginardi made Skye and Simon walk ahead of him, keeping his gun pointed at Skye's head and carrying the rifle under his left arm.

Skye's mind was working furiously. Should she pretend to trip? If Simon had freed his hands, this might be a good time to try to escape. Ginardi hadn't seemed to notice when she'd casually tucked the keys to the Navigator in her pants pocket.

Before she could decide what to do, they emerged from the trees into a small clearing occupied by a rustic cabin. Ginardi urged them up the steps and onto the small porch. He unlocked the door with a key he took from above the door-frame, and pushed them inside.

A thick layer of dust coated the meager furnishings, and the air was rancid with the smell of decay. Ginardi sniffed. "Rufus must not have cleaned up very well after his last kill."

Skye wondered if Ginardi was talking about deer hunting or something worse. It was time for a tactical reconsideration. She still couldn't tell if Simon's hands were free, but she'd have to take a chance, and soon. "You know, Bob, I still don't understand why you killed the Addisons."

"I did it for Lu, of course." He forced Simon to sit. "Tape his arms and legs to the chair."

"Because of the Instant Gourmet contract?" Skye asked as she followed Ginardi's orders.

"Barbie was bleeding us dry with that damn contract. I went over that day to get her to tear it up. She refused."

"That must have made you furious." Skye tried to keep him talking as she edged closer to the rifle he had set on the table near the door.

"Barbie was supposed to be Lu's best friend. She made Lu feel like an idiot for even wanting to read the contract before signing it. Lu can't stand feeling stupid, so she signed. Then when she realized what she had done, she got depressed, lost weight, couldn't sleep. If Barbie wouldn't tear up that contract, then I had to end it another way. She left me no choice. I had to terminate her before she killed my wife."

"Is that why you tore up the house? Were you looking for the contract?" Skye asked.

"Yeah, but I didn't find much. She must have kept everything on her laptop, and I destroyed that."

Skye didn't mention the disks they had found. Bob was the city attorney; if he knew about them he could easily make the disks "disappear" from the evidence locker. "But why did you kill Ken?"

"That was bad luck on his part. He came home unexpectedly, right after I put Barbie's body in the freezer. I had to kill him, too. I snuck up behind him, slipped the loop of ribbon around his neck, and pulled it tight." Ginardi paused, then smiled coldly. "Since you won't be telling anyone, I might as well confess. I was glad to see him dead. He had slept with my wife, while his wife was screwing her with that Instant Gourmet crap. They both deserved to die."

Skye felt the back of her leg brush against the table. She almost had the rifle.

Suddenly, Ginardi noticed what Skye was doing, and snatched the gun before she could nab it. Enraged, he swung the rifle stock at Simon's head.

Skye rushed toward him, but Ginardi grabbed her and threw her against the wall. Dazed, she watched in horror as blood spurted from Simon's temple and he sagged in the chair. He moaned, and then was silent.

Ginardi turned on her, still furious. "Go sit on the couch and shut up." When she was slow to obey, he jerked her to her feet and threw her on the sofa, then swiftly taped her hands, ankles, and mouth.

She had hit the wall hard. Her back hurt, and her ankle throbbed. Ginardi was really strong. He had picked her up as if she weighed less than a sack of potatoes. He had two guns, more muscles than Mr. America, and she was tied up tighter than a bale of hay. How could she possibly escape and carry an unconscious Simon with her?

"I'll be right back, and you'd better not have moved an inch." Ginardi grabbed a shovel from beside the door and stormed out of the cabin.

Oh, my God! He was going to dig their graves! Up until now she had been able to fool herself into thinking they

would be able to escape, but suddenly the realization hit her.
They would die in this awful little shack and no one would
ever know what had happened to them.

Where was the cavalry when you needed them?

The thought had barely crossed her mind when she heard
a splash, a scream, a couple of whooshes, and then thwacking sounds. Before she could figure out what was happening
she heard voices, but couldn't make out any words. A few
long minutes later the door swung open, and the Three Mus-
keteers charged inside, pushing and shoving one another out
of the way to be first.

Bunny won. She took one look at Simon and wailed,
"Sonny Boy, what has that awful man done to you?" She
rushed to his side and started tearing away the duct tape.

Justin and Frannie hurried over to Skye. Frannie pulled
the tape off her mouth, while Justin used a pocketknife to
slit the strips binding her hands and feet. Skye flinched as
the tape tore her skin when it was removed. "Where's Ginardi?" she asked.

"He's secured," Justin declared.

Skye was about to demand a more detailed answer when
she noticed Bunny had managed to free Simon and get him
to his feet. Skye ran over to him. "Are you alright?"

He started to nod, but winced. "I think I'm okay, but I
have a terrific headache. What happened while I was out?"

Bunny and the teenagers all tried to explain at once, but
Skye interrupted. "This can wait. We need to get Simon to a
hospital and Ginardi to the police." She put her arm around
Simon and started toward the door. "By the way, where are
we?"

"Near Pontiac," Frannie answered, then added, "Be careful when you go outside. The porch steps are real icy."

"Okay." Why were the steps icy? Had it started to snow?
Skye couldn't think of that now. She had to focus. "There's
a cell phone in Ginardi's SUV. We'll use it to call the police

while we're driving." Skye tossed Frannie the keys. "Phone and get directions to the nearest hospital."

"Tell me again why you took it upon yourself to get a suspected killer to confess," demanded the deputy sheriff who had met them at the hospital.

"No." Skye crossed her arms and leaned back in the molded plastic seat of the hospital waiting room. "I'll explain when Chief Boyd gets here. I've told you three times already, and you obviously don't believe me, so I'm not saying it all a fourth time."

"You'll talk to me here or down at the sheriff's office." A stubborn look descended on the man's face.

"Fine." Skye stood up. "Let's go. I can't wait to see the newspaper headline. Woman Captures Murderer. Police Drag Her Away While Fiancé Lays Dying."

"Sit down." The deputy swallowed. "The doctor said Mr. Reid is going to be fine. At most, he has a minor concussion."

Skye sent up a silent prayer thanking God for Simon's hard head, then raised an eyebrow at the officer. "I sure hope the doctor is right, but do you want to bet your career on it?"

Before he could answer, Wally strolled into the room and stuck his hand out to the deputy. "Chief Walter Boyd."

"Chief Boyd, nice to meet you. I'm Deputy Knox." He gestured to Skye. "Miss Denison has been trying to explain to me what happened."

"Simon okay?" When she nodded, Wally patted Skye's shoulder. "Caught yourself another one, huh?" He shook his head. "Is this what you call being careful?"

"Well . . ." Skye looked into Wally's eyes and saw resignation rather than anger. She reached up and squeezed his hand. "Let's just say it's a good thing I had a little help from my friends."

Deputy Knox asked, " 'Another one'?"

Wally sat down next to her. "Skye has helped the Scumble River Police Department with several cases."

Skye appreciated Wally's support, knowing he was subtly vouching for her to the other law enforcement official. "Shall I tell it from the beginning?" She smiled sweetly at Deputy Knox, who nodded tersely. "Well, it all started this afternoon when Bunny phoned to tell me about her gentleman caller." Skye finished her story with "Then the Scooby gang burst in and saved the day."

Wally's brow furrowed. "Scooby gang?"

"Bunny, Frannie, and Justin—you know, like on the cartoon *Scooby-Doo*."

He nodded, but didn't look enlightened. "How did they find you?"

"Deputy Knox hasn't let me talk to them since we brought Simon in, so I don't know. I was concentrating too hard on driving and finding the hospital to question them before we got here. I don't even know how they got past Ginardi."

"Where *is* Ginardi?" Wally looked at the other man.

The deputy answered. "They had him all trussed up in some kind of net thingy. He looked like a Thanksgiving turkey ready for the oven, and he was swearing like one of those rap singers. He's at the sheriff's office."

"I know this is your jurisdiction, but I sure would like to talk to the people who came in with Skye," Wally said.

"Let me call the sheriff. I'll be right back."

When Deputy Knox returned, he said, "Sheriff says this looks like your mess, and he's glad to hand them all over to you."

"Thanks. Tell Buck I owe him a beer." Wally turned to Skye. "I'll call Quirk to come get Ginardi. You sit still."

Several minutes ticked by, and Skye was wondering what would happen if she just got up and found Simon. Everyone kept telling her he was fine, but she'd like to see for herself. Wally's return, with Frannie and Justin in tow, foiled her escape plan. Both teenagers seemed excited as they sat on either side of Skye.

Wally asked, "How did you find Ms. Denison and Mr. Reid?"

"We followed them," Frannie said. "Miss Bunny used to date a police detective in Las Vegas, and she showed us how to shadow someone without them knowing it."

"But why did you follow us?" Skye asked. "And how did you get hooked up with Bunny?"

Justin leaned forward. "We couldn't decide what to do after we saw someone trying to break into Ms. D's cottage. Ms. D and Mr. Reid weren't around, Frannie didn't want to tell her dad, and I didn't think telling you would do any good, so we decided to tell Mr. Patukas. We know he kind of looks after Ms. D. He wasn't at the motor court, but Miss Bunny was. So we told her to tell him when he got back."

"Miss Bunny called us today after Mr. Ginardi visited her," Frannie explained, "and asked her to spy on Ms. D. So we decided the three of us would keep an eye on *him*. We staked out his office."

"All three of you?" Wally asked.

"Yep."

"Why didn't you come talk to me?" Wally demanded.

"Miss Bunny said she didn't have a real good relationship with the police, and that you wouldn't believe her. And I knew you'd never take a couple of teenagers seriously." Justin shook his head. "Anyway, when we saw Mr. Ginardi force Ms. D and Mr. Reid into his car, we followed them."

"Ginardi never noticed?" Wally asked.

"I thought I saw a pickup once," Skye said, "but then it disappeared."

"Frannie had her dad's truck," Justin offered.

Wally asked, "Why didn't you call the police station?"

"We didn't have time to stop and find a phone," Frannie answered.

"How did you capture Bob Ginardi?" Wally appeared as confused as Skye felt.

Justin smiled proudly. "I had a three-part plan. First, I found a couple of gallon containers of water in the emergency kit behind the seat of Frannie's dad's truck. I took one and poured it over the cabin steps. It's so cold outside it started to freeze right away, which was great because wet ice is the most slippery—"

Frannie broke in, "I took the other container of water and hid next to the stairs. We were going to make some noise in order to get him to come outside, but he came out on his own." Frannie beamed. "My job was to douse Mr. Ginardi when he ran out the door."

"But how did Ginardi get all tied up, and what's this about a net thing?" Wally asked.

"That was the third part of my plan," Justin answered. "Last week I got this neat self-defense device from a guy who used to work as an animal control officer. It's called a Webshot and looks sort of like a bazooka, but it shoots out this sticky Kevlar net. The manual says the criminal won't be able to move a finger. I hid behind a tree, and when Mr. Ginardi came out of the cabin, Frannie threw the water in his face. When he slipped on the ice on the steps and fell flat on his back, I blasted the Webshot at him. I used two cartridges just to make sure."

"What about his gun?" Skye asked.

"I made a tiny slit in the web with my pocketknife and grabbed it out of his hand," Frannie answered. "We weren't sure how long the netting would hold. As my dad always says, better safe than sorry."

"What was that thwacking sound I heard before you guys rushed into the cabin to rescue us?" Skye asked.

"Miss Bunny beating Mr. Ginardi with a stick." Justin looked sheepish. "Look, I know that beating him with a stick is pretty lame, and actually wouldn't do any good, but she really wanted to do something, and I figured she could handle stick duty."

Wally looked at Skye. "This could almost make you believe in miracles."

"I don't just believe in miracles," Skye answered, putting an arm around each teen, "I rely on them."

# EPILOGUE

*Things do not change; we change.*

—Henry Thoreau

"Where is everyone?" Skye asked as Simon turned his Lexus into the bowling alley's nearly empty parking lot. "Did they call off the league again this Friday?" They hadn't bowled the last two Fridays—first due to the Thanksgiving holiday weekend, then because of Bob Ginardi's arrest and Simon's head injury.

"I don't know." Simon's expression was innocent. "Maybe I missed something. Did you hear anything?" It had been a week and a half since Ginardi had assaulted Simon. The doctor had allowed Simon to resume his normal activities only as of yesterday.

"No. As far as I know, our Friday night bowling league should be starting in about ten minutes." Skye paused. "Unless the bowling alley was finally sold."

"Let's go in." Simon got out of the car. "The owner probably knows what's going on."

Inside, it was obvious that there was no league tonight.

The lanes were dark, the grill unoccupied, and the only illumination was over by the bar.

"We should leave," Skye said, tugging on Simon's sleeve. "Something's not right here."

"I can't believe you don't want to investigate." He tucked her hand into the crook of his arm and walked toward the light. "Let's see what's going on."

Skye looked at Simon. He sure was acting strangely. Had that blow to his head changed his personality?

No one was there, but the jukebox was playing, and there were plates of snacks on the cocktail tables, which had been pushed together in the center of the room. Simon went behind the bar. "What would you like?"

"You can't go back there." Skye was startled. This was not at all like him. "You'll get into trouble."

"I didn't realize rules meant that much to you." Simon grinned. "Don't worry. I'm a personal friend of the owner."

Skye frowned. Was he trying to use reverse psychology on her—show her how it felt to be the one pulled into a situation against her will? While she contemplated the idea, she heard the outside door open and then voices coming toward them. Uh-oh. Now they would be in deep dodo.

Charlie and Bunny were the first to appear, followed closely by Frannie and Justin, then Jed and May. Everyone had questions, but Simon ignored them and said, "Thank you all for coming to my party. What can I get you to drink?"

Once they were all seated and had a beverage, Simon stood, raised his glass, and said, "To family and friends."

After a brief hesitation, everyone followed suit, though they looked puzzled.

Simon took a swallow of wine and then a deep breath. "Living in Scumble River these past few years, and knowing Skye and her wonderful family, I've learned that sometimes you have to forget about the past in order for the future to be better." He paused and took another gulp of wine. This was clearly very difficult for him.

Skye watched as Bunny clung to Simon's words. Her expression was full of hope and fear, and mirrored her son's. Skye felt her chest tighten and knew these next few minutes could change everything, either for good or for bad.

Simon continued. "Last week, Justin, Frannie, and Bun . . ." —he hesitated, then corrected himself—"my mother saved Skye's and my life."

Bunny chimed in, "That's right. I beat up Ginardi and made sure he couldn't hurt Son . . . I mean, Simon."

"Thank you, Mother." Simon acknowledged Bunny, then continued, "My mother spent a lot of time with me while I was in the hospital recovering from my injury, and she and I had quite a few long talks, which made me realize that everyone makes mistakes, even me."

Skye took his hand and squeezed. "Although usually you let me make the mistakes for both of us," she said.

They all laughed.

He kissed the top of her head. "That's another conclusion I've come to. Skye, you add the adventure that had been missing from my life for a long time."

She blushed and ducked her head, not used to public compliments.

Frannie stared at the two adults and said, "Wow. Way cool." Then she shot a speculative glance at Justin, who had been looking at her, but turned away when she caught him.

"As I was saying, everyone makes mistakes, and everyone deserves a fresh start." Simon walked over to where Bunny was sitting and stood by her side. "With that in mind, I have a proposal—"

May gasped. Her face glowed. Clearly she thought Simon was about to ask Skye to marry him.

"Since it would be kind of hard to miss the big sign out front," Simon went on, "everyone knows that the bowling alley has been up for sale for the past year. This week I ha my Realtor put in a bid, and yesterday it was accepted. So I canceled the bowling leagues and invited you all here to hear my proposal . . ." He looked at May and amended his word choice. "What I would like to suggest is that my mother manage the bowling alley for me."

For a moment Bunny appeared to be stunned. Then she leaped from her chair and threw her arms around Simon's neck. "Yes, yes, yes!"

After Bunny stopped hugging Simon, Charlie pumped his hand and said, "Congratulations. This business could be a gold mine if it's run right."

Jed clapped Simon on the shoulder, and May kissed him on the cheek before turning to Skye and whispering in her ear, "Did you know about this?" When Skye shook her head, May said, "Bunny sticking around Scumble River is not a good thing. She'll bring us trouble. I can feel it in my bones."

Skye shrugged. May was probably right. She turned, noticing Justin and Frannie talking to Bunny. All three wore wide grins.

People stayed for hours drinking and eating and talking. They toasted Simon and Bunny, laughed at the picture of Skye dressed in wallpaper that May had gotten from Joy Kessler, and heard Charlie's story about his discovery that Bob Ginardi and Tony Zello had stuffed the GUMB ballot box in order to ensure Bob won the election. After the fake votes were discounted, Charlie had been the winner by a landslide.

As Skye and Simon cleaned up after everyone else had gone home, she said, "That was quite a change of heart you had."

Simon polished a wineglass and held it up to the light. "After hours and hours of talking to Bunny while I was in the hospital, I realized that part of my problem with her is that I wanted her to be the ideal mom. I wanted her to be

June Cleaver and Donna Reed, and when she didn't live up to the image I had in my head, I couldn't forgive her."

Skye nodded. "It's hard to give up our childhood dreams, but you're right to move on."

"Don't get me wrong, I'll never think what she did to my dad and me was right, but despite her faults I'm willing to start fresh because I do understand a little better now that appearances can be misleading." Simon shook his head. "Look at the Addisons and the Ginardis. They seemed to be living perfect lives."

Skye nodded again. "I liked what you said about fresh starts." She wiped off the top of the tables. "It's almost as if Scumble River is the place for people who need a second chance."

"Well, Bunny definitely needs that. She finally told me the whole story about her sudden urge to visit me."

"Oh?" Skye hopped up on a bar stool and leaned her chin on her hands. "Give."

"It seems she was in a bad car accident a couple of years ago and broke her pelvis. She couldn't dance anymore. An old friend who lives here in Illinois offered to let Bunny stay with her while she got back on her feet financially."

"I take it those living arrangements didn't work out."

"No. What Bunny didn't tell her friend was that while she was injured, she had been in a lot of pain for a long time, and she got hooked on prescription painkillers. Recently the doctor had refused to give her anymore. So, while she was staying with this woman, she tried to use a forged prescription. She was caught, and her friend kicked her out."

"How awful."

"Yeah. It was pretty rough." Simon came around the bar and sat next to Skye. "Bunny was sent to Drug Court."

"Drug Court?"

"It's a sentencing alternative. She has to report to the court every week for the first twelve weeks and then every other week for the next six months. And she must have a permanent address and a job."

"She was hoping you'd take her in, and she could find a job around here," Skye guessed. "Bunny's involvement with Drug Court explains her mysterious phone calls, and why she wanted proof she had attended Mass, too."

"Right. Because she has to attend Narcotic Anonymous meetings and they're held at the church. The bulletin lists the time and date."

They sat silently for a few minutes, then Skye asked, "Did you buy the bowling alley so she'd have a steady job?"

"Of course not." Simon's ears turned red. "It's just a good investment."

"I think you're the good investment."

Turn the page for an excerpt
from the Scumble River Mystery

# MURDER OF A PINK ELEPHANT

*Available from Signet*

The music struck Skye Denison with the force of an ax blow. She stood in the open door of her brother Vince's hair salon, with a cooler at her feet and a picnic basket in her arms, trying to determine if her ears would start bleeding if she ventured over the threshold.

When Vince had said his band was changing their name from Plastic Santa to Pink Elephant, Skye hadn't realized that they'd be changing the type of music they performed, too.

Now she understood why her mother had asked her to drop off the food at the rehearsal. Evidently May had heard Pink Elephant rehearse before.

A blast of frigid air blew a strand of Skye's hair across her face and reminded her that she was standing outside in the middle of one of the coldest Illinois Februaries on record. Steeling herself to the deafening sound, she kicked the plastic ice chest through the doorway and entered the waiting area.

White wicker chairs and settees, which usually held customers waiting for their turn to be cut, colored, or coiffed, were filled with instrument cases, amps, and cables. The stark black equipment was a jarring contrast to the sofa's

garden print cushions, and the glass coffee table that typi-
cally displayed *People*, *Cosmo*, and *Glamour* was littered
with guitar picks, sheet music, and drumsticks.

Skye paused at the entrance to the styling area. This was
the juncture where the noise level went from merely painful
to excruciating. She felt like there should be a sign saying,
"YE WHO ENTERS HERE, ABANDON ALL HOPE OF EVER HEARING
AGAIN," posted among the red hearts and shiny pink-foil gar-
lands that decorated the lattice archway.

The band members were scattered among the styling stations, curler carts, and freestanding hairdryers. The smell of
testosterone battled with the acrid odor of perm solution,
while the stink of cigarettes and beer lost the war to the
sweet aroma of floral shampoo and conditioner.

Skye blinked. It wasn't every day that she saw four
macho musicians performing against a beauty salon background of delicate mauves and pinks.

Vince was crowded up against the far wall between the
front windows, surrounded by drums of all sizes. Whenever
he lifted his drumsticks too high they got tangled with the
fronds of a potted fern on a shelf above his head. There were
beads of sweat above his green eyes, and his butterscotch
hair was tied back in a ponytail.

Opposite Vince, sitting at one of the freestanding
hairdryers and hunched over the keyboard in front of him,
was Finn O'Malley, a scruffy carrot top wearing faded jeans
and a tattered T-shirt. At some point the dryer's hood had
slipped down and covered the top quarter of Finn's head.

To Vince's left, Rod Yager concentrated on strumming
his guitar. Stringy brown hair obscured his face, and his blue
jeans and T-shirt were only slightly less frayed than Finn's.
At first glance it appeared that he was doing some strange
version of the Mexican Hat Dance, but then Skye noticed
that he was actually trying to avoid tripping over the cords
of the various hair styling implements that trailed across the
salon floor.

Center stage, silver blond hair trailing down his back, blue eyes blazing with emotion, the lead vocalist Logan Wolfe screamed out the lyrics to an acid rock hit from the nineties. His tight black tank top was soaked in sweat and his black jeans rode low on slim hips.

Skye closed her eyes and tried to hear why someone would like this kind of music. As a school psychologist, she often watched television programs, went to movies, and listened to CDs that she would never choose on her own, in order to better understand the teenagers she evaluated and counseled. But this noise masquerading as a song was beyond her comprehension.

As Logan's voice trailed off, Vince glanced up and waved Skye over. "What do you think of our new sound?" he yelled from across the room.

"It's . . . ah, loud." Skye tried to think of a polite lie but ended up saying, "I sort of liked the music you played before."

"We'll still play that when we do gigs for the older crowd."

Skye gave him a sharp look. Was he saying she was old? She was only thirty-two.

Vince got up from his stool and gave her a quick hug. With his arm still around her, he said, "Guys, you remember my sister, Skye?"

Rod and Finn grunted hellos.

As they wandered away to investigate the food, Finn said to Rod in what was clearly the continuation of an ongoing conversation, "I still don't understand why the chicks don't seem to dig me."

Rod slung his arm around the other man's shoulder. "It's how you talk to them, man. You gotta quit being so sexist. Broads really hate that."

Skye was still shaking her head at Dumb and Dumber's remarks when Logan strolled over, took her hand, and said,

"Of course I remember you. You moved back to town a couple three years ago, right?"

Skye shrugged. "It seems longer."

"Nope, it was two years ago last summer." He smiled seductively. "I keep track of all the pretty ladies in Scumble River—especially those with such beautiful emerald green eyes and sexy curls."

Vince frowned and removed Skye's hand from Logan's. "I'm sure your wife would be thrilled to hear that."

Skye shot her brother a puzzled glance. Considering Vince's own reputation as a ladies' man, she was surprised at his censure of Logan's behavior.

The singer shrugged, not bothering to respond to Vince's taunt. Instead he stepped closer to Skye and fingered a ringlet of her hair. "What color do you call this? It's not brown, but it isn't red either."

"Chestnut." She assessed the singer. He was handsome in a pop-idol sort of way. She could see the appeal he would have to a lot of women, but he wasn't her type. Piercings and tattoos left her cold. Not that she thought he was really coming on to her. He was obviously the kind of guy who flirted with every female he met.

Vince moved between them, forcing Logan to step away from Skye.

She could feel the tension between the two men, and wondered what was causing it. She didn't flatter herself that it had anything to do with the singer's behavior toward her.

Vince and Logan continued to stare at each other, until Skye took each of them by the arm and moved them toward the food. "Mom sent over some supper for you guys. Don't make me tell her you didn't eat every bite."

Skye watched as the men filled their plates, grabbed cans of beer from the cooler, and sat down to eat. It took her a few minutes to realize that they weren't talking to each other. Well, Rod and Finn were talking to each other, but no one else was. Logan had his back to the group and was staring at a poster of Monet's *Water Lilies*, and Vince had retreated to behind the reception counter. Was something wrong with the band?

The mood among the musicians concerned her. She had recommended the group to play at the high school dance Saturday night. What if they were breaking up? Everyone would blame her if there were no music at the Valentine's Day Ball.

Grabbing the manicurist's chair, she wheeled it over to where Vince was sitting, and asked in a low voice, "So, what's up?"

"Nothing. What do you mean?"

"You guys seem upset with each other or something."

"Nah, just a difference of opinion." He finished his sandwich and crumpled his napkin. "It'll blow over soon."

"Why were you so mad at Logan when he was flirting with me before?" Skye raised an eyebrow. "You know he wasn't serious, and even if he were, I can take care of myself with guys like that."

"Yeah. I know."

"Besides, he could never compete with Simon."

"I know," he repeated. "But the guy irritates me with his 'never met a mirror he didn't like' attitude."

"That's what you're upset about?"

"Nah." He didn't look her in the eye. "We're trying some new music tonight and it's just not sounding good. It makes me jumpy."

"So, why don't you just do the soft rock stuff you've been playing? The band sounded great at the last wedding reception I heard you at."

Vince rolled his eyes. "Let's just say we're tired of playing the 'Chicken Dance'."

Skye hid her grin and suggested innocently, "You could always do the 'Hokey Pokey' instead."

Vince swatted her arm. "Gee. Can we? Please?" Before she could return the conversation to why Vince was upset, he sprang up from his chair and said, "We need to get back to practice."

Skye was forced to let the matter drop. As long as the band showed up and played for the dance Saturday, she'd worry about their interpersonal relationships later. "Are you going to return the basket and cooler to Mom, or should I take them?"

"I'll bring them over tomorrow, before I open the salon." Vince moved back behind his drums, and the other guys took up their instruments. "Want to stick around and listen?"

"No, thanks. I'll see you guys at the school's Valentine's Day Ball. I'm one of the lucky chaperones."

"Right. I just hope we can get it together by then."

Skye put her coat on and moved toward the door. "Don't worry. By Saturday night I'm sure you'll knock them dead."